THE
GHOST
WHO SAID
GOODBYE

A MYRON VALE INVESTIGATION

THE
GHOST
WHO SAID
GOODBYE

A MYRON VALE INVESTIGATION

SCOTT WILLIAM CARTER

FLYING RAVEN

PRESS

THE GHOST WHO SAID GOODBYE

Copyright © 2015 by Scott William Carter.

Published by Flying Raven Press, April 2015.

FLYING RAVEN PRESS
4742 Libery Rd. S #382
Salem, Oregon 97302

For more about Flying Raven Press, please visit our web site at
http://www.flyingravenpress.com

ISBN-10 0692412530
ISBN-13 978-0692412534

Printed in the United States of America
Flying Raven Press paperback edition, April 2015

For Viola

Before

I WAS SEVEN YEARS OLD when I first held a gun.

First day of school. First kiss. First time making love. There are a lot of firsts in life, and I have memories of all those things, but none of them are as vivid as the night I snuck into my father's den—having recently discovered where he hid his desk key—to see if he really kept a revolver in the top drawer. I was doing it because of a kid named Kevin Blaine, a gap-toothed bully who always waited for me behind the big oak after school. I thought if I just held a gun once, if I could just feel its weight in my hand, its power, I could tell Kevin I knew what it was like—and that I could get to it if he ever laid his meaty hands on me again. When you had a gun, nobody could mess with you.

That's what I thought at the time. It was only years later, after everything that happened to me, when I discovered there were evils in the world no bullet could ever stop.

Awake in my bed, I waited until the grandfather clock in the living room gonged a dozen times before I crept to the door. Barefoot, in pajama bottoms and a thin cotton T-shirt, I felt winter's bite from all sides. It was cold in the house not just because the city outside was

1

covered in a white blanket, but because Mom, who already preferred the thermostat be set to a balmy sixty-two degrees, turned off the heat completely when she climbed into bed. No reason to waste money on gas when we could all put on sweaters, she'd say. This, coming from a woman who wore sweaters even in the dog days of August. In winter, she often wore layers of them.

School had been canceled for two days because of the snow, but I knew my luck was running out on that front. Even Portland, Oregon, a city that was lucky to get a dusting every other year, eventually got chains on the buses, meaning there was a good chance I would not only have to face Kevin the next day, but he'd be armed with plenty of snowballs.

I waited with my ear pressed against the door for a long time to make sure I didn't hear Johnny Carson. Mom often stayed up to watch him when Dad was working a night beat—or when he was out drinking, which he was doing that night. Which he'd been doing *lots* of nights lately, truth be told, a fact that Mom was none too happy about, considering how often I found Dad in the morning sleeping off the booze on the sofa.

With no sound at all coming from Mom's room, I opened the door and tiptoed to the edge of the hall. From this vantage point, I saw not only the sleek darkness of the back of the couch but also the glow of the streetlights outlining the curtained bay window, giving me just enough light to realize that there were no boots hanging off either end of the couch.

My heart rabbity-tapping away, I made my way to the den.

It was not a big house, just a two-bedroom bungalow off I-84 in the Rose City Park area, but it still felt like hours to cross to the other side of the living room. The hardwood floor was so cold my toes curled, and each creak set my heart racing faster. The place still smelled like the lemon chicken we'd had for dinner, and, glancing into the kitchen, I saw that Mom hadn't put away Dad's untouched plate.

I probably would have stood outside the den for an hour, stifling the urge to pee, but the sudden bark of a neighbor's dog so scared me that I bolted into the room.

It was even darker in his den. Leaning against the closed door, I tried to will my heart to slow down. The faint dark-chocolate scent of Dad's favorite cigars hung in the air. I didn't dare turn on a light, but I also didn't dare touch a gun in such utter darkness, so I felt my way past the desk to the window, opening the curtains.

The fluorescent security bulb mounted on the side of the neighbor's garage filled the den with plenty of light. The dust, catching this pale eerie glow, floated in the air. Icicles hung from the eaves outside like blue daggers. Swallowing away the lump in my throat, I found the book I was looking for, *Mastering Golf*, on the shelf in the corner, and opened it to the hidden compartment. There I found the key, as well as his passport and what was left of a rabbit foot I knew he'd had with him in Vietnam.

Dad hated golf. That's why, a week earlier, I'd taken the book off the shelf in the first place. Baseball and basketball were his sports.

Placing the book on the old cherrywood desk, I settled into the swivel chair, the thin cushion like cold concrete. I held my breath and slipped the key into the top drawer's lock. It took a bit of jiggling, but the key turned.

The drawer opened.

At first, I saw nothing but what you might expect to find in the top drawer of a man's desk: a medley of ballpoint pens, rubber bands, and wrinkled maps, a deck of playing cards picturing pinup girls from the fifties, half-empty packs of gum, loose Tic Tacs ... but something wasn't quite right. The drawer didn't open far enough. Then I found the levers in the back and, holding them down, slid the drawer open the rest of the way. There, in a compartment all to itself, was a black revolver on a folded white handkerchief, like a corpse in an open coffin laid out for a funeral viewing.

A Colt Python .357, I found out much later. When Dad went drinking, he never took it with him. I overheard him tell Mom that a cop who took his gun drinking was just asking for something stupid to happen—which was why I knew it would be in the drawer that night. Dad may have liked to drink, but he wasn't stupid. Everybody said he was the smartest detective on the force.

It took me a few long, agonizing minutes before I summoned the courage to even touch it—on the walnut handle, lightly. I traced my finger over the chamber and along the barrel, resting it there for a long time as if taking the gun's pulse. I shivered. Finally, I closed my fingers around the handle and lifted the gun, ever so slowly, out of the drawer. Did I feel its power? I have to say I did. I may not have decided I wanted to be a cop in that moment, but I did decide I wanted to own a gun.

I was pointing the revolver at the leather chair across from me, pretending to aim it at a bad guy skulking into our house to kill us, when I heard the rattle of our front door.

An icy dread shot through me. For just a second I thought it might really be a bad guy, and that would have been better, really, because I could almost imagine myself playing the part of the hero—swaggering out there with my gun like John Wayne, stopping the Terrible Burglar of Greater Portland from stealing Mom's china. Later, of course, in all the congratulatory fervor, nobody would think to ask me why I had been in Dad's office in the first place.

But the rattle of the front door was immediately followed by the murmur of voices, and even though I couldn't make out the words, I would have known my father's rough baritone anywhere, slurred as it was. And the other voice, slightly higher, slightly more clipped—I knew that one, too. His partner Sal.

My heart, which had finally slowed down, began to pound. There was still hope. If Dad crashed on the couch, there was a chance I could sneak past him once he was asleep.

Luck really must not have been on my side that night, because Dad was making some kind of fuss, and Sal was trying to shush him.

"Hank, quiet," Sal said, "you'll wake Eleanor and Myron."

"I don't care!" Dad said. "Listen to me. You should have let me take that guy."

"Hank—"

"Will you listen? One punch … I could have took him!"

"Shh! Hank … Hank, come on, pal. Okay, to your office. Let's talk about this."

"No—"

"Come on, you want me to listen. I'll listen. There you go. This way."

And that's when I knew, hearing their shuffling footsteps on the wooden floor, that it was over. I was going to be grounded until I was eighteen years old. The punishment for breaking Dad's No. 1 rule—to never go into his office without permission—would be severe enough. What would happen when he caught me with his revolver was unimaginable.

I had only seconds. I put the gun back in the drawer and closed it. I put the key in *Mastering Golf* and slipped it back on the shelf. The doorknob to the den was turning; I could clearly see that in the silvery light. Where to go? Where to hide? There was only one place—I dived under the desk.

Just in time. I heard the swish of the door as I slid to my knees. The overhead light flicked on, blindingly bright, and I squinted at the chair I'd been sitting in seconds earlier. Was it still moving? It didn't look like it.

"All right," Sal said, "this chair here. Let's have you take a load off, partner."

"I want to sit—sit at my desk," Dad protested, filling me with terror. While Sal was doing his best to talk in a whisper, Dad was practically belting out every word. "My desk—"

"This chair is fine," Sal said, and I heard the click of the door closing.

"No—"

"Sit!"

I'd never heard Sal talk to Dad this way, like he was a misbehaving child, and I didn't like it. Yet his stern tone must have worked, because the leather chair whooshed as Dad slumped into it. I heard footsteps and I tensed, but Sal didn't go far. The wooden desk creaked above me. A bit of dust rained down, and I pinched my nose, praying I didn't sneeze.

Dad mumbled something.

"What's that, partner?" Sal said.

"I said I coulda—coulda taken that punk," Dad replied.

Sal didn't say anything, the silence stretching for an interminable moment. "Be straight with me," he said finally. "This ain't about some drunk football fan with an ax to grind, is it?"

Dad didn't answer.

"What's this really about?" Sal asked. Then, after a pause, he spoke in a whisper I had trouble hearing: "It's about *him*, isn't it?"

"No," Dad said.

"Level with me. I'm your partner."

"Fuck you, Sal. I just don't like people insulting the Seahawks, okay?"

"Man, I didn't realize you cared about the Seahawks so much."

"Well, I do."

"You even watched a whole football game since that Super Bowl party at Ted's last year?"

"Fuck you, Sal."

"That's the second time you've said that to me. Making you feel better?"

"Fu … Whatever. I don't care. I don't care about anything. Just go home. It's nothing. I'll see you tomorrow. Just got to sleep this off, is all."

Sal took a breath and blew the air through his lips. "Fine. Tried my best. Pick you up at a quarter to eight. And I'm not waiting this time, so make sure you're ready."

Again, I was surprised by Sal's disrespectful tone. I'd always liked Sal—he usually had a pocket full peppermint candies he was more than willing to share—but I couldn't stand him treating Dad this way. One foot planted on the floor, the back of a shiny black boot, then Dad spoke.

"Wait," he said.

"What?"

"I just … wait a second, will you?"

Sal waited. His boot slid up and out of view, the heel banging against the desk. In the stillness, I could hear Dad breathing through his nose, a deliberate and labored breathing. I did my best to make my own breathing match his, but quieter, hiding the sound. It was as if Sal wasn't even there, just the two of us in that little room, Dad and me, breathing in unison. My bladder was like a water balloon stretched to the limit. I felt a twinge in my knees, growing into a painful ache, but I didn't dare adjust my position. The slightest rustle of my pajamas might alert them.

Still, this silence went on for so long that I was seriously thinking of outing myself—when something must have changed.

"Oh shit," Sal said.

"I'm sorry," Dad said. His voice sounded strange, gurgled.

"Jesus, man. It's okay."

"I'm just tired."

"Hank—"

And then I knew, because Dad wasn't even trying to muffle the sound now. He was *crying*. There was no other way to explain the sniffling, the shuddery breathing, the pitiful whimpering. Of all the things that happened that night, this was the biggest shock. Dad never cried. It just didn't happen. I cried. Once in a blue moon, Mom cried. Even Kevin Blaine cried when Mrs. Rooker sent him to the principal's office for shooting spitwads at the girls in our class. But Dad? No. He didn't cry any more than a lion did. Or a bear. Or a mountain. I may not have known much at seven years old, but I knew this much.

I felt a lot of things in that moment, in addition to shock. The worst of them, the one I'd tried to forget as much as I could in the ensuing years, was shame.

For the first time in my life, I was ashamed of my father.

"Man, take it easy," Sal said. "It's all right. Just let it out. You can let it out."

"No—"

"It's good to let it out. You can only keep it bottled up for so long."

"No, I'm—I'm all right. I just … Oh, boy."

"Hank—"

"It's okay. I'm okay. I've got it."

Finally, mercifully, Dad stopped crying. He sniffled a few times, cleared his throat, and that was it. It was like one of Portland's rare thunderstorms, here as fast as it was gone. He took a few deep breaths. I heard a rustle that might have been Dad wiping his face on his sleeve.

"Meds," Sal said.

"What?" Dad said.

"You asked how I handle it."

"I did?"

"You were about to. Meds. That's how I handle all this crap. I've started taking some meds. Right after we saw him, I started. It was the only way to make things feel right, you know. To make the nightmares stop. Don't tell anybody, okay? I don't want it getting around the station."

Dad was silent.

"You might want to think about taking some yourself," Sal offered. "I can recommend a doctor—"

"I don't need any pills."

"Yeah, that's what I thought, but—"

"No pills, dammit!"

"All right, all right. It's just a suggestion, that's all. It helped me, okay? You don't need to be an asshole about it."

"No pills."

"Fine, whatever," Sal said.

There was another uncomfortable silence, but thankfully there were no tears. The urge to pee was back, and this time it was so strong I had no choice but to cup my hand over my crotch.

"You have to let it go, Hank," Sal said. "There hasn't been a killing in months. The guy is gone."

"We don't know that."

When Sal spoke again, his voice took on a strange, tremulous quality, as if somebody put hands around his windpipe. "When we saw him … When we saw him, it must have, I don't know, spooked him. He must have realized how close we were getting. It was only a matter of time. He must have known that."

"Seventeen, Sal."

"I know."

"Seventeen murders. Seventeen in five years … and those kids. The kids of those first two victims. I still think about them, the way they looked at me. Their mothers were taken from them. And the one boy? I told you, he said he wanted to be a cop when he grows up."

"I know. But I'm telling you, Hank. The Goodbye Killer is gone. We've got to get on with things."

"There's got to be clues—"

"All of them have been dead ends, you know that. No fingerprints. No DNA except the victims. The national news has moved on. Even Portland is finally turning the page. I haven't seen a story on the front page of the *Oregonian* for over a week. Maybe he'll show up again, but for now … there's nothing to go on. And the only people who've even …" He trailed off.

"Who've even seen him are the two of us," Dad finished.

"Yes."

"But what did we see, Sal?"

"What?"

"What did we actually see?"

Even under the desk, I felt the mood in the room change, a subtle shift, a curtain of dread dropping over us. A wave of cold passed through me, and I felt something, a strange uneasiness that prickled the back of my neck. It was almost like there was something … there. When Sal finally replied, his voice was hoarse.

"I don't know," he said.

"That—that face—" Dad said.

"I don't know what we saw."

"I can't describe it."

"I know."

"It wasn't …"

Dad trailed off, his voice so anguished that for a moment, I was afraid he was going to cry again. Sal cleared his throat.

"Human," he said.

"Yeah," Dad said. "Human. It was like it wasn't human. Inside that hood … Then, when he turned away …"

"A hallucination," Sal said.

"What?"

"It's the only explanation. We were tired. Exhausted from a lack of sleep. It was late. Dark. The mind plays tricks. You know that, Hank. Think of all the crazy shit we've heard from drunks and crackheads over the years. You think any of that was real? It was in their minds. *This* was in our minds. Only explanation. Has to be."

"But if both of us—"

"A hallucination," Sal said firmly.

"He disappeared, Sal. He disappeared right in front of us."

"We imagined it."

"No."

"It has to be that way," Sal insisted. "Don't you see? It has to be. You have to convince yourself of it, Hank. If not with meds, then some other way. See a shrink. Drown it in Jim Beam if that's what you have to do, but just don't kill yourself. Clamp it down. It's going to eat you up otherwise. We *didn't* see that. We didn't see anything, just like we told people. It was just like the others. He was gone by the time we got there."

I heard Dad sigh. The desk creaked again, and the backs of Sal's heels appeared in the crack. I heard him pat Dad's jacket.

"I got to get home, pal," Sal said. "I'm already on thin ice with Maria. I know things ain't peachy with you and Eleanor either. Get some rest. In the morning, you'll feel better."

"Okay," Dad said.

"Quarter to eight."

"Right."

The doorknob clicked and a tiny jet of air flitted under the desk. "Sal?" Dad said.

"Yeah?"

"It was like he wasn't even there. It was like he was a ... *a ghost.*"

If Sal answered this, I didn't hear it. There may have been a head-shake, a frown, or some other unspoken communication, but all I heard were Sal's footsteps, then the door closing.

For a long time, Dad did nothing but sit there. I didn't hear him move. I didn't hear him breathe. Even though I was sure I'd heard only Sal's footsteps, I was tempted to lean down and peer through the crack to see if he really was gone, but I didn't dare. The slightest sound would have been a dead giveaway.

I prayed that he would get up soon and head for the couch, because if he fell asleep in the chair, my chances of sneaking past him were slim. And that's if my bladder could even hold for another five minutes. I was debating just peeing myself when the neighbor's dog barked again, loudly enough to rouse Dad from his stillness. He made a sound, half groan and half cough. *Oh please*, I thought, *please, please* ... Then there was the distinctive rustle of leather, the chair groaning as he rose out of it.

The door opened, he shuffled out, and the light clicked off. He closed the door behind him. I stayed under the desk for as long as I could, holding my crotch, rocking back and forth, praying for him to fall asleep fast. Maybe I'd even get lucky, and he would risk his life and go crawl in bed next to Mom. When I couldn't wait any longer, I crept from under the desk to the door, first on my knees, then walking, forcing myself to take my time so the floor wouldn't creak. I turned the knob slowly—not a sound. I opened it a crack and felt a stream of cool air against my nose.

His boots were at the edge of the couch, toes pointed to the ceiling. I could just make out his easy, regular breathing over the hum of the refrigerator and the ticking of the grandfather clock.

Tiptoeing with all the terror of a Marine traversing a minefield, I headed for the hall. The air, cooler in the living room, pressed my pajamas against my skin like a wet sheet. The cotton was damp, and I thought maybe I'd wet myself after all, but no, it was just sweat. Lots of sweat.

Halfway there. Almost. A little bit farther, and then I'd be to the bathroom door. If he woke then, he'd just think I was getting up to take a leak.

Then, like a ghost in the darkness, my father spoke to me in a voice that was not slurred at all.

"The next time you want to hold a gun," he said, "make sure you ask first. I might even let you shoot it."

Chapter 1

IF THERE WAS ONE THING I'd learned since becoming a private investigator, it was that when Elvis gives advice, you listen. It didn't matter that he was holding a hot dog with a pair of metal tongs or that he was wearing an apron stained with enough grease that it could have been displayed in Portland's Museum of Modern Art as an abstract painting. Or that he'd been dead for more than thirty years. The guy had an angle on wisdom that even the Dalai Lama couldn't match.Even if half the time, what he was saying didn't make much sense at first. Or ever.

"Frozen yogurt," he was saying to me. The smoke curling around his white chef's hat was so real it was hard to believe I was probably the only living person on earth who could see it. "I'm telling ya, Myron. That's the answer to all your problems. Frozen yogurt."

"Frozen yogurt?" I said.

"Yep. Money in the bank."

"I ask you how I can drum up more clients, and you tell me I should sell frozen yogurt?"

The expert way he rolled the franks on the grill, with such style, cooking them up to a nice golden brown, I could see the same echoes of flair and panache that had made him so famous in his music days. "You got it, pardner. Or coffee, I guess. But Starbucks has kind of got that one cornered. Frozen yogurt—that's your ticket."

I blinked at him through the haze. Was it some kind of Zen koan, or was he just messing with me? The smell of grilling meat, and the wonderful honey-mustard glaze that was his specialty, reminded me that I hadn't eaten anything since coffee and toast that morning. Even the sting of the smoke in my eyes was real, which still made no sense even five and half years after the shooting that made me this way, but it was one of the strange rules I'd been forced to live by. If a ghost could see it, hear it, or smell it, that usually meant I could, too.

Only touch. That was all that separated us. If I reached for them, they weren't there. I called it a hand check, and every now and then I was forced to use it just to keep what was left of my sanity.

It was not yet noon, but already the sun felt warm on my neck. We were still in early April, barely out of winter, and yet it was one of those bright, blue-sky days that were more common in Portland in June. My eyes felt heavy from all the pollen in the air, and no amount of Claritin or Allegra had done the trick. The Willamette Valley was ground zero for people with allergies. I didn't have problems with my nose or throat—thank God—but this time of year my eyes always felt as if they'd been replaced with ball bearings.

A homeless woman wearing enough clothing to stock Target pushed a rattling shopping cart past us, giving me a strange look. Probably a living person like me, though it was hard to tell. I adjusted my copy of *Willamette Week*, doing my best to hide my mouth while I chatted with Elvis.

The sidewalks on Burnside bustled with pedestrians, normal for a Saturday—grunge types on skateboards stopping at the vinyl shop across the street, a Vietnamese man cleaning the window of the laundromat, a burly guy with tattooed arms tinkering on his Harley in front of the closed bar, yuppie lovebirds decked out in J.Crew and Birkenstocks out for a casual stroll, parents with their kids coming out of the diner, old people holding hands sitting on the bench, waiting for the bus. There were stranger ones, of course, two boy scouts wearing uniforms and wide-brimmed hats in a style thirty years past its prime, a woman with a big red perm roller-skating in the middle of the street, a bearded man leaning against a brick wall, giving me the cold eye, his gray Confederate uniform stained with dirt. Or blood. It was hard to tell. There was no doubt, though, that the bayonet at the end of his musket was deadly sharp.

The strange ones were probably ghosts, but then without a hand check, *any* of them could have been ghosts. I'd learned that the hard way more times than I could count.

I didn't usually come to the office on a Saturday, but then I didn't usually have $32.18 in my checking account. Or credit-card companies filling up my voice mail with gentle reminders that I was sixty days past due.

"Frozen yogurt," I said again.

"Yep." He used one of the tongs to hold up a hot dog. "Want one?"

"You know I can't do that, Elvis."

"Ah, right. Sorry, pardner. You just seem so much like us that I'm always forgetting."

"I'll try to take that as a compliment, I guess."

"You should, you should. All my best pals are ghosts."

"That's because all of your best pals are dead."

"Hey now. No need to be rude … Uh-oh. Don't look now, but bad news coming your way."

He was gazing east on Burnside when he said it, his brow furrowed with concern. I turned, newspaper in hand, and followed his gaze up the crowded street. There, inside a group of fit twenty-something women in sports tanks and spandex, who jogged past him without taking any notice of him at all, was a lanky old priest. His white hair on top of his flowing dark robes was like creamer on black coffee. In the bright sunlight, his obscenely large cross shone like a beacon. There was no doubt, judging by the way he was hastily heading in my direction, that he was coming to see me.

From my past experience with him, this was never good. The

grumble of my empty stomach was suddenly replaced with queasiness.

"You don't happen to know his name, do you?" I asked Elvis.

"Oh, I know much more than that."

I looked at him, surprised, but Elvis merely returned his attention to his hot dogs. I waited for him to elaborate, but he didn't.

"Really?" I said. "You won't tell me anything more?"

"It's not about *won't*."

By then, the priest had reached us. Right away, judging by his grave expression—even graver than usual—I saw that I'd underestimated how bad his news was going to be. His face, with all its pockmarks and deep gouges, and with its weathered, grayish quality, reminded me of an old wooden fence. The lines in his face, once deep and sharp but now faded, were like graffiti carved with a knife by a teenager long ago.

"I need to speak to you immediately, Myron," he said, in his deep, James Earl Jones voice. He gave Elvis a perfunctory nod. "Hello, again. I trust you know better than to tell people I was here?"

Elvis, his attention fixed on rolling the hot dogs, replied with a grunt. The grill sizzled and spit out fumes of smoke, which plumed in the air.

"How do you know each other?" I asked.

"We've had ... past dealings," the priest said. "The rest is not relevant, except that I know that he can keep a secret. Can we go up to your office? We should speak about this in private."

I turned the page in my newspaper, suddenly very interested in the article about rezoning part of Martin Luther King Jr. Boulevard. "I'm actually pretty busy right now."

"You don't seem busy."

"Just came out for some air. Got a lot on my plate."

"Really? You haven't had even a small case in over a month."

"How do you know that?"

"Myron, please. This is quite serious, so let's skip—"

"Are you a paying client?"

"If we could just go upstairs to your—"

"I didn't think so."

"This one has to be off the books, Myron. When you hear why—"

"I don't need to hear why," I said. "I don't need to hear anything from you at all. Or the Department of Souls. Or whoever you actually work for. Whatever crap you're mixed up with, I don't want any part of it. Now, if you'll excuse me, I have to get back to work."

Folding my newspaper with a snap and tucking it under my arm, I turned to go. Myron Vale, exit stage left, with plenty of attitude— even if in reality all that was waiting for me upstairs was a half-finished game of Sudoku.

"Myron—" the priest called after me.

"Forget it."

"Myron, please. There was a murder. A terrible one."

"Not my problem."

"We need your help. When you hear the details—"

"Nope."

I was almost to the door. I didn't think there was much he could say to stop me, but of course I was wrong.

"It involves your father," he said.

UPSTAIRS, IN A MUSTY OFFICE no bigger than a solitary-confinement cell at the prison in Salem, I settled into the chair behind my metal desk and gestured for the priest to take one of the chairs across from me. He stood instead, peering at the picture on the wall over my computer, a gold circle with the letters *MV* in the center in a stylistic font, as if scratched on a medallion with a knife. It was a logo of sorts, *my* logo, with the city of Portland at night pictured around it, the glowing building windows reflected in the shimmering Willamette River.

"Interesting," he said. "Billie painted that one, right? What do the living say when they see that you have a blank canvas hanging on your wall?"

I put my feet on the desk and clasped my hands. I didn't want to talk about Billie with him. Really, I didn't want to talk about *anything* with him, but I especially didn't want to talk about my wife. Or ex-wife. I still wasn't sure what our marital status was, since she'd left over six months earlier, and it hadn't sounded as if she was planning on coming back. And of course she was dead. There was always that.

Since Billie had created the painting after she died, only the dead could see it. Except for me, of course.

"My father," I reminded him.

"Right, right," he said.

He began to pace, head bowed as if that massive gold cross were weighing down his neck. In the silence, I heard the Gregorian chants start up again down the hall—or not exactly Gregorian chants, but something that resembled Gregorian chants if the people doing the chanting were also doing jumping jacks. I never knew what to expect from the Higher Plane Church of Spiritual Transcendence, except that whatever they did would annoy me.

I was sitting there, waiting for the priest to get to the point, when I heard scratching on the window. Turning, I saw my furry partner sitting on the ledge—Patch, a black cat with a white starburst over his left eye. In the morning light, his fur appeared more charcoal than black, his body sleek and muscular. He tilted his head in that cocky way of his, as if I were nothing more than his doorman and I needed be snappy about doing my job.

When I opened the window, he stepped onto the windowsill inside the glass—and immediately hissed at the priest.

"Well now," the priest said. "Your friend appears to have a gift. He can see people like me."

"And the living," I said. "We're kindred spirits."

"An interesting talent. I'll have to mention this to SISAH. Have you heard of them? The Society for the Investigation of Strange Animal Happenings? There's still plenty of debate whether animals have ghosts, since nobody can see them, and they're always interested in—"

Patch hissed again.

"He doesn't seem to like me very much," the priest said.

"Well, he's a pretty good judge of character."

I petted Patch a few times, thinking he might purr, but he wasn't in the mood. Leaving the window open, the cool breeze flitting past my neck and the sounds of the street drifting up to the room, I turned back to the priest. Raised my eyebrows.

"Right," he said. "To the point."

"To the point," I agreed.

He swallowed. "You have to understand, this has all—this has me a bit rattled. Your father—Hank Vale. Do you remember a case he worked on when you were quite little? Seventeen—seventeen murders in Portland over five years. They called him the Goodbye Killer. Your father was one of the lead detectives on the case. You would have been, what—"

"Seven years old," I said.

"Right. So you do remember?"

Of course I remembered. How could I forget? Even though Dad knew I'd been in the room, we'd never talked about it, not once in the decades since. And now? With the condition Dad was in, a conversation like that wouldn't be possible.

"They never caught him," I said.

"No. Not yet."

"Not yet? That case has gone pretty cold." Then, realizing that this wasn't an academic conversation we were having, I leaned forward in my seat. "Something's happened. What is it?"

The priest started to answer, then shook his head and started to pace again. "Where do I begin? It's been so many years, and I never thought … well … you have to understand something, Myron. In my position, I have encountered evil in many different forms. And I have never … never felt what I felt the one time I was in the same room with this, this *thing*."

"You saw him?"

"No," he said, tugging at his collar. "No, it was too dark. I was just briefly in the same room with him. We—we had information that led us to believe he was hiding in an abandoned church in Sandy."

"We?"

"Yes, at the time I was part of the—" he began, then stopped and looked at me, as if catching himself. "A special group. A task force, if you will, whose purpose was to hunt down ghosts who had committed the most heinous crimes and transport them to Alcatraz."

"Alcatraz? That place is a tourist attraction."

"For the living," the priest said. "For ghosts … well, let's just say someone like you wouldn't want to go there, Myron. It would seem very … crowded. We have our laws, too, as I'm sure you know. The Ghost Reaper may never have been locked up there, but we still put away plenty of bad ones over the years."

"The Ghost Reaper?" I said. "That's what you guys call him?"

"He's had plenty of names, but that one stuck, mostly because of what he could do. Or seem to do. Nobody really knows, of course. And yet, by all appearances—"

"Just spit it out, for God's sake."

"He can kill ghosts, Myron."

"What?"

The priest made a face as if he'd swallowed some moldy Communion bread. "At least that's the way it appears. I have always been one of the last holdouts, refusing to accept it, but the facts have became increasingly hard to dispute."

"I didn't think ghosts could be killed—if that's even the right word," I said. "I thought once you died, you walked the earth forever. Isn't that the deal? Immortality, but no heavenly gates, no harps, no hellfire?"

"I wouldn't quite describe it that way," he replied, "but yes, something like that. Which is why someone like the Ghost Reaper can cause such panic among our kind. He … upsets the prevailing worldview, a worldview that might be the only thing keeping complete chaos from breaking out. Tell me, Myron, what do you actually know about him? The Goodbye Killer, as you call him."

Patch had obviously had enough, because after a final glare at the priest, he leapt to the windowsill and walked along the ledge out of sight. I watched him go, keeping my back to the priest. Across the street, in the window of the apartment above the bar, an old black guy wearing a wifebeater sipped a cup of coffee. A twenty-something black woman dressed in a Navy uniform stood behind him, looking over his shoulder. I knew the guy, Bud Kamen—he owned the bar. I knew the woman, too. Her name was Angie and she was his daughter.

Looking at her, you would never know that she'd been killed in friendly fire in the war-torn alleys of Baghdad.

"Seventeen murders in five years," I said. "This was the eighties, so before cable news, but it was a big enough story that Tom Brokaw and Dan Rather talked about it every night for nearly a year. Tons of pressure on the bureau. Like no pressure any cop had experienced, and Dad and his partner Sal were right in the middle of it. Dad never talked about it, but that's what I heard from some of the older cops on the force. The victims were men and women of all ages, all nationalities, no pattern anyone could detect."

"And?" the priest said.

"Yeah," I said, "the weird stuff. No cause of death could be determined. It was like their hearts just … stopped. People thought maybe poison, but the autopsies could never prove it. In fact, nobody might have thought they were murders at all except for the notes."

"Yes?"

"He left goodbye notes. To the victims. Or not really notes, but that's what people called them. They were written on whatever was … around. Dirty concrete. A dusty window. In the bark dust. On the snow. One time, that guy in the candy shop, jelly beans had been arranged on the floor. They didn't say much: *Goodbye, John. I will take you to a better place.* The only things different were the names. *Goodbye, Larry. Goodbye, Sally.* Creepy stuff."

"That's putting it mildly. Clues?"

"Nothing. Nobody could understand how he could leave these notes and not leave any trace of … wait a minute." I spun around and faced him. The long-ago case, brought into the perspective of my current life, made me see an angle I never would have believed when I was just another human blissfully unaware of the other world around us. "Wait, you're telling me you think—"

"We don't know what to think."

"—he's a ghost?"

"That's one of the prevailing theories. If so, he has enormous gifts."

"A funny word for it."

"Gifts can be good or bad, depending on how they are used."

"Are we back to riddles now?"

The priest sighed. "We're back to the unknowns. Myron, we don't know *what* he is. Or even if it's a *he*. She might not even be a ghost. She might be something else altogether. Whatever he or she or it is, I was never in the presence of something so evil, so depraved, as I was in the basement of that church so many years ago. That's the only way I know he was in the room. *The feeling.* So very cold. So very, very cold—not a physical sensation, but inside. In the soul."

Before the shooting, before the bullet that lodged between the two lobes of my brain somehow gave me this *gift*, I would have scoffed at such mumbo-jumbo metaphysical nonsense. But not now, of course. Now I knew what the priest was talking about, because I had felt it a few times myself—not to that extent, maybe, but enough to know that there were ghosts in the world that were not like the others. Some were dark. Some were *very* dark, which wasn't quite the right word, but there was no word for it. It was as if some ghosts, when they died, had a bit of mold about them, a whiff of sour milk or rotten meat, and like all things that turned bad, time only made it worse.

"But he got away?" I said.

"I hesitated," the priest replied. "I was ahead of the others, walking down the steps, when I ... when I felt it. I froze. It was only for a few seconds, but it was enough. A window shattered. There was ... I don't know, a *whoosh* of air, then he was gone."

"A breaking window? Doesn't sound like a ghost at all."

"Could be. Or it could be that he simply wants us to believe he's flesh and blood. As I said, we don't know."

"You don't really know much, do you?"

He grimaced. "You say that as if you enjoy it."

"I do. You've made me uncomfortable so many times, I like seeing the tables turned."

"Fine," the priest said, "but I wouldn't be too smug. The news hasn't gotten out yet in your world, but when it does ... well, it will be like it was in the eighties all over again, but this time with the twenty-four-hour news cycle and the Internet to ratchet up the panic a few more degrees. The police should be finding the body any moment."

"What body?"

"A young woman," he said. "A college student at PSU named Jasmine Walker. Her mother found her in her dorm room this morning, dead."

"If her mother found her, why didn't she call—"

"Because she's a ghost, Myron."

"Right. Of course."

"Her boyfriend is already worried, so it shouldn't be long before he gets campus security to open her door. If he hasn't already."

"You mean you don't know?"

He shook his head, not so much in answer to my question but in irritation. "You may find this hard to believe, but the organization that I work for doesn't know *everything*. There are limits."

"Well, that's a relief."

"When they see the goodbye message written on her mirror in lipstick, trust me, no one is going to be relieved."

"It could be a copycat killer."

"No."

"How can you be so sure?"

"Because sometimes," he said, measuring his words, "sometimes, but not always, he leaves ... traces of himself behind. It rubs off on people, like, I don't know, like cigarette smoke. The girl's mother certainly felt it. The feeling fades, but it was still there when I arrived on the scene a few hours ago."

For a moment, I was again transported back to that seven-year-old boy hiding under his father's desk. Hadn't I felt something like that when Dad and Sal were talking? I'd tried to tell myself it was just nerves, the fear of being discovered combined with the creepy stuff they were talking about, and over time, I'd almost convinced myself, but there was always part of me that didn't understand that weird moment when it felt as if someone else, or some*thing* else, was in the room.

"You know what I'm talking about," the priest said, surprised.

"Maybe. I still don't understand why you want me involved."

"Come now," he said. "I think you already know the answer to that question. Your ... talent makes you uniquely qualified to help, since you can talk to both the living and the dead. Unless you know of another Ghost Detective?"

"Dear God, don't call me that. I hate that that's the name your people have given me."

"God has nothing to do with the name people have given you. Or any of this. I wish he did, because he could certainly help."

"God doesn't exist," I said.

"He would beg to differ."

"Oh, you've talked to him?"

The priest, fiddling with his cross self-consciously, didn't answer. As if filling the silence, the chanting from down the hall grew louder. I actually felt the floorboards vibrate. If it went on much longer, I was going to have to do something, and the something I was imagining would mean I wouldn't be available to help the priest or anyone for quite a while. Twenty years at least, and that's if I had a decent lawyer.

"Didn't think so," I said.

"Myron, dying doesn't change that some of the biggest things in life require a leap of faith."

"Oh, not this nonsense again."

"Myron—"

I got up and went to the door. The paper-thin sheetrock that separated my office from the hall hadn't blocked the sound, but all that chanting still seemed much louder with it open, like the roar of a jet engine and a dozen jackhammers and some combination of Metallica and Yanni if they were both on acid.

I screamed some choice profanity down the hall. Like water on fire, the chanting sizzled to silence. I slammed the door.

"Obviously this has you rattled," the priest said.

"Oh shut up."

I started back to my desk, then thought better of it. I opened it and gestured for him to leave.

"We're not done yet," he said.

"Oh, yes we are."

"There is another, even more important reason we need your help. Your father and his partner Sal Belleni were the people who came closest to catching the Ghost Reaper. More than that, your father got the very best look at the killer of anyone, living or dead. He might know something, something that could help us. It might be something small, but we have so little to go on that—"

"My father can't help anyone."

"Myron—"

"When I'm with him, half the time he doesn't even know it's me."

The priest sighed. "I know where your father is. I know what condition he is in. But you're telling me, with all that's at stake, you'd prefer not to even try?" He gestured impatiently around my shabby little office. "If nothing else, it'll get you out of this place. Unless you have something more pressing to do?"

"Frozen yogurt," I said.

"What?"

"Never mind. Let me get this straight. You want me to help you hunt down one of the world's most infamous serial killers, who, it turns out, is even more infamous in the world of the dead than he is in the world of the living, someone who can not only kill people but destroy the ghost within them, too—which means, what, he could kill me twice? And the second time would be a trip to oblivion? Plus, just to put the cherry on top, you can't pay me for my services?"

He crossed his arms, looking at me. I shook my head.

"Do you really have to guess at my answer?" I said.

"Even in a situation like this, money is that important?"

"My landlord thinks it's important. He doesn't speak much English, but when I'm late with the rent, he demonstrates the full range of his vocabulary. Loudly."

The way the priest glowered at me, it was like how Mom used to look at me when I begged her for ice cream after dinner, like she was so disappointed I could even ask for something so trivial. With a sigh, the priest stepped past me to the window, gazing at the street. The light shone on his black robe so vividly, catching every wrinkle and every piece of lint, that it was hard to believe he was a ghost.

"If I pay you," he said, "it will draw a lot of attention from the Department. As you know, you have a fair amount of enemies. There are people in positions of power who are even more afraid of you than the Ghost Reaper. If they weren't more afraid of what you might become if they killed you, you would have been dead a long time ago."

"If I don't get to eat," I said, "they won't have to kill me. I'll be joining them soon enough."

"Fine. Your compensation will have to come through indirect channels, but I can probably arrange it."

"Indirect channels? What does that mean?"

"It means you'll just have to trust me."

"Ah, I see. Then no deal."

"What?"

"Any deal that requires trusting you is dead on arrival. Sorry. No pun intended. And it doesn't matter anyway. I don't care how broke I am, no amount of money is enough to get me mixed up with this."

"So it's fear that stops you?"

"Sure. As crappy as my life is, I'd still like to hang on to it for a while. That, and who would take care of Patch? He's very particular about the way he likes his tuna."

This whole time the priest had his back to me, meaning I saw no warning on his face when he shouted at the glass.

"You can be so infuriatingly difficult!" he cried.

A bit shocked at his lack of composure, I let his voice fade to silence. It may have been my surprise, or perhaps the stress, but standing there I suddenly felt the odd rush of blood to my head, the dizziness, the floor tilting like the deck of a ship—then the dull throbbing, of course, the terrible headache that started pulsing in the middle of my skull—where the .38 was still firmly embedded between the two lobes of my brain—and working its way outward until the ache and nausea spread to the tips of my fingers and the tips of my toes.

The migraines hadn't been too frequent lately, but when they did hit, they were particularly bad. I steadied myself with a hand on the desk.

"I wish I could help," I said.

"No, you don't."

"No, you're right. I don't. I was just being polite. You are a priest, after all, and I was always taught to be polite to a man of the cloth. Or is it just a costume? You never did show me your priest license."

He sighed, and it was the sigh of man who had plenty of practice with sighs, imbued as it was with frustration and meaning and even a bit of style. A man could go far with a sigh like that, in life or in death. I made mental notes, figuring I could practice it. Then, unexpectedly, when he spoke again, his voice took on a slightly more upbeat quality.

"Well," he said, "if you won't get involved to help me, maybe you'll get involved to help someone else."

"What?"

He glanced over his shoulder at me, raising his rather large, frosty eyebrows. With a sigh of my own—quite pathetic, really, by his standards—I braved the unsteady walk to the window, the headache mercifully already beginning to pass. There, parking at the curb in front of my building, was a blue Crown Victoria, an unmarked police cruiser judging by the lights I could see tucked just inside the windshield.

The doors opened and two people got out, a young redheaded guy in a suit a size too big even though he was quite tall, and, more importantly, a stunningly beautiful black woman in a suit that fit her all too perfectly. The guy I didn't know, but the woman I did. Alesha Stintson. My former partner.

"It looks like the police found the body," the priest said.

Chapter 2

"Have you checked the news yet?"

This was what Alesha said to me as she barged into my office. She blew in like a dust devil, the air from the door scattering the unpaid bills littering my desk, the lanky redheaded guy trailing cautiously behind her as if he didn't want to get swept up in the storm.

Her eyes were wide and dark, almost as dark as her skin, like shiny black chrome. The tiny sliver of white around them made the pupils all the more arresting. She was a beautiful woman, to be sure, but those eyes of hers could lasso a man's heart—and *had*, considering the countless number of poor male victims over the years who had the misfortune to love her and not be loved back. The leather trench coat and charcoal pants might have looked good on someone else, but not as good as they did on Alesha, hugging her slim but athletic frame. She'd been growing her hair out lately, and straightening it, and now it was long enough that she could pull it back in a tight ponytail. It was almost as long as Billie's had been, when we'd first gotten married.

"I avoid the news whenever possible," I replied. "Doing so brightens my mood. Instead I watch cat videos on YouTube. Hello, by the way. That's usually how we start these things. Conversations, I mean."

She dropped into one of the chairs across from me as if she owned it, which she practically did, considering how often she occupied it. The priest had left just moments before, telling me he'd be in touch soon.

"There was a murder at PSU, Myron," she said. "It's going to be big. Really big. You're going to crap your pants when you hear the details."

"Well, then I apologize in advance," I said. "For the crapping, I mean. You want to introduce your friend here?"

The redheaded guy, as if surprised that anyone would ever take notice of him, stood a bit straighter. His hair, a shade of orange somewhere between carrots and ketchup, was cut short, but not so short that it didn't curl. He had the boyish face of a high school freshman on his first day of school. I doubted he was older than twenty-five. He was tall but also rail-thin, which was why his gray suit hung on him like a sheet on a clothesline. He seemed to be trying to make up for the roominess of his suit by the tightness of his tie, which made his collar cut into his neck like a dull blade. I didn't even know how he could breathe—which, when he spoke, was actually how he sounded.

Alesha glanced at him as if she was surprised he was there, then looked back at me and rolled her eyes.

"This is Tim O'Dell," she said, not even bothering to hide the exasperation in her tone. "He just made detective last week. Tim, this is Myron Vale."

"Hello, sir," he said, and it was almost cute the way his voice cracked, even if his windpipe sounded so pinched that I wanted to loosen that tie myself. "I heard a lot about you, sir. Nice to meet you."

He stood awkwardly for a second, then, like an actor receiving whispered urgings from a stagehand, suddenly stuck out his hand. I reached across the desk and shook it. The handshake surprised me. I'd been expecting a wet sponge and got polished granite instead.

"So you're Alesha's new partner," I said.

"Yes, sir. Just a week now, sir."

Alesha rolled her eyes again, but I found his earnest demeanor endearing. I'd had a little of that myself when I started, which—fortunately for me—Alesha had never witnessed, because she was seven years younger and didn't join the bureau until after a few dozen meth heads and child abusers had sucked the earnestness out of me.

"Let's stop with the *sir* business," I said. "It's making me feel like I'm your father, and I'm not old enough for that."

He looked like a slapped golden retriever, his expression equal amounts surprise and shame. "Sorry, um, Mr. Vale."

"Just Myron."

"All right."

"Great," Alesha said, "now that we've got that fun stuff out of the way, I need your help."

"My help?" I said. "I don't work for the bureau anymore."

"Yeah," she said, "and one of these days you're going to come to your senses and get your ass back on the force. I don't even know what you do with your time. You talk about cases, but there's never anybody here. It's like your clients are invisible or something."

"Only about half of them," I said.

"What?"

"Nothing."

She searched my eyes, and I caught that old flicker of attraction, that thing that had always been between us but that we'd never been able to grasp. We'd kissed once, shared a few intimate moments, and last year, after Billie left, I'd actually thought I was ready to take it to the next level with her. Yet we hadn't. Why? I told myself it was because I was afraid of being just another man laid to waste in her wake, but I knew that wasn't the real reason. There was no reason. We just didn't. There was plenty of beer and pizza and pool and late nights arguing about music and one long moment shivering in the cold outside her condo, when I couldn't look anywhere but at her lips, but still, it didn't happen. Why do some people get together while some don't? Alesha and I were opposites in so many ways, and there was no logical reason why we *should* be together, but some deeper, animal instinct in me sure didn't know that. I was fairly confident the same was true for her. One of these days, the animal instinct would win. It just hadn't yet.

Alesha didn't know about my condition. I'd thought about telling her many times, but whatever was holding me back from going to bed with her was also holding me back from telling her about the world I lived in now.

"Tell me why you need my help," I said.

Her gaze lingered on my eyes for a few more seconds, then she nodded. "I'll tell you about the case," she said. "Then you'll *know* why I need your help."

I gestured impatiently for her to proceed. I didn't need her to tell me about the case, of course, but she didn't know that, and she did manage to fill in some details. She told me all about the death of one Jasmine Walker, age twenty, African American, originally from Seattle and on a full-ride basketball scholarship at PSU. Poisoning or strangulation was speculated, but so far no cause of death was obvious. The boyfriend was being held for questioning, but it was doubtful he was a suspect unless his imploring the dorm's resident assistant to open the door was a superb bit of acting. Alesha held the critical detail to the end—the goodbye message scrawled on the bathroom mirror—then leaned back in her chair and watched me.

I did my best to look like I'd just realized what it all meant.

"The Goodbye Killer?" I said.

"Bingo," Alesha said.

"Impossible. How many years has it been?"

"It's true it could be a copycat," she said. "That's the way Chief Branson wants to treat it, but the media has other ideas. That blond chick on CNN is already going nuts, and it hit the wires less than an hour ago. But even so, I have a gut feeling it's the same guy."

"Not seeing where I come in," I said.

With some apparent reluctance, she jerked her thumb at O'Dell. "Blame him if you want. He's the one who remembered that your dad and his partner were the lead detectives on the Goodbye Killer case."

I looked at him. "Were you even born yet?"

"No, sir," he said. "Myron, I mean. I wasn't. But I like—I some-times read the cold case files. That one was very interesting."

"You need a new hobby," I said, and to Alesha I added, "and I still don't know what you think I can do."

"I want you to come with me when we talk to your dad," she said. "Maybe he'll remember something that can help us. And Sal Belleni, his partner. I looked him up. He still lives in Portland."

"You're not fucking talking to my dad," I said, surprising myself with the bite in my reply. "That's off the table right now."

"Hey," she said, "I'm not trying to—"

"He doesn't remember anything."

"Myron, I know he's—"

"You don't know anything, Alesha. You don't know anything at all. You haven't even met him."

"I know, but—"

"He barely remembers me, let alone his cases. He's not himself. He's not anyone. He's just … there. Okay? Leave him out of this. You barge in there and bully him with all your questions and you'll upset him. He doesn't need that."

She frowned. "I *wouldn't* bully him."

"Yeah, well, I've seen the way you question people."

"Oh, is that so? And you're so different?"

"I know how to shift gears better than you. You go at people with one speed—hard, all the time."

She pursed her lips into a rigid line. When she spoke, her voice cut into me like barbed wire. "I'm so glad you're so aware of all of my flaws. You should write a book about them. You certainly seem to have the time. You know, you have been off the force for over five years. I might have learned a thing or two. It's just possible, you know."

"Sure, and pigs could fly."

"Jesus, what is it with you?"

We glared at each other across the desk. So much for the flicker of attraction. I was aware that my fists were clenched. Down the hall, the chanting started up again, a low murmur this time, but I knew the volume would only grow. Of course that would be the case. The sun rose in the east, set in the west, and the Higher Plane Church of Spiritual Transcendence existed for the sole purpose of annoying me. Where *was* all this hostility coming from? I looked at Tim. He offered a weak smile, then studied his shoes.

"Maybe I just don't want to put my dad through the meat grinder," I said.

"You know," Alesha said, "I don't need your permission to talk to him."

"Yes, that's true."

"I could do it without you."

"Yes, you could."

"You're saying the word *yes,* but I'm hearing the word *no.*"

"Perceptive," I said.

"Man, you really did take the asshole pill this morning, didn't you?"

"Are we done?"

"You're really not going to help me?"

"Nope."

Alesha leaned back, shaking her head at me, then gave Tim a *What can you do?* sort of look. He swallowed as if trying to force down a mouthful of rotten eggs. Must have been tough for him, seeing his parents argue like this.

With a sigh, Alesha brushed off her pants and stood. She regarded me as if I were one of those new age crystals she liked so much, the ones she told me she bought for contemplating the mysteries of the universe. Then she turned her gaze to the room, scanning its contents, settling on what must have appeared to her to be a blank canvas hanging above my computer.

"You know," she said, "around the force, nobody really gets what you're doing here."

"Good to hear," I said.

"You're something of a ... I don't know, a joke."

"Glad I amuse people."

"Not everybody. Some people actually worry about you."

In my present mood, I didn't know what to say to this, so I said nothing. She shrugged, walked to the door, and opened it. Like a puppy, Tim followed and nearly banged into her when she stopped in the doorway, speaking over her shoulder.

"When you change your mind," she said, "give me a call."

"I'm not changing my mind."

"Oh, yes, you will. Because I know your flaws, too, Myron."

"Oh yeah?"

"Yeah," she said. "If somebody really needs help, you can never say no."

Before I could offer a response, she left.

AFTER SHE'D GONE, I jumped on the computer. It was like she'd said. CNN, NBC, Yahoo—the death of Jasmine Walker, and more significantly, the goodbye message scrawled on her dorm-room mirror, was already all over the news.

If I listened intently, straining to hear above the chanting down the hall that had once again reached a dull roar, I could almost hear the clicking of hundreds of keyboards all over the country as reporters booked their flights to Portland. By the end of the week, it was going to be a media madhouse. Why would I want to get mixed up with all that nonsense? And yet an hour later, I was still on the Internet, having followed some of the links in those news articles to older articles about the case and books on the subject, ending up on Wikipedia.com, devouring everything they had before following even more links.

There were half a dozen true-crime books on the subject. I bought all of them. Only one was available as an e-book, another was still in print as a paperback, and the other four I purchased from an out-of-print website. There were hundreds of amateur web pages about the Goodbye Killer. Most hadn't been updated in a long time, but one was particularly disturbing: The Goodbye Killer Will Return Fan Club. It wasn't just current, but it even had links to most of the news articles about Jasmine Walker I'd just read. There was a very active forum.

I found lots more: a Facebook fan page, YouTube videos, three fake Twitter accounts, and a merchandise site that would sell you a T-shirt with the goodbye message on it replaced with your own name. *Goodbye, Myron. I will take you to a better place.* I knew there was a whole subculture that revered serial killers, but I'd never immersed myself in it until now. I read about women who wrote to serial killers in prison and eventually married them. I read about Ted Bundy, Charles Manson, and Jeffrey Dahmer. I even stumbled across a twenty-page academic paper on the difference between the terrorist and serial-killer mind-sets. I wondered if those who flew the airplanes into the World Trade Center were whittling away eternity as ghosts in Alcatraz.

After a few hours, my empty stomach couldn't be ignored, so I hopped downstairs. The sun still shone brightly, and the crowds were even thicker than before. A couple of nuns saw me and cut a wide swath to the other side of the street. Must have been ghosts. My fame had been growing, of course, and many ghosts were truly terrified of me. I also had my own fans, though I don't think they were capable of creating websites, and none had written to me proposing marriage.

My lime green Prius was parked just around the corner, in front of an old Lutheran church with a mossy stone facade. Pink petals from the nearby cherry-blossom trees, now in bloom, dotted the hood. The way the sun glared on the glass, it took me a moment before I saw somebody in my passenger seat, a young woman dressed in a denim jacket and a baseball cap, her blond hair pulled out the back. My patience for this sort of nonsense was always minimal, but today it was precisely zero.

I used the remote to unlock the car, then jerked the passenger door open.

"Get out," I said.

If I had been in a slightly more charitable state of mind, I might have been at least a little dazzled by the young woman who leaned out to look at me. *Girl.* She was definitely more girl than woman—twenty-two, tops, with a face that could have passed for sixteen if not for the purple eye shadow, the ruby lipstick, and the gold piercing over her left eyebrow. Of course, based on the sixteen-year-olds I'd seen lately, that was pretty much normal attire. This one wore acid-washed jeans and an acid-washed denim jacket over a black Michael Jackson *Thriller* T-shirt, something I might have seen back in the eighties when I was a kid. I wondered how long she'd been dead. She was an itty-bitty thing, but if her face was more sixteen, her body definitely wasn't. There were a heck of a lot of curves packed into a tiny frame.

She was chewing gum—smacking it, more like, and obviously had been doing it in the car a while, because I got a good whiff of strawberry when I opened the door. I saw a bit of a dragon tattoo on her forearm, peeking out of the sleeve of her jacket.

"Heya there, Myron," she said, as if we'd been friends for years. The pink wad of gum I glimpsed in her mouth was almost as big as her tongue, and she moved it from side to side when she spoke. "Nice car. Kind of surprised a private eye would dive a hybrid, but hey, I'm all for breaking stereotypes."

"I told you to get out," I said.

"Yeah, you did. Why don't you get in instead?"

"Who the—wait, forget it. I don't care. Just get out."

"Hey, chill. Don't you want to know who I am?"

"No. Get out."

"Aww, don't be that way," she said. "Name's Jak. Jacqueline Worthe, actually, but everybody just calls me Jak—that's Jak with a *k* and no *c*, in case you were wondering. Come on, just five minutes to hear my pitch. We can talk on the way to your dad's. You get tired of me, you can just drop me off on the side of the road."

"I'm not going to see my dad," I said.

"Sure you were. Where else would you go? That's why I'm waiting for you."

Most ghosts didn't like to be touched by the living—they usually found the experience extremely unnerving, which was why they walked around us rather than through us—and what little patience I had for Jak's antics was already gone. I put my hand on her leg.

Fully expecting her to yelp and jump out of the car, I was surprised when instead my hand stopped at the denim pants.

"Oh," I said

She smiled impishly. "You always this forward with people?"

"You're real," I said.

"LOL," she said, spelling out the letters. "What, you thought I was a dream?"

"I just assumed …" I began, then realized, because I was dealing with a flesh-and-blood human here, that I was about to spill my secret to a total stranger. "Wait a minute. The car was locked. How did you get in?"

That impish smile of hers broadened. "Let's just say I have many talents, not all of them legal."

"But the car was locked with you in it."

"Sure. I locked it. You see all the nuts in this neighborhood? A hot woman like me sitting alone? You can never be too safe."

"Your clothes. They're kind of … an older style."

"Yeah, I like to go a little retro. You getting in, or are you going to cop a feel of my boobs next?"

I stammered some kind of response, then shook my head and slammed the door. Walking to the other side, I took the opportunity to gather myself a bit, since she'd managed to fluster me. When I climbed into the driver's seat, I found that she'd pulled out a black smartphone as big as her hand and was tapping away on it. Granted, she had fairly small hands, but the phone was still enormous. My parents' first television was probably smaller.

"Twitter's going nuts with this thing," she said. "It's not trending yet, but I bet it will be in another hour."

"Who the *hell* are you?"

Her fingers flew across the little keyboard, typing twice as fast as I could have typed on a full-size keyboard, and I wasn't a half-bad typist. "You on Twitter?" she said. "Give me your handle and I'll follow you."

"I asked you a question," I said.

"I've got over 100,000 followers, but only a few hundred I follow myself. So it's not like I just auto-follow every—"

"Answer me!"

"Huh?"

"You asked for five minutes," I said. "I'll give you thirty seconds. Tell me exactly who you are, or I'm going to call the cops."

She raised her eyebrows. With the deftness of a circus knife thrower, she twirled the phone into a side pocket of the denim jacket, then swiveled so she faced me. She tucked her legs up—she was small enough that she could get away with this—and wrapped her arms around them, resting her chin on her knees. She stopped chewing her gum and just stared at me.

Her eyes were a shade of green that made me think of mint tea. Before, I'd been irritated when she wasn't giving me her full attention, but now that I had it, it was a bit unnerving. She wasn't just pretty. She was drop-dead gorgeous, not like a movie star, a supermodel, or some other celebrity-infused, Photoshopped fantasy, but in the way that only a teenager's first crush can be so beautiful. The touch of rebelliousness, the eyebrow stud, the tattoo, all the attitude—it only added to her allure. *Dear God, she's a knockout.* The thought just leapt into my brain, and I knew right then this girl had some kind of hold over me. My mouth felt dry and my neck burned.

I swallowed, and in the quiet of the car, it was comically loud. She took note of it and smiled. Her teeth were perfectly white and straight, which meant braces and crowns, which also meant that at some point in her life, either now or growing up, she'd had money. She was at least ten years younger than me, and she didn't seem like my type at all. She chewed her gum a few times, then swallowed it.

"Um," I said, "you just swallowed that gum."

"Yeah, I like to swallow." She winked at me.

"Ah…"

"Hey! Lighten up. Jeez, most guys talk with all kinds of sexual innuendo, but a girl makes one little crack and they turn as red as their little toy fire trucks. You're not some kind of prude, are you? That would make this totally lame."

"I'm not—"

"You're an eye guy," she said.

"What?"

She studied my face, as if reading something there. "Some guys like boobs. Some guys like legs. You like eyes. I can tell. You keep coming back to them, really looking at them. Don't worry, it's a nice quality. In my experience, eye guys are always really good lovers."

"Oh."

She giggled, and it was such a girlish giggle, such a contrast to her cocky demeanor, that it was a bit jarring. "Okay," she said, "I'm coming on a little strong, aren't I? Really, I'm not hitting on you here. I know it seems that way. I mean, if it happens, it happens, because you're pretty damn hot yourself and all, but it's not why I'm here. I'm here because of the blog."

"The blog?"

"Yeah. You haven't heard of me, huh? I guess that's not a big surprise. Your generation isn't quite as wired as mine."

"My generation! I'm not *that* much older than you."

"Sure," she said, "whatever you want to tell yourself. I don't see age anyway. I mean, you know how some people say they don't see color? Which is total bullshit, of course, because how can you not see color, but I still kind of get it, because I don't see age. You could be fifty and I'd still think you'd be hot. You're not fifty, are you?"

"No!"

"Good. Just because, well, *I* don't care, but it's a bit better when people at restaurants don't think I'm a guy's daughter. If you were fifty, though, you'd be a damn good-looking fifty, I tell you that. I'd wonder if you had some work done or something."

The temperature in the Prius must have been climbing, because I felt sweat forming on my back, underneath my leather jacket. "The blog," I reminded her.

"Right," she said, with another one of those girlish giggles, "the blog! Sorry, I'm not usually so scatterbrained. You obviously got in my head a little there. Kudos to you. Most guys can't do that. Maybe it's your eyes, huh? They're pretty blue. Anyway … yeah, the blog. I've got a website called UndercoverGirl. It's about all the hidden worlds people don't see."

"Hidden worlds?" I said, my interest piqued. "Like what?"

"Oh, you know, all the subcultures that are all around us, some of it online, some of it in meat space. D&D groupies, Second Life addicts, poetry slams, AA meetings, dog shows—"

"Dog shows!"

"Sure. Anything that people could immerse themselves in and disappear. I just kind of drifted from world to world, you know? I was kind of like an undercover cop, disappearing into each one, dressing the part when I had to, and it turned out I had a knack for really making readers feel like they were *there*. At least, that's what my PayPal account told me, because once I put that on there, the donations really started coming in. I'm almost embarrassed by how much money I make now."

"Really."

"It's a lot."

"I'm still not getting why—"

"Well over six figures. Like more than double."

"I see."

"Almost triple, really. That's if you add in the Google ads, the T-shirt sales, the e-books—it really does add up. Lots of income streams. I've got so much money, my accountant keeps giving me brochures on how to invest. He works for A&M. Heard of them? Huge CPA firm in town. Only people with big bucks use them. I never even went to college! Well, except for that series I wrote about sorority life for a few weeks. You wouldn't believe how much sex some of those girls have. You think boys are the bad ones? Uh-uh. Not all of them, of course, but there are some who—"

"I'm still not understanding why, exactly, you're taking an interest in the Goodbye Killer."

"Honestly?" she said. "I don't know yet exactly. I just get these hunches. Normally, I don't go anywhere near the really big news stories. Why compete for eyeballs, right? But when I saw some tweets about it this morning, I just knew I had to put myself in the middle of this one. I might write about serial killers, or serial-killer groupies, or maybe I'll write about cops. I don't know. I'm also thinking it would be fun to walk a mile in the shoes of a really cute investigator." She winked at me.

"Hmm. You know, I'm kind of a private person."

"Aw," she said, and waved her hand dismissively. "Privacy is way overrated, trust me. Nobody really wants to be private. People want to be *understood*."

"Is that so?"

She nodded.

"Well," I said, "let's see if you understand me, then. I find what you do very interesting, but I'm not going to be part of it."

"But you already are," she said.

"No, I'm not."

"Yes. You *are*. I've already blogged about it this morning, about going to see if I could meet you."

"You *what?*"

"And I tweeted some things just a minute ago, when you walked around the car."

"I don't believe this."

"Don't worry. If we eventually have sex or something, I don't put any of that online. I do have *some* fade-to-black moments. My regular readers are always pushing me to write more about my kinky side—and believe me, I have a *big* kinky side—but I just give them hints. Honestly, I think that makes them want to read even more, because their imaginations—"

"Look," I said, "I don't want to be part of this. Got that? Any of it. If you make me your story, you're going to be very disappointed. The city might go nuts because of all of this, but my life is going to be very boring."

"Oh, I'll make sure it's not boring." She grinned.

I sighed. "Jak—"

"I really like you saying my name."

"Jak, please get out of my car."

"Aww …"

"I'm going to lunch."

"Okay, I'll come. And I'll buy!"

"No."

"You're turning down a free lunch? Even if I toss in … dessert?"

I tapped my hands on the steering wheel, waiting. She waited back, searching my face with those mint-colored eyes. A couple of old guys in tuxedos and bowler hats walked past on the sidewalk across the street, but I didn't look. Jak was paying such close attention to me that if I even glanced that way, she would look, too, then wonder what exactly I had seen. I had to be careful with this one, or she would broadcast my secret world far and wide.

The tension between us, sexual and otherwise, didn't just smolder. It crackled. I was caught between two competing impulses, both equally powerful. On the one hand, I wanted to throw her out of the Prius. On the other, I wanted to rip off her clothes and make wild and passionate love to her. I didn't care if people saw. I needed her. *Now.* That animal impulse was so powerful, so unlike anything I'd felt before, that it scared me. I was aware of my beating heart, the sweat sticking to my eyelids, the dryness of my throat. I'd been in love with women. This wasn't that. This was lust, but it was a gripping, powerful, all-consuming kind of lust, a tsunami of desire that would swamp every other part of me if I even flirted with giving in to it.

This time it was Jak who swallowed in a comically loud way. I found myself moving from her eyes to her lips, studying them with intense scrutiny, all the little lines and creases in that ruby lipstick, watching them part.

"You know—" she began.

"Please go," I said.

"Maybe we should just—"

"*Please.*"

I faced forward and gripped the steering wheel, doing my best to avoid the temptation. Finally, she sighed.

"I'm going to write about this, Myron," she said, and this time her tone was all business, the Portland hipster girl gone. "This is what I do. If you work with me, I'll let you have some say in things that involve you. Trust me, that's something I never do. But I'm going to write about it either way. I think it would be better for you—better for both of us—if you didn't fight me on it."

I looked at her. She didn't say it like a threat. She said it like it was a fact. Even her physical demeanor had changed, the casual cockiness replaced by a dead-eye seriousness. That's when I realized just what a chameleon this girl was. *Woman.* I had to revise my estimation of her. This was a woman, not a girl, despite her youthful appearance. There were layers to her. She wore the casual, carefree cockiness like just another outfit, putting everyone at ease, making people think she was just some kid playing around with a laptop and a smartphone, when in fact there was a ruthless businessperson under that facade.

"I need to go," I said.

She shrugged and got out of the car, shutting the door with a bit too much force. She started to walk away, mercifully taking all that coiled sexual energy with her, then turned back suddenly. With a grin worthy of the Cheshire cat, she leaned forward and then, with delib-erate slowness, puckered her lips and planted them on the passenger-side window. When she pulled back, I could still see the imprint her lips had left on the glass.

Then, with another grin, she tapped the window where she'd kissed it and walked away, giving me just enough sway of her hips to set my mind on fire.

Chapter 3

AFTER SWINGING through Burger King, I unwrapped my chicken sandwich and devoured it while heading over the Morrison Bridge. Maybe it had something to do with trying to feed a different kind of hunger, but I couldn't eat fast enough. By the time I headed west on Highway 26, the sandwich was gone, and so were the fries. Jak Worthe was right about one thing. I was going to see Dad. There was no sense in lying to myself about it, even if I was still completely convinced that I was going to have nothing to do with the Goodbye Killer case. Not in a million years.

The sun, in all its glory, glared brightly on the back windows and trunks of the cars ahead of me. Traffic was heavy, mostly heading the same direction I was—beach runners, probably, making a Saturday jaunt to Seaside or Cannon Beach. I cracked the windows open, partly to clear the greasy smell, but also to clear the sexual tension that permeated the inside of the Prius. Was that her strawberry gum I still detected? I kept flashing back to those green eyes. Each time I did, the same unquenchable desire took hold of me.

Easy, Myron. That woman is trouble.

Picking up speed on the highway, the gasoline engine took over from the electric one—the roar a reminder of just how silent my car was at low speeds. I was glad for the sound. That, along with the wail of the wind in the open windows, was a welcome distraction from my twisted pretzel of emotions. I didn't want to think about Jak. I didn't want to think about Alesha. I especially didn't want to think about Billie, who—almost six years since I'd been able to touch her and six months since I'd heard her voice—still haunted both my dreams and my waking thoughts. In the morning, I still reached for her side of the bed and felt the terrible clench of disappointment when she wasn't there. In the evening, when I returned to my house in Sellwood, I still sometimes called out, "I'm home!" And only when I was met by lonely silence did I remember that she was no longer part of my life.

Yet she was. They all were.

When I arrived at the Forest Grove exit, I was a feeling a bit better. A few turns, a few stoplights, and I'd reached the Mistwood Senior Living Center, a series of tan brick buildings a block off Pacific Avenue. Evenly spaced dogwood trees, expansive lawns laced with pristine sidewalks, and dozens of duplexes surrounded the larger central building. Half the time, I expected to find kids playing volleyball on the lawn, the place had such a college-campus feel.

I parked on the street, in the shadows of the white-blooming dogwood trees. A young man riding a Wright brothers–style bicycle with an enormous front wheel, his brown pants rolled up and his white socks reaching his knees, pedaled past me. When I watched him, our gazes locking, he swerved violently and nearly crashed into the Prius. An old woman using a walker to inch along the sidewalk, however, barely took notice of me, and certainly didn't notice the man on the bicycle. I knew her. Her name was Bethany Calhoun, and she lived two doors down from Dad.

On my way to the main building, walking on concrete so new it shone like fallen snow, I came upon a familiar old man sitting on a wooden bench next to the lion fountain. He was dressed, as always, in a black tuxedo and red bow tie, his walnut cane with the brass handle leaning against the wrought-iron side of the bench. He rested his wrinkled hands in his lap and smiled down at his shoes—black wingtips polished to such a shine that the sun reflecting on them was nearly as bright as the real thing.

Usually when his attention was elsewhere, I would just walk past, but his smile caught my eye. I couldn't remember him ever smiling. Two Hispanic guys in overalls were trimming the boxwood hedge on the other side of the lawn, too far away to hear me but close enough that they might think it odd if I stood there talking to what appeared to be an empty bench, so I took a seat. I could spare a few minutes. Heck, I could spare the whole afternoon. It wasn't like I had a case.

"Hello, Bill," I said. "You seem in a good mood."

He jumped a little, looking at me, his face clouding for just a second before his eyes softened and the smile returned. That smile, even with all those yellowed and gold-capped teeth, took a few decades off his face. I was just glad he wasn't scared of me. It might have been the senility, but I'd take it.

"Well, hello, sonny," he said. "You going to the ball tonight?"

"Not this time, I'm afraid."

"Well, that's too bad. Supposed to be a good one. Can you dance the Charleston?"

"Can't dance, period, Bill. Wasn't blessed with the genes."

His frosty white eyebrows furrowed. "What do jeans have to do with anything?"

"Oh. Nothing, I guess."

"We're not talking pants! We're talking *dancing!* Agnes can dance the Charleston like nobody's business. She should be along shortly. Just went to visit with some old friends. We're going together. Never miss the ball. Not once."

I nodded and said nothing. What could I say? He'd been dead for over ten years, and Agnes, I knew, had died two years after him—disappearing on Bill shortly thereafter. Maybe it was his senility, or maybe, like many married folks who saw an eternity staring them in the face after they died, she realized she couldn't quite imagine spending that much time with her dearly departed husband. If he'd gone from hoping Agnes would return to actually imagining she had, I couldn't blame him, even if I found the whole affair depressing. How far away was I from such a total mental collapse? I reached to pat Bill on the shoulder, then of course realized I'd only find empty air.

Inside the main building, I checked in at the reception desk, then steeled myself for the inevitable crowd. The place was always packed with people—most of them dead, of course. Today was no exception. The main living area, with plush furniture, soft green carpet, and walls the color of caramel, was filled with people.

The floor-to-ceiling windows, looking out on a pond ringed with cherry-blossom trees in bloom, filled the area with a gauzy pink glow. Two old codgers dressed in matching red suspenders played chess while a half-dozen other old men watched. Another crowd, most-ly old women draped in shawls, played pinochle. At another table, three women assembled a puzzle of the Eiffel Tower while still more watched. Reading books, flipping through magazines, chatting in hushed tones—the people were everywhere, filling every couch and chair, standing in every corner, at least a hundred, maybe more. Most were certainly ghosts.

I smelled mothballs and peppermint and bourbon and freshly baked cookies and the pine air freshener I knew the staff used, at least one odor I knew was real, an assault on my senses that always took a few seconds to absorb. A few people looked younger than the rest, some even in their twenties, but most were of the old and wrinkled va-riety. Knowing better than to linger with this crowd, I made a beeline for Dad's room, but not fast enough. A burly old black man in dirty overalls and a sun-bleached Shell baseball cap, his face pockmarked and sporting white tufts of hair in odd places, stepped into my path.

"Um, howdy, Mr. Vale," he said, his accent imbued with echoes of the Deep South. As rich as his voice was, though, he spoke in a halt-ing, strained manner, as if he wanted to be anywhere but talking to me. "I been—I been hoping you might stop by to see your papa. I hear you might be able to help me. If—If you're obliged, that is."

Heads turned to look at us. I kept walking, conscious of the Asian girl at the desk behind me, knowing how strange it would look if I stopped to chat with an invisible person. Or was he invisible? With a slight wave of my hand, I brushed his arm—and *through it.*

I'd barely grazed him, but any kind of hand check was enough to elicit a slight electric jolt—for both him and me. The difference for me was that even if I still may not have been completely used to the jolt, I at least expected it. The old black guy, however, jumped back as if I'd poked him with a cattle prod.

"Hey now!" he exclaimed.

"Excuse me," I mumbled, and veered around him. I knew to the living people in the room, my walk would come off as a drunken stagger, but I couldn't help it. It was one thing to touch a ghost, quite a bit more unsettling for me to do the full pass-through.

He rubbed his arm and glared. "I just want you to say a few things to the missus for me! Wouldn't take but a minute!"

Not answering, I beat a hasty retreat down the hall to the private rooms. I felt his rage burning into the back of my neck, and I felt bad for turning him down, but I'd learned from my mistake a few months earlier. At Mom's urging, I'd agreed to act as a sort of celestial translator for a friend of hers on the second floor, a garrulous Jewish woman who desperately wanted to comfort her depressed husband. Before I'd even left the building, I'd been practically mobbed with similar requests—this despite the fact that the encounter with the Jewish woman's husband had been a complete disaster. Not only did he not believe me, no matter how much private detail I gave him fed to me by his wife, but he actually tried to strangle me. If he'd been just a little bit stronger—as strong, maybe, as the burly black guy I'd just passed—he probably would have succeeded.

No, I wasn't doing that again.

Before I even reached Dad's room, I heard one of those bombastic financial gurus shouting "Buy! Buy! Buy!" Stepping inside, I found Dad where I always found him, hunkered in his worn leather La-Z-Boy, his attention riveted on the television mounted in the corner. Just for a moment—a second or two that always made my breath catch in my throat—he looked at me. It was not much more than a glance, but it *was* more, so much more, his eyes fixing on my face, seeing me, recognizing me, *knowing* me—and then it was gone. Whatever part of him that knew me as his son disappeared into the fog.

When he turned to the screen again, I felt the terrible sadness that was the chief reason I didn't visit more often.

"Hi, Dad," I said, trying to sound cheerful.

He didn't answer. Physically, he was a pale shadow of his former self, that big cop with the lumberjack build, and he looked so much older than my last visit, so much more sunken and wrinkled. He was still tall and lanky, the recliner barely containing him, but the powder blue V-neck sweater over the crisp white dress shirt, which would have once strained against his broad chest and thick arms, collapsed on his body.

Before the disease hit, people often assumed he was ten years younger than his actual age, but now the opposite might be true. What was left of his hair, a fringe around his scalp, was now silver where it had been brown. His complexion, which had always been a bit rough, had at least sported a healthy tan; now it was a chalky, uneven white, as if a blind man had tried to apply makeup to his face. The bags under his eyes were like dry arroyos that hadn't seen water in eons. Someone meeting him for the first time might have thought he was in his nineties instead of his seventies.

The financial guru jumped up and down, honking a red horn. I watched the screen with Dad, hoping it might afford us some connection. No such luck. His place was as clean and spartan as a hotel room—the twin bed neatly made, the top of the dresser bare, the bathroom counter, or what I could see through the open door, unblemished by even a toothbrush. He had a couple of framed photographs of Multnomah Falls, one of Dad's favorite places to hike, but that was the only sign of personal decoration. In the beginning, we'd had lots more—pictures of me and Mom, some of his medals from his time in Vietnam, other mementos—but over time we'd had to remove them.

In the beginning, these nostalgic reminders of his life comforted him. Later, they agitated him. Still later, they sent him spiraling into a deep and lasting depression.

"Looks like stocks are up today," I said.

He didn't answer.

"Mind if I turn it down?" I asked. "Just for a minute. Love to chat."

No matter how distant he seemed, I always waited long enough for him to respond, even if he didn't. Smiling at him, I turned the television down to a low murmur, but he went on looking at the screen as if nothing had changed. I wondered how long it had been since we'd had anything resembling a real talk. Weeks? Months? I couldn't remember, and that scared me.

He was fading away before my eyes. For a few years, the fade had been slow, the day-to-day loss so gradual that it was hard to notice, but now it was accelerating. It was impossible to lie to myself about it any more. How much longer before his mind gave up on his body, too, I didn't know, but it couldn't be long.

"Cherry blossoms are in bloom," I said. I almost asked him where Mom was, but of course that would have been silly, since he couldn't see her. "You hear the Blazers are doing well? Seems like they've been bad forever. Everybody says they might go deep into the playoffs this year. You remember when …"

I trailed off, because I remembered the last time I had asked him about our outings to Blazer games. It had not gone well.

"Business is good," I said, and then, because I had a hard time lying to my father even in his present condition, I had to correct myself. "Well, slow, I guess, but that's okay. Gives me time to brush up on my private-eye skills, you know, take a few online classes from University of Phoenix." I chuckled. He didn't, his face as fixed as the pictures on the walls. "Hey, you want to look at the fountain? Be glad to go on a little walk with you."

It was like talking to a mannequin. The doctor had told me it was crucial for me to keep up the pretense of having a normal conversation, as much for me as for him, but it was getting to be a strain. I was struggling for something else to talk about when Mom spoke to me from the other side of the door.

"Vinnie?" she said. "Vinnie, is that you in there I hear? Open this door."

The sound of her voice prompted me to reflexively grab the back of Dad's chair. Her calling me Vinnie, a shortened form of my middle name, Vincent, was her lifelong protest against my dad, who'd insisted on naming me Myron after an Army buddy of his—one of the few arguments with her he'd won, as far as I knew. For some reason known only to her, she'd always wanted a son named Vinnie. I'd long since given up convincing her that I preferred Myron, but I still liked to make my displeasure known from time to time.

"Nobody in here by that name," I said.

"Vinnie," she admonished me. "*Vincent*. Please. It's cold out here. Let me in."

"It's no colder out there than it is in here."

"Open this door right now, young man!"

Taking my time about it, I got around to opening the door. With a single distasteful glance in my direction, she swooped into the room, her long black shawl pluming on either side of her like a raven's wings. She was small and compact, her face full of hard edges and distinct lines, everything about her chiseled and distinct. She had a penchant for monochrome, and today was no exception. Underneath the black shawl, she wore a long gray dress buttoned to the nape of her neck, black heels that still left her a head shorter than me, and white pearls that were still darker than her skin. Her black hair was shiny as polished obsidian, not a hint of gray or white, which was no surprise, since she'd been dying it since I was ten. Even her searing eyes appeared black. It was only when she stood in bright sunlight, which she seldom did, that you could see that her irises were actually a deep chocolate brown.

"Why didn't you just walk through it?" I asked her.

She glided to Dad, tipped her head from side to side as if inspecting him, made a few clucking sounds of disapproval, then perched behind the chair.

"Walk through *what?*" she said finally.

"The door, Mom."

"What? Don't be ridiculous. What kind of silly thing is that to say?"

"You're a ghost, Mom. You can walk through anything."

"Don't be crude! I told you not to use that word with me."

There was no use treading down this path again, so I let it drop. Dad went on staring at the TV. The financial guru was wearing a green foam hat shaped like a dollar sign and clapping his hands. I always felt a little bad talking to Mom in front of Dad, since he couldn't see her, but then most of the time he didn't seem to be able to see anyone. On top of that, ignoring Mom even for a moment took her—and me—to heights of hysteria I tried to avoid. Billie used to say that when I argued with Mom, she could see two words floating behind my eyeballs: *justifiable asphyxiation.*

"Where were you?" I asked.

"None of your business," she said.

"It's just—I don't remember the last time I showed up and you weren't in here."

"I was playing bridge with a few friends upstairs. Am I not allowed to have any fun at all?"

"I'm just surprised, that's all," I said, then couldn't stop myself from deploying her own favorite weapon against her: the sharp knife of guilt. Her manner was so strangely evasive that it practically invited it. "It's just not like you to leave Dad alone. What if something would have happened to him?"

"Really!"

"He could have fallen."

She stared at me with those piercing black eyes. If I strained, I could just make out a bit of rouge creeping into the chalky white skin stretched over those sharp cheekbones. "Well!" she sputtered, fingering the pearls on her neck. "Well! Isn't this just fine! My own son, casting judgment against his mother! Is that why you showed up today? I thought it might just be to visit, but then you never visit, do you?"

"I was here last weekend," I said.

"You were not. It's been at least a month. Maybe two."

"I came on Sunday. Don't you remember? I joined you and Dad in chapel."

"I don't remember. It's hard to remember anything in this place."

Here it comes, I thought. The begging, the pleading, the repeated requests to take her away from this awful prison. Ever since I'd moved Dad into the Mistwood a few years ago, she'd been desperately trying to get me to change my mind and have them move in with me. She was both relentless and impervious to reason on the matter.

Yet instead of tacking in that direction, she surprised me.

"We used to play bridge," she said, so softly that at first I thought it was part of the murmur coming from the television. "Do you re-member?"

I did remember, but I was surprised she did. It hadn't lasted long, a few months when I was eight or nine years old, and it had been during the time when Dad was out late drinking a lot. She'd played bridge forever, usually with her Tuesday group, but she'd never asked me to play until she surprised me one night by asking me if I wanted to learn. I'd said yes before I even knew what bridge was; I'd always assumed it was a construction game, like Legos or Tinkertoys. Even when I'd realized it was a card game, I'd been so delighted that she'd wanted to spend time with me that I didn't care. Even when she wasn't the most patient teacher in the world, and even when she admon-ished me for the slightest mistake, I went on looking forward to our games—and I was sad, a few months later, when she stopped asking if I wanted to play.

"Yes," I said.

"Those were good times."

"It was just … one summer."

"Still. Still. We had fun, didn't we? I thought we did."

"Sure."

"Maybe—maybe we could play again."

It would have been easy to hurt her, to cut her down to size, to do what she so often did to me, but her unexpected vulnerability was disarming, even if I still suspected she was trying to manipulate me somehow. I was trying to imagine how we might play bridge, since she could no longer hold the cards, when there was a strange, low hum below us. I thought it might have been a pipe beneath the floor. It was such an odd sound, almost mechanical, that it didn't occur to me that it could come from Dad until I looked down at him. Not only was he producing the sound—a rhythmic, moaning *uhhhhh, uhhhh*—but he had his arms folded so tightly against his chest that he might as well have been wearing a straitjacket. His face, already pale, had gone ash white. His eyes bulged and twitched.

I looked at the television. A square-jawed newscaster in a dark suit was talking underneath a *Breaking News* banner—and there, next to him, was a fuzzy photo of a bathroom mirror taken at an angle with a cell phone, only the person's hand and a bit of pink sweatshirt visible in the reflection. A message was scrawled in red lipstick on the mirror: *Goodbye, Jasmine. I will take you to a better place.* The photo was replaced by a young black woman with braided hair, her PSU basketball jersey crisp and vibrant.

"What is it? What is it?" Mom cried. "Hank—"

"It's the news!" I said.

Dad's moaning grew into grunting shouts. He pointed at the screen, jabbing at it repeatedly. Mom, never good in a crisis, burst into tears. I lunged for the television and smacked it off, hoping that would stop his antics, but his hysteria actually increased. He kept jabbing at the screen, each punch of his arm rocking him out of his chair.

"Dad, Dad, it's okay—" I tried to soothe him.

"Make him stop!" Mom pleaded. "Oh, it's awful! Make him—"

"Dad—"

"Why is he doing this?" Mom said.

Dad's rhythmic shouting became a full-throated roar. I crouched in front of him, shushing him as I might a baby. It had no effect. In my panic, I grabbed his arms and tried to hold him, knowing this was wrong, that this was something you should never do to someone having a violent episode, but it terrified me to see him acting this way.

Two male orderlies in blue burst into the room, a nurse in gray following right on their heels, all of them descending on Dad like a swarm of bees. The more people who tried to comfort him, the more violent he became, swinging his arms, punching at random, displaying a strength I didn't even know he had anymore. Despite their best efforts, soon he was on the floor, kicking and wailing, thumping his head against the low-nap carpet, teeth bared, his pupils dilated, his whole body trembling and shaking and—

And then it stopped.

As if someone had flicked a switch, he went limp. Even his ragged breathing immediately steadied. The rest of us were the ones gasping for air. The loudest person in the room was Mom, crouched in the corner and crying, but of course neither the orderlies nor the nurse could hear her. Someone asked me what happened, the nurse maybe, but it hardly registered.

I was looking at Dad because he was looking at *me*, directly at me, seeing me in a way he hadn't in years.

"Myron," he said.

It was spoken in a whisper, but there was no mistaking what he'd said. Everybody looked at me—the nurse, the orderlies, and people in the doorway, too. I was conscious of an audience of older people there, at least half a dozen, all of them gaping at us.

He whispered again, but this time I couldn't hear it at all. Weakly, he lifted his hand and beckoned for me to come closer. I did. He beckoned again and I lowered my head, meeting his gaze briefly before bringing my ear to just above his lips. I felt his warm breath on my cheek.

"Myron," he said, so softly I doubted anyone else in the room could hear him, "you have to stop him. You have to stop him before it's too late."

Then, while I was still digesting the meaning of this, my father did something even more unexpected.

His bony fingers curled around my neck, and, in an affectionate, caressing way that had never been his style when I was a boy, he kissed me on the cheek.

AFTER THAT, he was gone again. He gazed at the blank television while the rest of us crouched in front of him, anticipating more mortar fire. It never materialized. Mom, hugging herself and keening softly, watched from within the little bathroom. After some conferring with the medical staff about what triggered the episode (I lied and said I didn't know), everybody dispersed, including our audience in the hall. I waited a while longer, talking soothingly to Dad, making sure he was okay, then turned my attention to Mom. It took a while to talk her down from the ledge, but by the time I left, she was back to pleading with me to take her and Dad away from this vile place.

I told them both I would be back soon.

The room had been shrinking, the walls closing in on me. I needed to get out—somewhere else, anywhere else—because I sensed what was coming. I felt the first tremors behind my eyelids when I was still in the hall outside Dad's room. By the time I reached the reception area, the tremors had turned into a pulsating ache in the center of my skull. Nobody bothered me this time. Overcome by both dizziness and nausea, I stopped at the lion fountain, bracing myself with a hand on the stone rim. The splashing water billowed wet air on my face. Soon the worst of the symptoms passed. The throbbing was still there, of course, and would be for hours, the smallest trigger ready to set it off, but I was fine for now.

Or was I? When I blinked away the stickiness in my eyes, I saw old Bill still sitting alone on the bench, all dressed up in his tuxedo for a ball that was always on the verge of happening, waiting for a dance partner who would always stand him up. All at once, I saw myself in Bill, flashing forward forty or fifty years, me sitting on that bench, my mind gone, hopelessly chasing the shadows of the past in search of … what? What was I after? Was I still waiting for my wife to return? Was I still hoping for a miraculous cure for my ghostly affliction? Was

I still desperately trying to prove myself to my father, but for some reason always shying away in the big moments when my mettle would truly be tested?

Dad had asked for my help. So had Alesha. The priest, as much as he annoyed me, had made it clear that my unique talents could make a difference. It was time to make a decision, a real one. To look at Bill, so full of hope in his obliviousness, I couldn't help but feel hopeless. What was the point of it all, if in the end I was just left alone and confused?

I didn't think I was waiting for a sign, but I probably was. While I watched Bill, an old woman in a green dress approached from the street, her face shadowed by a white bonnet. Her dress, an intricate pattern of sequins and satin, was showy without being gaudy, the color brightening to a vibrant aquamarine when she passed out of the shadow of a dogwood tree and into the sun. It was the kind of dress a woman might wear to a ball, especially one held many decades ago. When she tilted her head back, I saw that she had tried to hide her age, all those wrinkles and moles, under enough makeup to frost a cake. I also saw that she was crying, the tears sliding over that sheen of makeup like beads of water on ice.

Seeing her, Bill broke into a wide grin. I could see it on his rumpled old face, all that joy, all the relief that his years of hoping had finally paid off. Even with his cane, though, he struggled to rise, knees wobbling violently.

He might have gone down if not for the old woman—who was now at his side, her hand extended to him.

Chapter 4

By the time I parked the Prius in a metered spot near the farmers' market on Montgomery, it was going on three o'clock. The sun had already started to duck behind the buildings to the west, and the first hint of urban dusk had settled into the city, a haziness in the shadows, a little more nip to the air as the fleeting warmth of the spring sun retreated. The Broadway Building—the dorm where I was headed—was on the south side of the PSU campus, a walk of five or six blocks, but I'd already caught a glimpse of the media madhouse waiting for me and didn't dare try to park over there.

The campus itself, though, was strangely deserted. I walked alone on Park Blocks, the wide pedestrian boulevard lined with pin oaks. The trees, late in getting their leaves compared with the rest of the city, sported only the tiniest buds, and the canopy of bony branches and gnarled twigs loomed over me like the fraying remains of an abandoned circus tent. All the benches were empty, as were the steps leading into the campus buildings. The fading sun gave everything, at least for the moment, a sepia hue. I caught the scent of barbecued chicken and stir-fry from the food stands I knew were a street over, but here, alone on the boulevard, I could have been in one of those last-man-on-earth movies.

No living people or ghosts? It was odd: the campus, with something always going on even on the weekends, was usually a popular place for both the living and the dead. Even the sound of street traffic was strangely muted.

Halfway across the boulevard, though, I experienced a sudden reminder of *why* the campus was probably deserted.

It came on fast, as if I'd passed into a jet of cold air—an abrupt shift in the mood, an unsettling feeling that raised the hairs on the back of my neck. It was as if something awful was about to happen. Was it just my imagination, or were the shadows a bit deeper, the silence a bit more profound? I stopped and with a quickening pulse searched the trunks of the trees, drawn to the shadows, my mind fleshing out the details of a person wherever even the hint of a person could be seen. There was something there. Some*one* was there. I may not have been able to see him, but he was there. He was watching me.

Then it was gone, the feeling fading so quickly that a second later, I was left wondering if I'd felt anything at all. I heard sounds that may have been there all along—birds chirping, some girls laughing up ahead. A man on a ten-speed rode past, a leather satchel slung over his shoulder, then two boys in denim on skateboards. These were living people, I was sure of it, because I realized now why the ghosts were avoiding campus. *They were afraid of the Ghost Reaper.* They felt what I felt: the uneasiness, the dread of some impending awfulness. But did the living feel it, too, even on some deep subconscious level? Maybe that sense of dread was not quite as intense, but it was enough to repel most of them from campus.

I saw no one hiding behind the oaks, and, minutes later—when I passed through some of the brick buildings and came upon the half-dozen television trucks parked near the ten-story Broadway Building, as well as the gaggle of reporters and looky-loos gathered outside the double glass doors—the unsettling feeling was gone altogether. It baffled me how I could feel such oppressive loneliness just fifty yards away, when here there was nothing but the hum of activity, reporters talking into microphones, television vans puffing out clouds of diesel, the excited murmur of the students lining the sidewalk. Judging by the number of people holding paper coffee cups, it was a good bet that the Starbucks on the first floor was doing well. A couple of cops stationed at the door occasionally barked at a reporter to stand farther back. A KATU helicopter buzzed overhead.

Alesha, scrutinizing her phone, waited for me on a concrete bench near the back of the L-shaped building. I always liked seeing her before she noticed me, because something always changed when she saw me, some strange self-consciousness that robbed her of some of her natural cockiness. Sitting there, elbows on her knees, her eyes as intense as those of a raven that had spotted a field mouse from afar, I could admire her in her natural state—if only for a second.

Seeing me, she shoved her phone into the pocket of her leather jacket.

"Told you so," she said, her smile just as smug as her tone.

"You did," I said. "Where's your partner?"

She wrinkled her nose. "Don't call him that."

"Well, isn't he?"

She smoothed out the wrinkles in her charcoal slacks and got to her feet. Standing toe-to-toe, she wasn't much shorter than me. "Not for long. He's already up there talking to the forensics team. Come on, let's go. I figure I can get you in there for about two minutes, that's it. If the chief finds out I'm doing this, he'll probably suspend me."

"Even for me, one of his old detectives?"

"Especially for you."

She didn't elaborate and I didn't ask. It was no secret that Chief Branson, who'd been a great admirer of my father's when Branson was but a lowly traffic cop and my father was a lead detective, didn't think highly of the son. It hadn't always been that way. When I'd joined the force, he'd done so much to help my career—fast-tracking me to detective—that there were grumbles of favoritism in the locker room. It was only later, after the bullet in my brain made it impossible for me to go on carrying that badge, that his attitude toward me changed. As long as I was on the force, I was the son he never had. Off the force, I was a joke and a disappointment.

It had gotten to the point where I actually considered telling him the truth about my condition. But then, if I couldn't even bring myself to tell Alesha, how could I tell him?

I followed Alesha not to the front of the Broadway Building, where the crowds were gathered, but to a service entrance on the back side. Alesha punched in a combination on an electric keypad and the door buzzed open. We passed through a narrow hall with exposed metal pipes that smelled faintly of laundry detergent, entered a concrete stairwell, walked up to the studio apartments on the next floor, and punched a button for the elevator. A door opened down the hall, and an Asian girl leaned out, saw us, and quickly closed it.

Inside the elevator, Alesha punched the button for the top floor. While the elevator hummed its way up, Alesha narrowed her dark eyes at me.

"You saw your dad, didn't you?" she asked.

"Yep."

"Figured you would."

"Just a social visit."

"Uh-huh. Maybe I could talk to him, too?"

"I told you. I already did."

"Yeah, but—"

"There's nothing to learn there."

She let it drop, though I sensed she didn't quite believe me. The elevator doors opened to a nondescript hall with thin blue carpet and the kind of nonthreatening watercolor paintings common in hotels. I heard activity down the hall—the rumble of cop voices, the shuffle of footsteps, nervous laughter. The flash of a camera flickered on the plain white walls. I started to step out and Alesha blocked me with her arm.

"One question," she said.

"Yes?"

"Why the urgency in seeing the crime scene? I told you there's nothing here."

"Maybe I need to see that nothing for myself."

She shrugged and dropped her arm. As we stepped into the hall, I felt a nervous anticipation take hold, mouth suddenly dry, pulse beating hard enough that I could feel it behind my eyeballs. I knew what I was after. I wasn't looking for clues. I was looking for that *feeling*—a rising dread, a lurking evil, an impending sense of doom, all of it at once and more.

Two uniformed cops stood guard next to an open door in the middle of the hall. The voices and camera flashes came from the room. Halfway between us and the door, a short, stocky man in a plaid blazer and wrinkled tan chinos talked to a tall black woman dressed just as sharply as the man wasn't—in a bright navy blue suit and heels that boosted her an extra few inches when she clearly didn't need the help. Hearing us, the plaid-jacket guy turned abruptly from the woman and stepped into my path. He was bald except for a few sweaty loose threads of hair that were combed to create maximum coverage, and his skin had a strange orange pallor that seemed even more orange because of the amber-tinted glasses hanging low on his nose.

"Mr. Vale!" he exclaimed. He had the kind of fast, squeaky voice that instantly made me want to punch him in the face. He adjusted his glasses nervously. "I'm Eddie Quincy, the true-crime writer. You've probably heard of me, right? *Right?* Love to ask you a few questions, about your father, the case, you know."

The second time he said *right,* his voice cracked like a boy going through puberty. He had a bad overbite and the yellow teeth of someone who usually either had a cup of coffee or a cigarette in his hand. Judging by his awful breath, it was probably both. I looked at Alesha.

"Branson would throw a fit if he knew I was here," I said, "but you let this guy in?"

Alesha eyed me curiously. "What guy?"

I realized then my mistake. Eddie Quincy was a ghost, as was the black woman leaning against the wall behind him—Jasmine's mother, most likely. I should have known that, because the priest had told me that Jasmine's dead mother was the first one to find the body.

"Oh," I said, "yeah, I just meant—never mind."

Embarrassed, I stepped quickly past Eddie, trying to avoid contact, but in the narrow hall and with Alesha at my side, I couldn't quite manage it, and the left side of my body passed right through him. There was the predictable electric jolt and both of us jumped a little— him to the side, with a yelp, me forward, trying not to trip.

"What's gotten into you?" Alesha said.

"Not cool, man," Eddie said, rubbing his side, "not cool at all. No reason to zap me like that, right?"

The cops by the door took all this in as if I were a carnival act. Here I was stopping for no reason, making a comment about someone who wasn't there, then weirdly turning my body as I hurried forward. There would be more talk about me at the station, that was for sure. One of them, who had the kind of square jaw and broad shoulders that made him seem as if he'd been picked out of a Cops "R" Us catalog, blocked me from entering with his well-muscled arm.

"Hey there, pal," he said. "Where you think you're going?"

"To look at the crime scene," I said, leveling my gaze at him. He may have been tall and muscular, but I'd handled plenty of guys taller and more muscular than him. *"Pal,"* I added.

"Let him inside, Marskon," Alesha said. "He's with me. Doing some consulting on the case."

"Unless the chief okays it," the cop said, "that's a negative."

"That's a negative?" I said. "Is that the way you think cops are supposed to talk now?"

"Myron," Alesha warned me.

"I'd like to ask you some questions," Eddie said to me.

I ignored Eddie, but his comment a few seconds earlier gave me an idea. "Hey," I said to Markson, "you don't want my help, that's fine. I'll just tell the press that the son of the lead detective on the Goodbye Killer case, and a former detective himself who was nearly killed in the line of duty, offered his services to the Portland Police Bureau and one Officer Markson said, 'That's a negative.'"

Alesha sighed. I was eagerly awaiting Officer Markson's response when a baby-faced tech with an SLR camera slung around his neck sheepishly squeezed past us—and I used him as a shield to dart into the room. "Hey!" the other cop at the door exclaimed, but Alesha was there between us, telling him she'd take responsibility for me. I didn't care. I'd actually been hoping he'd throw a punch.

Tim O'Dell was in the room, chatting with the lead forensic expert, an older guy named Harvey Rosin who'd tried to make up for his round, rather featureless face with a thick-as-a-rug goatee, but it had a glued-on look that wasn't helping him. He'd been there when I was detective, knew me well, and only nodded when he saw me.

The room wasn't at all what I'd expected. It didn't smell as if someone had died. It just smelled vaguely of Chinese food. Knowing that Jasmine Walker was on PSU's women's basketball team, I expected something of a shrine to basketball—posters of the great players, a miniature hoop attached to the door—or at least some clues of a jock in residence. There was nothing of the sort. There was, instead, a different kind of shrine. There *were* posters, but they were posters put out by Amnesty International, the Peace Corps, and Doctors Without Borders: pictures of starving African children, street protests in Iran, and a man in full combat gear praying on his hands and knees in the crumbled remains of a church. There was no bed, just a cot with some rumpled green wool blankets. The desk was a couple of apple crates joined by what appeared to be a metal RV door. A longboard skateboard plastered with stickers leaned against the wall next to the cot. There was no dresser, just two beat-up suitcases so big they could have doubled as a lifeboat in a pinch if they'd been lashed together.

It wasn't until I saw the goodbye message scrawled in ruby lipstick on the mirror on the wall to the right of the door (*Goodbye, Jasmine. I will take you to a better place.*) that I finally caught a mental whiff of the same feeling I'd experienced minutes earlier. It was very faint, more of a vague uneasiness than anything resembling terror or dread. I didn't know what I'd been hoping to learn, but whatever it was, I was disappointed.

A mousy young woman wearing blue plastic gloves was dusting for prints on the desk and the things on it—a picture of a young white guy who must have been Jasmine's boyfriend, an iPod, a Dell laptop adorned with stickers much like the posters on the wall. Another tech, a guy, was bagging her pillowcase.

"Where was she found?" I asked Alesha.

"Just lying in bed," she said.

"No sign of struggle?"

"None. She just ... didn't wake up."

Hearing us, Harvey piped up with his brusque baritone. "We won't know anything for certain until we do an autopsy. We'll try to get the toxicology report done as quick as possible."

"In case it was poisoning," Tim explained.

"I know what a toxicology report is," I said.

"Oh," Tim said, "I was just—"

"Is her boyfriend still being held for questioning?" I looked at the picture on the desk. He had long dirty-blonde hair that fell over his blue eyes, yin-yang earrings in both ears, and handcrafted wooden beads around his neck. "Or is he around someplace where we can talk to him?"

"He was released," Alesha said. "I think his parents picked him up—from Vancouver, I think."

"That boy didn't do this," a woman said behind me.

I turned and saw the black woman from the hall, Eddie standing just behind her scribbling something in a little spiral notebook. She held her head up as if it took great effort to do so, and even though she was doing everything to keep her reddened eyes fixed on me, I could see that looking at *me* was the last thing she wanted to do.

"What are you staring at?" Alesha asked.

"Huh?" I said. "Oh, nothing. Just thinking."

"Ben is a good boy," the black woman said to me, ignoring Alesha. "I didn't like him so much at first, thought he was just another skate-board loser like all the skateboard losers Jasmine dated in high school. But he's sweet, a real sweet boy. He—he didn't do this, Mr. Vale. He always brought Jasmine flowers. She told him it was a stupid waste of money and he should stop, but he brought them anyway."

"Well?" Alesha said. "Earth to Myron … care to clue me in? What are you thinking about this time?"

"The mother," I said. "What was her name?"

"Um …" Alesha began.

"I'm Loretta," the black woman said.

"Loretta Walker," Tim said.

"Loretta Walker," Eddie piped up, at almost the same time. He was studying his notebook. "Died when Jasmine was twelve. Was a few weeks shy of her thirtieth birthday when she passed. Lived in Seattle. Worked as a receptionist at an insurance—"

"How did she die?" I asked, still looking at Loretta.

"Why's that matter any?" Loretta asked.

"How did you know she died?" Alesha asked.

"I don't know," Eddie said. "I was just asking her that when you showed up."

I looked at Alesha. It was always difficult in situations like this to remember who could hear whom. "Heard it on the radio just before I got here," I lied.

"A domestic-violence situation," Tim said. "Apparently Jasmine's father, who'd left when she was a baby, came back into her life when she was about ten. He beat Loretta a lot. Apparently one time she'd had enough and tried to use a kitchen steak knife to defend herself. He used it on her instead."

Alesha rolled her eyes. "What, did you look all this up on Wikipedia?"

"There was no Wikipedia article," Tim said, clearly missing her sarcasm, "but I did find an interview with Jasmine in the student newspaper. She opened up about some of this."

"Fascinating," Eddie said, scribbling in his notebook.

"I don't know why we are even talking about this," Loretta said. "It don't matter! My little girl, she was a sweet angel. Even after I passed, she just became that much sweeter. I don't know how, 'cause my sister was something awful to her, but she just took it all in and always came back smiling. She just wanted the world to be a better place. She didn't deserve this! Mr. Vale, you got to find the one who done this! You got to!"

Her voice took on an edge of hysteria. This was bad enough—it was never fun to have a ghost screaming at you—but then a bit of blood appeared at the corner of her mouth. I stepped back, but she took this as an invitation to take several steps toward me, leaning in close enough that I saw blood pooling in her eyes, too.

"Find her!" she screamed. "You find her, Mr. Vale! Where is she? She's not nowhere! That's what they're all saying, but she can't go nowhere. She got to be around. I told her we'd be together again. I told her so!"

There was blood on her teeth. There was blood trickling from her ears. There was blood blooming from behind her blue jacket, spreading fast on her white blouse. She started to speak again, but instead of words, out came more blood, enough to darken her chin with a red beard. I heard Eddie say, "Oh boy," and I caught Alesha looking at me with concern, but then I was hustling out of the room, barely managing to say, "Excuse me, gotta go," before I fled out the door. Loretta clawed at my arm with bloodstained fingers, and the jolt was enough to make me hurry that much faster, making a beeline for the elevator. The cops at the door, oblivious to this madness, laughed at me.

I was inside the elevator when Alesha finally caught up with me, hopping in just before the doors closed. As the elevator started down, Loretta's shouting faded above us.

"Whoa," Alesha said. "What was *that* about?"

"Just got to go, that's all."

"Come on. You looked like you'd seen a ghost or something."

Her remark, even if it was just an expression, was so spot-on that I stared at her.

"What?" she said.

"Nothing," I said. "When was that article published?"

"What?"

"The one Tim mentioned. About Jasmine, in the student news-paper."

"I don't know. Why?"

"Can you look it up?"

"Why don't you look it up yourself?"

"You know I don't have a smartphone."

"Yeah, and maybe you should change that."

"Maybe I should."

With an exasperated sigh, she pulled out her iPhone. One of these days I would have to get a smartphone, but the idea of adding such an expense to my already overtaxed bank account wasn't something I could seriously consider right now. When the elevator doors opened, Alesha was studying her phone's tiny screen. Seeing the lobby tiled in faux stones and, beyond it, the glass windows filled with people, I im-mediately realized my mistake. I'd forgotten our back-door entry and punched the button for the lobby. Now they all spotted me. Reporters pointed. Cameras flashed. A television camera was aimed in my di-rection. The uniformed cops manning the door turned and saw me.

"Looks like it was published just this past Thursday," Alesha be-gan. "It's kind of long, but … Oh, crap." She'd finally looked up.

"Well," I said, "now they've got my picture. When they dig up who I am—"

"Cops upstairs would have leaked it anyway, but let's not make it easy for them."

She hit the button for the second floor. With all the faces gaping at me on the other side of the windows, I felt like a goldfish who'd been hauled into kindergarten for show-and-tell. The elevator doors were nearly closed when I happened to look past the crowd, above their heads and beyond, at the brick apartment building across the street.

There was someone standing on the roof.

Not just someone—a man in a dark cloak, watching me.

The hazy, late-afternoon air robbed what I was seeing of some of its detail, its distinctness, and so even as odd as this person was, it still took a moment to register him. When I finally did, I felt the same fear I'd felt earlier on the pedestrian boulevard—but much sharper, like a blade shoved straight into my gut. I stuck my hand between the closing doors.

"What?" Alesha said.

I started to answer, but my throat clenched up on me. What could I say anyway? She obviously couldn't see him. It was hard to tell how tall he was, because he stood alone on the roof and the lower half of his body was hidden behind a brick barrier, but I got the sense that he was *very* tall. He was thin, too, as thin as bones, judging by the way that cloak billowed against his body. His cloak was more like a series of layered gray rags than one solid garment, with faint gray plumes wafting from it. But that wasn't quite right, because the clouds weren't so much smoke as they were bits of himself, disintegrating before my eyes.

He turned away, disappearing from view, the gray fog trailing after him. I was finally able to get myself moving, darting from the elevator toward the glass doors.

"Myron!" Alesha called after me.

The people beyond the glass were no longer staring at me. They were turning the other way, and at first I thought that they'd seen the cloaked figure, too, but they weren't looking up. They were looking behind them, all the cameras turning, the reporters shouting, and then I saw the stern-faced man in the blue police uniform emerge from the crowd. He was distracted, his head down and his hands up, as if to ward off the questions. It wasn't until the cops opened the door for him that he looked up and saw me.

"Chief Branson," I greeted him.

Chapter 5

His gaze fixed solidly on me, his face awash in both confusion and anger, Chief Clive Branson advanced into the Broadway Building. Like a boxer in retreat, I couldn't help but back up a few steps. The doors swung shut, and though the glass somewhat muted the reporters behind him, it didn't stop them from shouting their questions. Branson was shorter than both Alesha and me, shorter even than Eddie Quincy upstairs, but he had such a presence, I always got the sense that I was looking up at him.

His dark blue uniform was so vividly bright, so clean and wrinkle-free, that it looked as though he'd just bought it at the store. The two silver stars on his collar sparkled. His beard was finely trimmed, with perfect symmetry on both sides. Not all men looked good in beards, but Chief Branson, from the few photos I'd seen of him in his early days when he'd dared to go clean-shaven, looked much worse without one; the beard gave his round, oversize face some desperately needed definition. Without it, his head would have looked like a basketball with a dusting of snow on top.

"Detective Stintson," he said, still glaring at me, "just what the hell is going on here?"

"Sir—" Alesha began.

"There better be a damn good reason you ignored my order," he said.

"Sir—"

"Because I remember explicitly stating that no one not authorized by me was to be allowed on the premises."

"Sir," Alesha said, "if you'll just let me explain."

Finally, with the reluctance of a hunter who'd had his aim set on his favorite stag, Branson turned toward Alesha. Ordinarily I would have managed some kind of witty remark, but my mind was still in a fog from spotting the cloaked figure on the roof across the street. The Grim Reaper. Those were the words that kept repeating themselves in my mind. I'd seen the Grim Reaper. The rational part of me—and there was a big part of me that was still rational, despite everything— dismissed this as fairy-tale nonsense. Sure, when people died, they walked the earth as ghosts. I'd accepted that this wasn't just a mass delusion on my part. But the Grim Reaper? He was no more real than God.

But then what had I seen on the roof?

My rational brain may have tried to dismiss it, but my heart, thundering in my ears, had its own ideas. While I stood there, dazed, Alesha argued to Branson that I could be a valuable asset on this case. It wasn't so much her voice that reeled me back into the present moment as it was Branson's smell—a strong minty odor. It hadn't been until the doors closed behind him, cutting off the afternoon breeze, that the smell reached me. His hair may have gotten whiter since I'd left the force, but he was still wearing the same cologne.

"I know perfectly well who Myron's father is," Branson said. "Hank Vale was a hell of a detective. A *hell* of a detective. Probably the best the bureau has ever had. Dedicated, focused, disciplined. I'm not sure how bringing his son down here helps at all."

He glanced at me. He may have been complimenting my father, but it sounded more like he was lambasting me instead.

"Myron might be able to talk to Hank," Alesha insisted, though I could already hear the fight in her voice waning. "With the condition that his father—"

"I know what Hank's condition is right now," Branson said. "I saw him myself recently."

This caught me by surprise. "When was this?" I said.

"A few weeks ago," he said. "What, are you trying to keep your father locked up in a dark room? You don't want people to know he's got Alzheimer's?"

"Of course not," I snapped.

It may have been my imagination, but I thought I detected the first glimmerings of a smile on Branson's face. He was enjoying this. What did I ever do to him to deserve this? I could understand his being disappointed when I'd turned in my badge, but it had been *years*. The reporters outside the window had suddenly gotten louder in their shouted questions, so I leaned in a bit closer. "Alesha asked for my help," I explained. "I don't need to be here."

"Good," he said. "That means we're in agreement."

"I've got plenty of work waiting back at the office."

"Oh, I'm sure you do. There's always another cheating husband to chase around."

"I was just trying to help out an old friend. Because, you know, that's what friends do. They help each other."

He winced. It was gone in a blink, but it was there. We'd been shadowboxing, and I'd finally landed a glancing blow. "Well, then let me make this clear," he said, leaning in a bit, his tone more menacing. "You're not helping. You can only get in the way. I don't know what you're doing with your life, and I don't care. Whatever. But you don't get to play the part of a real detective when it suits you." He turned toward Alesha. "I don't want to see him anywhere around a crime scene with you again, got it?"

"Sir—" she began.

"Detective Stintson," Branson said, "you *have* a partner. Maybe you should spend a little time actually treating him like one."

Alesha snorted dismissively. "O'Dell is just a kid."

"Yeah, so were you once. He puts up with a lot of crap from you.

Never complains. In fact, he does nothing but praise you to high heaven. Did you know that? Didn't think so. I just want to ask you one thing. When you were starting out, what if you were saddled with a senior partner like *you?* How would you feel about it?"

There'd been a sharp-edged retort loaded up and ready to go, I could see that in her eyes, but then she stopped. It took her a moment to summon a reply.

"No," she said, "I can't imagine it, because I got real lucky. I had a *great* first partner. Taught me everything I know."

She shot me a meaningful look, then returned her attention to Branson as if challenging him to contradict her. For a moment, I thought he actually might, but then he grimaced and stepped past us to the elevator.

"I'm wanted upstairs," he said.

THERE WAS NO one on the roof of the apartment building across the street.

I'd been pretty sure that was going to be the case, but I still had to see for myself. After the elevator closed with Branson inside, we took the stairs to the second floor, traversed the hall to the north side, then took the back stairs to the same service doors we'd come through earlier. To make sure none of the reporters spotted us, we had to circle over a block, burning up even more time, but I doubted it made any difference. On the roof, where the late-afternoon breeze ruffled my hair, there was no one there. Three white reclining lawn chairs sat empty. A couple of raised garden beds, the rich, fertile soil recently tilled, were unattended. I checked the greenhouse and found no one inside.

There was, however, a feeling when I placed my hands on the brick wall where the cloaked figure had been—not a strong one, but it was still there, a bit of uneasiness, a dark echo of something terrible.

Alesha wanted to get a pizza, maybe shoot some pool and talk about the case, but I begged off. She threw a little fit and said I shouldn't let Branson dictate what I could and couldn't do, but I told her I was just tired. That was only half a lie, because I *was* exhausted, but I also didn't need to get Alesha in more trouble than she already was.

I also wanted to think.

Instead of going back to the office or to my house in Sellwood, I had dinner by myself—at the bar at Jay's, one of the most popular sports grills downtown. I couldn't afford it, but what the hell, there was just enough room on one of my credit cards if I had just one beer. The Blazers were playing the Celtics in Boston, making the restaurant even more raucous than usual. It might have seemed odd to others that I chose such a busy restaurant for some alone time, where the blare of the wall-size televisions was only barely louder than the din of alcohol-infused chatter, but I liked the place specifically because it *was* busy: with flesh-and-blood types. One of the things I'd learned early on about ghosts is that they tended to avoid areas crowded with the living, mostly because of the greater likelihood of inadvertent contact.

While most people didn't get quite the same jolt when a ghost passed through them—they might feel a bit of a chill or get goose bumps on the backs of their arms—the dead couldn't say the same. They felt just as intensely uncomfortable with the experience as I did, which was why, in a world filled with at least 100 billion ghosts, there wasn't a heck of a lot more ghost-to-living contact.

Clinking glasses. The scent of grilled hamburgers. Boisterous laughter. The odor of garlic practically oozing from the fat guy next to me in the black-and-red Blazers jersey. Sipping my frothy porter and doing my best to avoid looking in the mirror behind the bar, I tried to lose myself in the sensory overload. There weren't many ghosts in the room, but every now and then I still caught sight of a weird one flitting through the crowd—an old man in a fireman's outfit missing half his face, a little black girl with icicles hanging from her eyebrows, the kinds of ghosts who seemed oblivious to the disadvantages of getting too close to the living—and it always went better for all involved if we didn't make eye contact.

There were disadvantages to my choice, of course. When the

Blazers hit a long three-pointer at the First-quarter buzzer and everyone erupted in cheers, the fat guy swung his arms wide and jostled my
shoulder. Beer sloshed over my fries.

"Oh, sorry, buddy," he said.

"It's okay," I said. "I'm sure they'll taste better soggy."

If he caught my sarcasm, he didn't show it. He'd already gone back
to watching the game. On most days, I might have been interested in
it, basketball being one of the few sports I could actually tolerate without suffering an acute case of boredom, but I was too preoccupied by
what I'd seen on the roof of the parking garage to care much about tall
men trying to put a ball through a metal ring. Who could care about
that when they've seen the Grim Reaper? Or Ghost Reaper. Goodbye
Killer. Whatever name he—or it—went by. For all I knew, it may have
been just a guy in a cloak with a touch of special effects to give himself
a supernatural appearance.

But if so, who was he? For a little while, I actually entertained the
idea that Branson himself was the Goodbye Killer. He'd certainly been
around Portland long enough to commit the murders all the way back
to the beginning, and his police skills would come in handy in not
getting caught, but he had arrived on the scene so quickly after the
cloaked person had disappeared from the rooftop that it didn't seem
possible.

I shook my head and took another sip of my beer. The idea was
nuts. Branson may have been an asshole, but I couldn't wrap my head
around him being one of the weirdest serial killers the country had
ever seen. No, I just *wanted* Branson to be guilty. I wanted it for the
same reason I still wanted Billie to show up on my doorstep, begging
for me to take her back. Because it would make me happy.

"Hiya!" a man exclaimed.

He said it into my left ear as I was midsip, and this time it was
me who got my fries extra soggy. I thought it might have been the fat
guy, some weird joke on his part, but it was Eddie Quincy. He smiled
around the cigar in his mouth. His mostly bare scalp glistened, and
the collar of his shirt was soaked with sweat.

"Christ," I said. "Don't do that!"

The fat guy on the other side of Eddie gave me an odd look. "Dude, I already said I was sorry."

"I wasn't talking to you," I snapped at him.

With a shrug, the fat guy went back to watching the game. Eddie, his eyes gleaming behind those orange lenses, exhaled plumes of smoke around the cigar. I caught a good whiff of dark chocolate and espresso and was immediately transported back to my father's study as a boy.

"You saw him, didn't you?" he asked.

The fat guy, his back turned toward me, was now so fully engrossed in what was turning out to be a close game that I could lower my voice and speak to Eddie without drawing his attention.

"Have you always smoked those cigars?" I asked.

"For a while now," he said. "It's an Oliva. A good brand, right?"

"My father smoked those."

"I know, I know."

"You know?"

"He had good taste. In lots of things."

"How did you know?"

Smiling, Eddie dropped the cigar on the hardwood floor and ground it out with his foot. The Celtics center blocked a shot and the people around us groaned.

"How did you know?" I repeated.

"You should read my book on the Goodbye Killer, Myron. That's the title. You know I'm the one who gave him the name, right? In the first article I published in the *New York Post*. It's what led to the book. It's what led to everything. Big-time, baby! Before then, I was just a lowly staff reporter for the *Statesman Journal* in Salem. Legislative meetings. Little League games." He stuck his finger in his mouth, as if gagging.

"You interviewed my dad?"

"Oh, sure. And his partner. Loads of people. Even your mom."

"My *mom?*"

"Sure. Lovely lady."

"We are talking about my mom, right?"

He grinned his yellow teeth at me. "I wanted to know more about the lead detectives. You know, their personal lives. What made them tick. Your old man was a tough nut to crack. The only way I could get him to open up to me was if I agreed to give him whatever info I found out about the case. I mean, all of it, lock, stock, and barrel. Your mother … she was actually real chatty about your dad. Kind of unloaded about him. I don't think their marriage was going so well at the time, so she wanted an excuse to vent with someone."

"I don't think I like the direction this conversation is going," I said.

"No? Hey, no marriage is perfect, kiddo. The ones that last are just the ones where the people in it don't have any other better options."

"That's pretty damn cynical."

"Yeah, well, I'm a cynical guy. I gotta be, the kind of work I do, right? And your parents, they were—"

"I don't want to talk about my parents' marriage."

"But—"

"*No.*"

I said this loud enough that more than a few people turned their heads. Fortunately, the Blazers had just fouled for the third time in a row, so everyone probably assumed I was just another pissed-off fan. Eddie stared at the side of my face. I would have frozen him out completely—my mild disdain for him was quickly metastasizing into outright contempt—but the rational part of my brain knew that Eddie Quincy was a possible fountain of information about the Goodbye Killer, a source my unique ability gave me access to that the cops didn't have.

"What do you want?" I asked.

"Touchy, touchy," he said. "I get it, sure. Must have been tough growing up with a father like Hank Vale."

"Tell me what you want or get the fuck out of here."

"Hey, hey, calm down. I meant no offense, Myron."

"Eddie—"

"Same deal," he said. "That's all I want. Same deal as the one I had with your dad, only this time with you. Quid pro ... what is it? Well, you know. I give, you give, right? *Right?* We can both help each other out. I don't have all the same connections as I had when I was ... well, you know. I mean, I *have* the connections, but I don't, right? I can't talk to anybody who's not pushing up the daisies. But you, you can talk to people, living people. And you can talk to me."

There was a note of worry in his voice that I hadn't picked up on before. I looked at him and he wilted back a step. Now I knew why he was sweating. He might have needed me, but like most ghosts, he was also at least a little scared of me.

"What do I get out of it?" I said.

"Information."

"You found out new things about the Goodbye Killer since you wrote your book?"

"Well ..."

"Because if not, I can just read your book. I'm sure they have it in the library."

"Oh, don't do that," he said. "At least buy it from Amazon, so the foundation gets a little money from royalties. Heck, there's even a Kindle edition."

"*You* have a foundation?"

"Okay, it's not technically a foundation. It's my estate. But the money goes to a scholarship fund for kids interested in writing."

"You're joking."

"No, no. Totally serious. It's real important to me."

"I'm still waiting for you to tell me something about the Goodbye Killer."

Eddie raised his hand to his mouth as if to smoke his cigar, then realized he didn't have one and let out a nervous giggle. "Well, I'm not going to unload everything at once, right? I mean, if I do that, then what reason do you have to talk to me?"

"I think I'm going to call for my tab," I said.

"Wait, wait, hold on, buddy. I'll tell you something if we have a deal."

"I'm not going to agree to anything until I have at least some sense I'm going to get something out of it."

"All right, sure, fair enough." He leaned in conspiratorially, his face so close to mine that I saw the scratches in his orange lenses, the veins in his eyes, the hairy mole at the end of his nose. "He might be an un-ghost."

"A what?"

He glanced around us, checking to see if he'd been heard, then continued in a whisper even quieter than before. "An un-ghost," he said. "It's something I found out about after I … well, you know. Stopped paying taxes. Un-ghost is a term they use to describe—"

"Who's they?"

"You know. The Department of Souls. It's the term they came up with, but I don't know how many of them still use it. That's the English word, but the term itself actually dates back to Roman times. I found out about it when I visited HAGS."

"Hags?"

He shook his head. "Man, I thought by now you'd know more about us. Historical Archives of Ghosts and Spirits. They've moved the place around from time to time, but for the last couple hundred years it's been in the second basement beneath the Library of Congress in D.C. I first saw mention of it in a book about Alexander the Great, about a wraithlike warrior who was killing Alexander's enemies in his sleep. The Department—back then it was known as the Order—called it an un-ghost. Actually, it was *non phantasma*, but that's what the Latin means, I take it. It was a ghost and it wasn't."

"I don't even know what that means," I said.

"Well, nobody else did either. The English word showed up in another book about Jack the Ripper. There was speculation he was an un-ghost. That's why both the living *and* the dead couldn't catch him. He didn't really belong to either camp."

"Then why did he stop killing?"

"Well, that's the thing. Maybe he didn't. Maybe it's the same un-ghost. Maybe he's like a cicada or something, emerging every so many years to kill before going back into hibernation."

"Seriously?"

"Hey, I don't know! I'm just saying it's possible. It sure would explain why nobody can catch the guy."

"That's not very comforting."

"I know, right? Okay, now you gotta promise me two things."

"I'm not promising anything."

"First," Eddie continued, ignoring me, "that you'll spill the beans when you learn something new. And second, you'll let me go with you when you do your investigation thing."

I slid my beer glass back and forth between my fingers, then pushed it forward on the bar. I took a couple of bills out of my wallet and placed it next to the glass. Standing, I towered over him, and he wilted away from me. "How about this?" I said. "You definitely can't come with me."

"Aw—"

"And if I *decide* that there's something worth telling you, then I will."

"Myron, buddy, come on—"

"I'm not your buddy."

"I know, I know. Look, I'm trying to help you out. I just want some help in return."

"And I told you, I *will* help you. If I think it's appropriate. And if I think you're not holding out on me, which is kind of how I feel right now."

"I'm not—"

Before he could finish, I walked away. I'd raised my voice enough that even over the din I'd drawn a fair amount of attention. Who was this crazy guy talking to? I could see it in their eyes. I wove through the people and reached the door before I realized that Eddie was right behind me. I spun around and pointed a finger in his face.

"That thing about not going with me?" I said. "It starts right now."

"Hey, hey, I'm just—"

"Now, Eddie."

"Okay, okay."

He raised his hands in surrender. I glared at him a few more seconds, half the room now glaring right back at me, then opened the door. Walking toward the street, I was still looking over my shoulder, making sure Eddie wasn't following, when I ran right into what felt like a brick wall.

Only it wasn't a wall. It was a person.

A very *large* person.

After I'd recovered, bouncing back a few steps, I was looking up at one of the most formidable men I had ever seen. If he wasn't seven feet tall, then he was very nearly that height, obscenely muscular, dressed all in black right down to his impenetrable black sunglasses. It was a good contrast with his skin, which was the kind of white that was usually reserved for dead bodies, circus clowns, and bars of soap. He was as sleek on top as a volleyball. I couldn't see his eyes, but judging by his frosty white eyebrows, the guy was probably an albino. His black T-shirt was so tight that it looked like it had been spray-painted on his chest, every muscle so sculpted to hard-edged precision that even Michelangelo would have been impressed. His biceps and forearms were thicker than my waist.

"Myron Vale?" he said.

His voice gonged like a church bell, so deep I could actually feel the sound wave hitting me in the chest. Behind him, idling at the curb in the brisk night air, was a black stretch limo with the back door open.

"Darth Vader?" I said.

He grabbed me and threw me in the limo.

Chapter 6

STUMBLING INTO the limo, I told myself that if I hadn't had that beer, I would have put up a bigger fight. But who was I kidding? I'd just been manhandled by a human mountain.

I slid face-first on the smooth leather seat. By the time I got my arms under me, the big guy had slammed the door. The dark interior became opaquely dark. It was so quiet and still, no engine hum or other vibrations, that if I had just awakened, I would have been hard-pressed to say I was in a vehicle and not in a cave far beneath the earth's surface. In addition to the strong scent of new leather, I also smelled scotch and a type of cologne that made me think of a winter breeze. Still, despite the cologne, I didn't think anyone was in the limo with me until my hand brushed through something that gave me an electric jolt. A *familiar* electric jolt.

Moving slowly, not showing any signs of panic, I sat up and leaned away from whoever was there. As if choreographed for maximum impact, a dome light clicked on and illuminated a small old man dressed in a white suit and a white bowler hat. He rested his chin on his clasped fingers, studying me with blue eyes flecked with green, like the ocean water over a shallow coral reef. He wasn't quite a midget, but if his feet touched the floor, it was only barely. He had a long, beaked nose and cheekbones sharp enough to draw blood. His beard—no mustache, just a thin white band from one sideburn to the other across his chin—was so faint I didn't notice it at first.

An ebony cane topped with a tiny white skull rested against his lap.

"Yes, Mr. Vale," he said, "I *am* a non-corporeal human being. We might as well get that little detail out of the way."

He smiled primly over the tops of his clasped fingers. He spoke in a British accent, with just a hint of cockney, so faint that I guessed he'd strived hard to rid himself of it. He also had the kind of slithery, I-have-an-evil-plan voice usually heard only in *James Bond* films and *Saturday Night Live* sketches making fun of *James Bond* films, and I found myself waiting for him to cap off his statement with a sly cackle. I was to be disappointed, alas. There was no cackle, only a glimmer of amusement in his eyes.

I felt a slight lurch. It was the only sign that the limo was moving, because I felt nothing after that. I couldn't see anything outside, only my own reflection and the reflection of the limo's interior. The black leather seats wrapped all the way around. There was a minibar done in mahogany and ivory, flat-screen televisions mounted in each corner, and a wall between us and the driver that looked like polished granite tiles. A trifold of small computer monitors was mounted on stands immediately to the man's left, and each of the screens was buzzing with hundreds of windows full of scrolling newspaper websites, stock tickers, weather updates, and Twitter feeds.

"Who are you?" I said. "Do you always greet people by kidnapping them?"

Now I did get a bit of a laugh, but it was more of an embarrassed chuckle than an all-knowing cackle. "Oh, come now, Mr. Vale. Kidnapping? That is a bit daft, wouldn't you say? I am sorry about the fairly abrupt method that Fist employed to assist you in joining me, but time is of the essence."

"Fist?" I said. "His name is Fist?"

"That is what he is called, correct."

"Is it his first name or last name?"

"Mr. Vale—"

"I just want to know the kind of parents who would name their kid Fist."

"Mr. Vale, please. Try not to get too cheeky. My corporeal assistant is of no concern. What *is* of concern is that we get right down to the business at hand. My name is Winston Hopner. Perhaps you've heard of me? No? I am the Associate Director. I tell you this not to impress you but so that you understand immediately what an urgent matter the Department considers your … latest case."

"The Department?" I said.

"*The* Department, Mr. Vale."

"Oh. That one."

He lowered his hands into his lap and watched me take in this news. The Department was the Department of Souls, the quasi-governmental organization that oversaw the affairs of ghosts everywhere. They were huge, bureaucratic, and full of so many divisions, departments, and offices that they made the United States government look like a small-town Elks Club by comparison. The Office of Otherworldly Transportation. The Council on Apparition Affairs. The Invisible Trade Commission. It seemed like every day I was hearing about some new board or bureau that was yet another tentacle of the Department. *Why* so many ghosts wanted to go on working, especially for something like the Department of Souls, when they didn't need food, shelter, or any of the other things that regular flesh-and-blood people needed to sustain life was beyond me.

Then again, much of their world was beyond me. The dead had their own ways and their own purposes, and no one could truly ever make sense of it, not even the dead themselves.

"The Associate Director, huh?" I said.

"That's correct."

"You have a human working for you."

"*I'm* human, Mr. Vale, despite what some of my employees sometimes claim." He chuckled. "But if you mean I have a corporeal human in my employ, yes. I have many. Fist is just one of them."

"How many?"

"Many."

"And they can all … see you?"

"Oh no," Hopner said. "Most can't see or hear us at all. They simply work for the Corporeal Division of the Department. Most are true believers in the non-corporeal afterlife, committed enough in their beliefs that they are … recruited to help, especially if they believe without any other religious dogma getting in the way. Some, like Fist, can hear us, even sense us a bit, but we are still invisible to them. A few have a direct connection to a single ghost, and some of these work at the highest levels of the Corporeal Division … No one, other than you, can see and hear *all* of us, *all* of the time."

He'd hesitated before telling me the last bit, as if he'd been unsure of whether he should. I remembered what the priest had told me, that many in the Department were afraid of me because of my unique abilities. He'd said that even though they perceived me as a threat, they wouldn't do anything about it because they feared I might be even more powerful when dead. I didn't know how much leverage that gave me, but it had to give me some.

"What do you want from me?" I asked.

"To work for us, of course."

"Right. I should have guessed."

"We want you to report your findings on this case directly to us—and to no one else. Whatever you find should be kept confidential. We will compensate you handsomely."

"Of course you would."

"*Quite* handsomely, Mr. Vale. You have no idea how many resources we have at our disposal. I merely need to say the word and a substantial sum can be transferred into your account. We know your financial situation is … dire."

"Well," I said a bit huffily, "I wouldn't quite put it—"

"*Dire,*" Hopner repeated, cutting me off. "You hardly have enough money to even fill the gas tank of your Prius, and that's a small tank indeed. Another few weeks of this and you will be evicted from your office." He leaned forward, lowering his voice. "Let us speak frankly. This … Ghost Reaper has many people on both sides of the divide quite rattled."

"Why are you whispering?"

"Our usual methods are proving ineffective," he continued. "I'm sure this is obvious, or I wouldn't be asking for your assistance, but I say it only to tell you why, exactly, I must use all my powers of persuasion to enlist your help."

"No one outside can hear us. You really can speak up."

"Mr. Vale—"

"I just don't like unnecessarily whispering."

"I truly wish—"

"It's a pet peeve of mine."

He stared. For just a second, the pleasant, beguiling mask slipped away, and I got a fleeting glimpse of what lay beneath: eyes as cold as an assassin's, face as chiseled as stone, an air of smug superiority that made me feel like an ant looking up through the magnifying glass at a cruel face. It was only there for an instant before the facade returned, but it was enough for me to know why, exactly, Winston Hopner had ascended all the way to second in command of the Department. Smiling furtively, he leaned back and gave his clasped hands a purposeful shake.

"Humor," he said. "I wish I was better at it, but I daresay it is one of my failings. Can I jolly well get to the point, Myron? Is it all right if I call you Myron? You may call me Winston, of course. We should think of ourselves as chaps, Myron, and chaps help one another. You see, we are in a bit of a precarious position. If things weren't so botched, I could give you a bit more leeway on such a matter, but I really must insist that you help us."

"Oh, insist."

"It is of vital importance."

"Well … You are just the Associate Director. If it's that important, maybe I should be talking to the Director himself."

"*No one* talks to the Director," he said coldly.

"Even you?"

"Even me."

"Then how—"

"I have no time for this bloody nonsense. You *are* quite special, Myron. You know that. Perhaps not as special as you think you are, but your abilities do give you an edge that no one in either of our worlds has. I know I am not the first from our side to approach you asking for your aid." When he saw my surprise, he smiled thinly. "Of course I know about him. I know all that happens within my organization, even certain rogue elements that are not nearly as rogue as they would like to think they are. It is why I am where I am."

"In Portland?"

"Don't be a twit. I'm speaking of my position within—"

"I don't care. I'm not working for you."

"You should reconsider."

"No."

"You *really* should reconsider."

"Or what?"

"Or else."

"You're threatening me?"

"Not you," Hopner said. "I'm sure you have surmised by now that we are ... uncertain of what would happen if you were to expire. It's not something we are prepared to deal with at this time."

"Oh, that's comforting."

"But ... there are others in your life, Myron. Others who are important to you. Take Alesha Stintson, for example. It's dangerous work, being a detective. It would be bloody awful if something were to happen to her."

This was a threat I wasn't expecting him to make, and I realized I was an idiot for thinking I had any kind of leverage. My face suddenly felt warm, my throat parched. Either the limo was rounding a corner or I was feeling off balance, because I had to put my hand on the leather seat to steady myself. Hopner studied my face, clearly enjoying my distress.

"Nothing untoward has to happen to her," he said softly.

"Right."

"And in addition to the … *extra safety* we will provide those important to you during your investigation, you will also be compensated handsomely, as I indicated. Enough that you wouldn't have to worry about making rent for a year at least. How does that sound? When you have been mostly surviving on Campbell's Soup and peanut-butter sandwiches, it sounds quite good, I imagine. So, we have a deal then? You will try to discover who, or what, this Ghost Reaper is, and you will report your findings to us and only us. I will give you an email address for your updates, and if need be, I may stop by to see you from time to—"

"I want something," I said.

"What?"

I took a moment to quash the worries that had thrown me off balance before looking him squarely in the eyes. Behind him, the computer monitors were alive with a flurry of scrolling text and pictures, windows rapidly popping open and closing, a contrast to how still Winston Hopner was across from me. In the silence, I heard Dad's warning rise up from the deepest corner of my mind: *Myron, you have to stop him. You have to stop him before it's too late.*

"I want something else," I said. "In addition to the money. And to leaving Alesha alone."

"I hardly think," Hopner said, "that you are in a position to make demands."

"No? Well, I'm still making one anyway. My father—I want you to help him."

"I don't know what you mean."

"Oh yeah? I thought you were all-knowing, all-powerful—"

"Don't be ridiculous."

"You know the condition he is in. I want you to do something about it."

Nothing I had done so far had truly thrown Hopner off balance, even when he had seemed irritated with me, but I could see that this had really surprised him—and not in a bad way. There are people in positions of power who don't like surprises, but I could see that Hopner was not one of them. His eyes, those cool blue eyes flecked with green, betrayed no emotion, but the corners of his lips curled up in a hint of a smile.

"The Alzheimer's," he said.

"Yes."

"You're hoping we can do something about it."

"I *know* you can do something about it."

He shook his head. "Myron, I take it as a compliment, but you vastly overestimate our abilities. We can do even less about your father's mental state in our world than you can do in yours. People with your father's condition … we can't make them better, alive or dead. When they eventually enter our world, they are no different. Alas, their minds continue to … deteriorate."

I tried to mask my disappointment, but it was extremely difficult. Not only was Hopner telling me he couldn't do anything about the Alzheimer's, a crushing blow by itself, but he was also taking away *all* my hope. I'd been clinging to the idea that if I couldn't have Dad back while he was still alive, then I'd at least see the real him when he became a ghost. What I felt was deeper than disappointment. That cold desolation burrowing into the pit of my stomach was the worst thing I'd felt since Billie left me.

"You're lying," I said.

"You know I'm not."

"You're lying and you know it."

"Myron—"

"You either help him, or … or …"

I trailed off, unsure. Hopner's smile widened a bit. I wanted to punch him in the face, and it only enraged me that I couldn't.

"Or what?" he said. "You'll put Alesha's life in jeopardy?"

"No," I said.

"I thought not."

"But—but my heart won't be in it. You want my all, really want my all, you can't just threaten me. "

"Hmm. Well, I daresay you should give us your all anyway. If you don't, there could be consequences. There are other ways we can … encourage you."

I had no answer. He had me beat and he knew it. I had never really had any cards to play. I wasn't going to sacrifice Alesha's life just on principle. I wasn't going to sacrifice her life no matter what, and Hopner knew that. He observed me silently for few seconds, then closed his eyes and tapped two fingers to his temple. Immediately, I felt the limo slow.

"I think we're done here," he said. "We've been circling your house for the last five minutes. Time for you to get out."

"But my Prius is back at the bar."

"You will receive an email from us tomorrow morning," he said, ignoring me. "When you have an update, simply reply to it. The email will go directly to me, bypassing all lower channels. Myron, please don't judge us too harshly. Ordinarily, we would not go to such lengths to enlist your help, but, well, desperate times and all that. You *will* be compensated well, I assure you. We are good on our word."

"What about my car?"

The door opened, letting in a rush of cool night air. Fist loomed before me, his blocky face so white it glowed except for his black band of sunglasses. It seemed odd to be wearing sunglasses at night, but then he was an odd sort of man—if he could be called a man at all. He was like King Kong. Except white. And hairless. Sure enough, there was my little house in Sellwood behind him, the porch light shining on my tiny covered patio and the potted geraniums, the streetlamps casting their golden glow on my recently mowed lawn, my nicely trimmed azaleas, and my blooming rosebushes. I'd always liked gardening, and when Billie left me, I'd found I liked it even more. Or maybe *like* wasn't the right word. What do you call something you do to forget about the things you used to do?

Fist reached for me. Before he got his hands on my jacket, there was a series of electronic beeps from the monitors—a rhythmic pattern, like a cell phone's ringtone.

"Wait," Hopner said.

I turned and saw Hopner peering closely at one of his monitors. Plain green text on a black background had appeared in one of the windows, the kind of thing that used to be common when computers were new. I was too far away to read the words, but they didn't even look like words, just long strings of characters. Hopner hovered his hand over the keyboard and a short string of characters appeared. A response popped up almost immediately, another few lines of text. Hopner shook his head, then turned to me. His prim smile was still there, but it was like the afterglow of the old television I used to have sitting on my dresser, a fading visual echo that remained on the screen a few seconds after I'd turned it off. He adjusted his bowler hat a little and swallowed.

"Well," he said, "it seems I may have spoken prematurely. That was the … Director."

"I thought you said nobody speaks to him."

"Nobody *does* speak to him," Hopner snapped. "Not in person. A few claimed to have talked to him on the phone, but I'm not so … Anyway, it doesn't matter. He says he agrees to your terms."

"What?"

"If you help us," Hopner said, "he will also help you."

"My father?"

"Yes."

"So it can be done."

"Apparently."

"Apparently?"

"Because he is the *Director*, Myron."

He flicked his fingers dismissively, then abruptly faced forward as if I'd already left. I started to ask him another question—this thing with Dad was too important to just take on faith—but I heard a menacing grunt from Fist. I turned and there he was reaching for me again, hands big enough to knock down buildings or to reduce mountains to rubble. In the reflection of his sunglasses, I was an inconsequential speck.

"But my Prius is parked at the bar," I protested.

He threw me out of the limo.

Chapter 7

I SLEPT LIKE THE DEAD. That was true at least metaphorically, although in my experience the dead didn't sleep any better than the rest of us. It might be better to say I slept like a corpse, but then corpses don't sleep at all. They're just corpses. Once they're separated from the ghost that used to inhabit them, they're nothing but a shell, one that their former selves often find unnerving to be around. Which is why, if I really want to go someplace that is free of ghosts, I sometimes hang out in graveyards. It had occurred to me that if I wanted to keep ghosts out of my house, I could scatter a few corpses around, kind of a homemade funeral parlor. But the bullet lodged between the two lobes of my brain had left my olfactory senses completely intact, and there was nothing quite as off-putting as the scent of rotting flesh.

Still, when I finally opened my eyes Sunday morning and saw Jak sitting on the edge of my bed, I wondered again what I had to do to get ghosts to respect my privacy. Then I remembered that she wasn't a ghost. She was real, just very good at picking locks. And she had her hand on my leg.

"Good morning, handsome," she said. "You sure are a heavy sleeper. I guess you had a long day, though."

"What the hell!"

I sprang out of bed like a cat that had been doused with cold water, my heart pounding, all my senses alive. The blinds were closed, but the morning light around the edges was bright enough that it still took a few seconds for my eyes to adjust.

There was no doubt, just based on the voice, that the grinning young woman sitting cross-legged on my blue comforter was Jak, but if I had seen her first, I might have said otherwise. She'd undergone something of a transformation since I'd last seen her. Gone were the baseball cap, the acid-washed denim clothes, and the gold piercing over the eyebrow. In their place she wore a pink cardigan sweater over a white blouse, a black skirt, and black leggings that hugged her calves. The blond hair was loose and combed smooth, held in place by a couple of pink clips that matched her pink hoop earrings. She looked like was she about to book a flight to Martha's Vineyard, where she would play tennis with guys whose crew cuts never got mussed and whose egos matched the size of their trust funds.

"What are you *doing*?" I shouted at her.

Still grinning, she touched the pearl necklace around her neck, clicking the beads together. Even the dragon tattoo I'd seen yesterday was gone; her forearm was a smooth, buttery brown. I stole a quick glance at the digital clock next to my bed. 8:25. For an early riser like me, that was practically noon.

"You can't—you can't keep breaking into my places!" I insisted.

"Hmm," she said.

"It's rude! And this is my *house*!"

"Hmm."

"Ever heard of knocking, for God's sake?"

"Hmm."

"Will you *stop* that!"

"Hmm?"

"That! That *hmm* business! It's annoying! Say something!"

"Oh," she said, her smile showing even more of those pearly whites than before. "Sorry. I was just having a hard time following you. Too busy enjoying the view."

She raised her eyebrows. That's when I realized I was standing there in nothing but my underwear. I grabbed my green cotton robe out of the bathroom and slipped it on, tying the sash. The hardwood floor felt as cold as ice against my bare feet, but I couldn't quite bring myself to put on my felt slippers in front of her.

"You need to leave," I said.

"I was kind of hoping you slept naked," she said.

"Now," I insisted.

"You talk in your sleep, by the way."

"What?"

"Billie was your wife, right?" she said. "The one who passed away?"

"We're not talking about this. We're talking about your penchant for breaking and entering."

"I didn't *break* anything."

"Trespassing, then."

"I brought your car back to you, by the way."

"What? *How?*"

She examined her fingernails. I noticed they'd recently been painted pink, the same color as her earrings and her hair clips. "I'm good at picking locks. I'm good at hot-wiring cars. I've got lots of talents … So, have you slept with anyone since she left?"

"Let's stay on the car for a second. You *knew* it was at Jay's? What, were you following me?"

"Sure," she said. "You're my story now, Myron. You and the Goodbye Killer. Plus, I'm kind of obsessed with you already." She laughed. "Just kidding. I'm not going to go all *Fatal Attraction* on you or anything. You want me to make you some coffee? I can't cook for shit, but I can make a mean cup of coffee."

She'd said the part about being obsessed with me as a kind of joke, but her eyes said something different. There was a vulnerability, a nervousness glimpsed behind all of her cockiness and bravado. She *was* obsessed, it was obvious, but I wasn't getting a *Fatal Attraction* vibe from her at all. Or if I was, it was mutual. Now that my initial shock at waking up to find her in my room had faded, that magnetic attraction was back, stronger than ever. Lust. Desire. Whatever it was, it was real and undeniable, and we were both very conscious of the bed between us. I found myself imagining unbuttoning her blouse, slipping my hands down the arch of her bare back, pressing her body against mine—

"You're welcome," she said.

"Huh?"

She swallowed. "For your car. For bringing you your car."

"Oh. Right."

"And sorry. For not knocking."

"Yeah. You—you really have to stop that."

"I know. I will."

"Okay."

"Myron."

"Yeah?"

But she didn't say anything. We merely looked at each other across the bed. I was conscious of her every movement. The parting of her lips. One hand sliding on top of another on her lap. This was crazy. If I really wanted to be with someone right now, it was Alesha—beautiful, bold, and brilliant Alesha—not this … this … *lovely, lovely creature.* She rose, smoothing out her skirt without looking away from me, eyes like portals into another universe. All those luscious curves moved and swayed inside her clothes. A few buttons. A zipper or two. The obstacles were few and insignificant. My fingers twitched in anticipation.

I hadn't noticed that she was moving toward me, but she must have, because she suddenly reached for the sash of my robe.

"Coffee," I said.

"What?"

I brushed past her quickly, making a beeline for the kitchen before I could change my mind. Morning light shone through the stained-glass butterfly hanging in the window, spreading a fan of rainbow color on the granite countertop. The vinyl floor was cool enough to curl my bare toes. The dishes that had been dirty in the sink the night before now sat clean in the drying rack. Had she? I glanced at Jak and saw her smiling. She had. Shaking my head, I got out the bag of coffee beans and plugged in the grinder. I'd never really cared whether the coffee was freshly ground or not, but Billie had preferred it, and it was another one of those things that I just kept doing out of habit.

"You're not wearing your wedding ring," Jak said.

"Huh?"

"It's by your nightstand. But you didn't put it on. And you weren't wearing it yesterday."

"I still wear it."

"Do you?"

"Sometimes."

"Sometimes," she repeated.

I poured the beans, dark and gleaming, into the grinder. Already the acrid smell was sharpening my senses. Maybe that was why I caught the murmur of voices, faint as they were, coming from the street in the front of the house. The clang of metal. Something scraping along the street. Even back in the bedroom, I'd heard something, but I'd assumed it was my retired mechanic neighbor down the street, who often got up early on Sundays to tinker in his garage. Now I sensed that those sounds weren't quite the same. I looked at Jak.

"What's that?" I asked.

"Hmm?"

"Out front. That noise."

"Can I ask you something? You've got two other bedrooms."

"Did you see something going on out there when you came in?"

"One of the bedrooms," Jak continued, "is completely empty. That's kind of weird, but okay, not everybody uses all of their rooms. But the other one … it's set up like an art studio, but the canvases hanging on the walls, on the easel, all of them … Myron, they're *blank*."

I was trying to think of what to tell her when a car door slammed out front, then another. Jak, as if just now remembering my question, glanced toward the front door.

"Oh yeah," she said, "the press."

"What?"

"The media types. Newspapers, TV crews, a whole bunch of them. Mostly local, but I saw that chick from ANC out there, the one with the big ... you know." She gestured in front of her breasts. "A couple other national reporters, too."

"No way."

"Oh, come on," she said, "you knew it would happen. As soon as somebody saw you at PSU and made the connection with your dad. What a story! The son carries on where the father left off! Add in the stuff about your shooting, your wife's suicide—ratings gold, baby! And what else are they going to focus on right now? But don't worry, I told them you would be making a statement later, and that if anyone stepped onto your property, you'd call the police. Bought you a little time, at least."

"You did *what?*"

She smiled impishly, and no amount of country-club attire could hide the troublesome vixen she really was. I would have slapped her if I were the kind of guy who slapped women. Part of me still didn't believe her, so I marched past her to the front door. She called after me, warning me, but it was too late. I already had the door open.

Lightbulbs flashed. People yelled out questions. Three television news vans and another half-dozen cars lined the street in front of my house. A motley group of reporters—the television folks sharply dressed in suits, the newspaper types in frumpier attire—stood at the edge of my driveway like a human barricade. The woman from ACN, her lemon yellow blazer cut low enough to reveal plenty of cleavage, jumped up and down, trying to get my attention. A pudgy guy in greasy overalls stood next to her, so close as he ogled her bouncing that I figured he had to be a ghost.

Sure enough, my Prius was parked in the driveway.

The chilly air flitting past my bare legs reminded me that I was standing there in my robe, getting my picture taken for tomorrow's paper. I felt Jak brush up against me, shoulder to shoulder as she peered at the reporters, and that photo became even more vivid. Who was this mystery woman with the great detective? I hoped they would put in the part about me being a great detective. It wouldn't quite make up for the awfulness of being in the paper in the first place, but at least *great* was a word my mother could underline. If she read the paper. Or still retained the ability to underline words.

Feeling queasy, I started to close the door, but then Alesha slipped between two reporters and headed my way.

She was saying something over her shoulder to Tim. As usual, she looked stunning in her black leather jacket, powerful while still stylish. She was halfway across the driveway when she finally turned and saw me—and, of course, Jak next to me.

Alesha already looked annoyed talking to Tim, so it was hard to tell just how much further Jak's presence annoyed her, but she definitely reacted. A hitch in her step. Some pain in her eyes. *That* hurt me, too, because I the last thing I ever wanted to do was hurt Alesha, but it also annoyed me: How dare she assume anything was going on between me and this pert little blonde? Leaning against me. Inside my house. With me wearing a bathrobe. Obviously, there was evidence that could lead to some conclusions, but that didn't stop me from feeling indignant. What, Alesha could use up men faster than she used up incense, but I couldn't have a one-night stand with a woman who did my dishes and retrieved my Prius?

"Hello," Alesha said. This was directed at Jak, not me. It was said with all the warmth of a master gardener greeting a newly sprouted weed. "I don't think we've had the pleasure."

It was subtle, but I felt Jak press just a bit closer to me. "Jak Worthe," she said, and there was something strained in her own voice as well, an unnatural lilt. "You're his former partner, aren't you? Allison Stetston?"

"Alesha Stintson."

"Right."

"I'm Tim O'Dell," Tim said.

Everybody ignored him. There was an awkward moment, then Alesha raised her eyebrows at me. I cleared my throat.

"She, um, brought my Prius back," I said.

"She what?" Alesha said.

"He left it at the bar last night," Jak said.

"Uh-huh," Alesha said. "That drunk, huh?"

"It's a long story," I said.

"I'll bet."

"Not *that* kind of story."

Alesha shrugged. "Whatever. Look, I know it's Sunday, but Sal Belleni said if we want to talk to him, it would be better today. The deli is closed on Sundays, and he's short-staffed this week."

"Dad's former partner owns a deli?"

"Oh, I want to come," Jak said.

"No," Alesha said.

She surprised all of us with her bluntness. Jak had been pretty unruffled so far, but I actually detected a bit of a flush. Her skin was pale enough that even a bit of pink was noticeable. Tim studied the shine of his black boots. I wondered just how I'd managed to be standing outside in my bathrobe having this conversation in front of clicking cameras.

"Excuse me?" Jak said.

"Oh, I'm sorry," Alesha said. "Are you a detective?"

"Let's keep our voices down," I said.

"I'm a *writer*," Jak said.

"Ooh, a writer," Alesha said.

"An independent journalist."

"Speaking of journalists—" I began.

"What does that even mean," Alesha said, "you post on Facebook or something?"

This must have hit a little too close to home, because Jak's flush deepened. There was something fascinating about two highly attractive women arguing in front of me—and it would be hard to pretend it wasn't about me in some way—but I wasn't about to let this little tiff go on in front of the media. I put my hand up before Jak could offer up another retort.

"I need to go with them," I said. "How about I see you later?"

I don't know why I said the last part. I suppose I meant it as a consolation prize of sorts, because despite my mixed feelings about Jak, I knew she would feel left out and I didn't want to hurt her. But there was a double meaning in my question I hadn't intended, and both she and Alesha quickly picked up on it. The hurt in Jak's eyes flitted away in an instant, replaced by a kind of smugness I might have found off-putting if I didn't find her so inexplicably attractive. Alesha's reaction was quite the opposite, a smoldering anger that perked up all my cop's instincts for impending violence.

Making matters worse, Jak leaned in and pecked me on the cheek. Making matters *even* worse, I didn't do anything but stare at her stupidly.

"All right," Jak said with a smile, "how about I pick you up at eight o'clock?"

"Um," I said.

"Dinner's on me. I won't even make you feel guilty about it. Or feel guilty myself. I'm a postfeminist modern woman, you know."

With that, she practically skipped her way down my driveway. It may have just been a coincidence, but she managed to elbow past the big-breasted television reporter on her way.

Chapter 8

A HALF-HOUR LATER, after I had a shave, a shower, and some coffee and toast, we were on our way to see Sal Belleni.

"She's way too young for you," Alesha said.

She hadn't said anything about Jak—or really, much of anything—since the incident on my front porch. I slouched in the passenger seat of Alesha's unmarked police cruiser, a big black Crown Victoria that drove like an ocean liner. She was driving. The seat belt pressed against the Glock in its holster underneath my black leather jacket, its presence bringing me comfort. Whether the Goodbye Killer was a ghost or not, after yesterday I wasn't going anywhere without it. Like a sulking kid, Tim O'Dell rode in the back. Or maybe he wasn't sulking. He might have just been quiet, since it was hard to tell with him. He could have been our son. If he were younger. With darker skin. And less Irish. Just the family, out for a ride.

The sun shining through the windshield was bright enough that I wished I'd brought my sunglasses. Alesha noticed my discomfort and, with a sigh, flipped down the visor. Now I felt like the child. Maybe *I* should have been the one in the backseat.

"I agree," I said.

"Okay. Then why are you dating her?"

"I'm not dating her."

"You're going on a date with her tonight."

"No. I'm not."

"If it walks like a date, and talks like a date—"

"Okay, fine. Call it a date then. I don't care."

"Have you slept with her yet?"

"Jesus. *No.*"

"Liar."

"Guys," Tim said from the backseat, "I'm still here."

"I don't see why it matters," I said to Alesha, though I realized it could have been taken as a reply to Tim, as well. "What if I *had* slept with her? Do I have to get your permission?"

Alesha snorted. "Of course not."

"Good. Because I don't remember you asking permission on all the many guys you dated."

"What do you mean, many?"

"I think you know what I mean."

"You mean I'm a slut or something?"

"Oh, for Christ's sake," I said.

"Maybe we should talk about the case," Tim said.

"Shut up, Tim," Alesha said, all the while directing her cool gaze at me. "No, I'm serious. You think I sleep around too much, that it?"

"I think you can do whatever the hell you want, Alesha. That's the *point.*"

"Oh, great. Glad there's a point."

"So we agree that our personal lives should be off-limits then?"

"Okay. Whatever."

"Good."

"You still slept with her, though."

Tim reached between us and turned on the radio. Some hideous noise that resembled monkeys screeching over harmonicas blasted from the speakers. I would have guessed the sound to be a product of a bad signal, maybe two stations mixed together—if I didn't know Alesha's taste in music. I turned it off. Alesha turned it back on. It being her car, we listened to monkeys screeching the rest of the way.

We passed three men in tan, colonial-era outfits riding horses. We passed an old milk truck parked at the curb and a milkman placing bottles outside a Starbucks. We passed road construction with guys working with jackhammers and guys in 1920s attire working with pickaxes. There were ghosts everywhere. Ten minutes later, I would have gladly talked about my nonexistent sex life again if only Alesha would promise to turn off the radio, but she mercifully parked in front of a slumping two-story building a few blocks off Belmont, where old Victorian houses in various states of disrepair or renovation lined the south side and businesses lined the other. Up the road a bit, on the corner, was an empty four-story warehouse with a big *For Sale* sign on the side that was so old, part of the letters had completely faded, spelling *F r ale*. I remembered the place being empty even when I was a teenager.

In the place before us, there was a laundromat, a used bookstore, and a bookkeeper. At first glance, I missed the sandwich shop, but then I spotted it between the laundromat and the bookshop—a glass door and a window hardly wider than the door with the word *Maria's* on the glass in white stenciled letters, part of the *M* missing. The deli was probably half a mile from my office, but I never knew it was there. Since Alesha had said it was closed Sundays, I'd figured we were headed to Sal's residence, not his business, but it turned out I wasn't wrong.

"He lives above the shop," Alesha explained, pressing the button next to the glass door.

If there was a doorbell, we didn't hear it. We waited a minute, then Alesha pressed it again. Still nothing. I tapped on the glass, loudly. No response. I tried the door. Open. We looked at each other, shrugged, and stepped inside.

The sandwich shop, no bigger than my bedroom, was dark and quiet except for the humming cooler to the right of the counter, full of plastic bottles of Coke, 7 Up, and various fruit punches. The light from the inside of the cooler, pale and harsh, shone on the dusty floor, the vinyl peeling back along the edges of the wall. It was hard to see how Sal could have been short-staffed, since there was hardly enough room behind the counter for one person, let alone two. The scent of freshly baked bread, which hung in the air, made the place seem at least slightly more inviting.

There was a door in the back, past a locked restroom, marked *Private*. I opened it and found steep stairs leading up to a landing.

"Sal?" Alesha called.

Her voice echoed off the walls. I tried the light switch, but it didn't work.

"Hey, Sal!" Alesha yelled.

No answer. With a shrug, Alesha started up the creaking stairs, with Tim and me behind her. The hall smelled faintly of moldy drywall. She was a few steps ahead of us, rounding the corner on the landing, stepping into darkness. It wasn't until she was at the door that I felt it—the same uneasiness I'd felt back at the university, first on the pedestrian boulevard, then later at Jasmine Walker's apartment building. It was like a poison, this fear, the way it froze my joints and tightened my muscles.

Consciously, by force of will, I reached for the Glock underneath my leather jacket.

The door at the top of the stairs was slightly ajar, a sliver of pale light falling across Alesha's face and illuminating the dust suspended in the air. Shaking her head, visible mostly as a silhouette, she reached for the knob.

"*No!*"

It was me, a whisper that was like a shout in the enclosed space. She froze, hand just over the knob, and looked at me, puzzled. The whites of her eyes were bright. The puzzlement changed to recognition when she saw that I was easing my Glock out of its holster.

"Myron?" she said.

"Don't," I said.

In a blink, she had her Glock out, as did Tim. I wanted to get ahead of her, but it was too late; she was already entering the apartment. Gun raised, easing the door open with her back, she was the picture of the perfect kick-ass cop, the kind the bureau should have put on recruitment posters. The door creaked in protest, light brightening the stairwell. Before I was even in the room, she was already reacting to whatever she saw.

"What the hell!" she cried.

I bounded in after her, Glock raised, my heart kicking into another gear. She sprinted to the left, toward an open bedroom door. I took in the cramped and cluttered apartment in a glance—stained green carpet, a futon covered by a black sheet, a kitchen nook buried in dirty dishes—as I pursued her. The place stank of cigarettes. An exposed bulb lit the room. The bedroom door was open, and I saw a man's hairy leg hanging over the side of a bed. The room was darker than the living area, lit only by whatever daylight was reaching it from the window.

"Hold it!" Alesha shouted.

She yelled this as she entered the room, once again too late for Tim or me to stop her. She swept her gun back and forth, first at the man in the bed, then to the right—before bolting that way. When I caught up, she was at the open window, leaning outside with her gun pointed below.

"Who—?" I began.

"I don't know," she said.

"You saw somebody."

She was still peering out the window, and she didn't answer. The bathroom off the bedroom was so small that with the door open, I could see everything, especially since the tub lacked a shower curtain, but I still ducked my head inside to make sure no one hid behind the door. Pill bottles littered the flaking green tile around the grimy sink, some over-the-counter, some prescription. Curious, I looked closer. I saw doxazosin and Lexapro. I knew doxazosin was for prostate issues. Lexapro was an antidepressant, if I remembered correctly. The doxazosin bottles were empty.

The man in the bed, which was the only furniture in the room unless you called the piles of clothes in the corners furniture, was Sal

Belleni—or at least someone who looked very much like Sal Belleni. I hadn't seen him in over four years, and that had been very brief—at a citizens'-brigade event back when I was still doing things like that in a misguided effort to hang on to parts of my old life—but I was still shocked by how much he had aged. The man I had seen back then, smiling and nodding at the mostly octogenarian crowd who took their neighborhood-watch duties very seriously, had been a swarthy, broad-shouldered man with a deep tan and a thick salt-and-pepper beard to go with a full head of salt-and-pepper hair. This person was a shrunken version of that man, like a blow-up doll that had been left outside to shrivel and fade. His driver's license might have said he was in his mid-sixties, but he looked more like eighty to me.

The bedroom smelled even stronger of cigarettes than the living area—cigarettes and stale sweat. He was naked except for a pair of blue-striped boxers, but his chest, arms, and legs were so covered in white hair that they almost qualified as clothes. Gone was the beard and most of the hair on his head, a few white tufts remaining on the sides of his scalp. Except for a puffy redness around his eyes, he was so pale I thought there was a chance he might be dead, but then he moaned.

"Sal?" I said.

As if the movement took a great effort, he brought his hands slowly to his face and rubbed his eyes. Alesha turned from the window, holstering her Glock. Tim and I also put our weapons away.

"Gone?" I said.

She nodded.

"So what was it?"

"I don't know."

"You saw—"

"I just saw something. A jacket, maybe. Or …"

"Or?"

"Maybe nothing. I don't know."

"Do you want to do a sweep of—"

"No."

"Alesha—"

"Later," she said, then shook Sal's leg. "Belleni, come on, wake up. You've got some visitors."

Sal let out a belch of beer-infused breath. I could tell Alesha wasn't quite right, that she had seen something that had really gotten to her. I felt a dryness in my throat and a tightness in my stomach, because I had a pretty good sense of what that something was, the same something that Sal and my father had gotten a glimpse of years ago. If so, what did it mean? Did it mean the Goodbye Killer had been coming for Sal? And why? That would have been a hell of a departure from his usual routine.

Or was he just taunting us?

Alesha shook Sal's leg again. He slurred something that resembled hello. His filmy eyes slid open like a lizard's, the whites bloodshot.

"Maria?" he said.

"It's me," Alesha said. "Alesha Stintson. I'm here with Myron Vale."

"And Tim O'Dell, sir," Tim piped in.

He rubbed his eyes some more. Maria. It took me a second to remember the name. His wife. Where was his wife, anyway? Passed away, now that I thought about it, not long after my mom died—breast cancer, if I remembered correctly, and it had been a long and ugly battle. By then, Sal had long since left the force, but I'd heard about it from someone at the bureau. I recalled thinking I should reach out to him, express my condolences, but I'd been too wrapped up in my own troubled marriage to turn such impulses into action. I felt bad about that now. It was true that the first year after the shooting was lost in a murky bog. What was also true, and what I seldom told people, was that the five years or so before the shooting were just as blurry.

Maria also wasn't *here*. If it wasn't just a temporary absence—that also said something. She hadn't stuck around after she died.

Sal rolled onto his side and started the arduous process of getting himself upright. He swayed like a ship on the high seas, and Tim steadied him with a hand on his back. A breeze ruffled the curtains, providing welcome relief from the stench. As I waited for Sal to become fully conscious, I drifted to the window to satisfy my own curiosity, looking out from the second story at the narrow alley between two buildings. Other than a gray cat nosing around behind a Dumpster, there was no one down there. Not even a ghost.

When I turned back around, Sal was staring at me, fully awake.

"Myron," he said.

"Hello, sir," I said.

"Been—been a long time."

"Too long, sir."

"What's with this sir business? Just Sal." His voice was throaty and thick, and I detected a hint of his ancestry in his voice. Usually he spoke with the clipped, perfect annunciation of a major-network news anchor, but every now and then his Italian roots showed themselves. "You know you can call me Sal."

"Right. Sal. It's good to see you."

He smiled ruefully. "I'm sure I look like crap. Wait a minute. You didn't all just kick down my door, did you?"

"No, it was partially open," Alesha said. "I thought there was … I thought there was someone in your apartment."

"Huh?"

"Mr. Belleni," Tim said, "did you, by chance, have any visitors staying with you last night?"

Sal rubbed his beard stubble, fingers scratching against skin like sandpaper on concrete. I thought I saw fear flit across his face. "Visitors? What kind—what kind of visitors?"

"Just one," Alesha said. "Maybe."

"Maybe?"

Sal's eyes were focused on Alesha with laser-like intensity, and it was clear that he *was* afraid. She was trying to be nonchalant about the whole thing, but his reaction was giving her pause.

"I don't know what I saw," she said. "I just thought… Maybe it was nothing. It was probably nothing. I just imagined it." She shrugged.

"Was it … a man in a cloak?"

The words choked off at the end. Alesha didn't respond at first, but the answer to his question was still plainly obvious on her face. That was *exactly* what she had seen. Sal, looking even paler than before, rose and shuffled to the bathroom, his boxers hanging low enough that his butt crack was visible. He reached behind the door and retrieved a powder blue terrycloth robe, slipping into it and tying the sash. It barely fit. The material was frayed and badly stained, the light blue bleached to white in a few places, but the cut and color were clearly intended for a woman. There were tan makeup stains around the neck. I wondered how long it had been since a woman had actually worn it.

"Maybe," Alesha said finally.

Sal swallowed hard. "So it's true. He's back. The killing at PSU—it was him."

"I don't know what I saw," Alesha insisted.

"You saw him. He was here."

"I don't know how. Where would he have gone? He didn't have time—"

"You know he's not human. You know that."

Nobody said anything. Sal stared out the window, then closed it, the aluminum screeching enough that everyone except Sal flinched. He stood like that, with his back to us, staring out the dirty glass. "I thought he might be watching," he said quietly.

Alesha and Tim didn't seem to know what to make of this, and I didn't blame them. If I didn't have a little inside information—not just about the Ghost Reaper, but about what happens to all of us when we die—I probably would have been just as stumped. Still, I wasn't quite sure how to go about questioning him, since I didn't want Alesha and Tim to think I was nuts. They may have already thought I was nuts, but I didn't want to conclusively prove it to them.

"I'm sorry about Maria," I said.

Sal's shoulders slumped, but he didn't say anything or turn around. I'm not sure why I said it. I certainly hadn't planned to say it. He scratched his rough chin, nodding, looking like he was trying to find something to say in response. Instead, he headed for the kitchen.

"I need some coffee," he said. "You guys want some coffee?"

"Love some," I said.

While he banged around in the kitchen, we settled behind a decoupage table with fifties-era newspaper front pages underneath the glass, Marilyn Monroe and James Dean smiling up at me. The table was small enough that our knees bumped. The tiny window was closed, but I still felt jets of cool air slipping through the cracks. Unable to find any clean mugs, Sal retrieved four of them from the landfill that was his sink, cleaned them with a rag that looked like it had been used on a chimney, and set them down in front of us. Mine was pink and decorated with purple fairies. Tim said he didn't drink coffee, but Sal ignored him. He turned back to the counter, watching the steam rise from the coffeemaker.

"We saw him, you know," he said. "Me and Hank."

"The Goodbye Killer?" Alesha said.

"One time," he said. "It got to Hank right away, but I didn't think it got to me so much. But it did. It just went deeper. I had terrible nightmares. Eventually ... eventually I told Maria. I had to tell someone, and she knew something was wrong, even when I wouldn't admit it to myself."

Nobody said anything. Alesha spun her mug, which pictured Clint Eastwood from *Dirty Harry*, the top half of his face rubbed away. Outside on the street, I heard children laughing. I wondered if they were alive. Nobody else seemed to acknowledge them. When Sal spoke again, I could barely hear his whisper over the percolating coffee.

"The nightmares were awful," he said. "I'd open a door, come around a corner, turn my head, and there they were. All the people he had killed ... Excuse me. I'll—I'll be right back."

He bolted from the room. We exchanged glances, but nobody rose. I heard him running the sink in his bathroom. Alesha started to rise, and I held out my hand for her to wait. He returned a moment later, wiping his mouth with the sleeve of his robe.

"Sorry about that," he said. "I just remembered my pills. Maria gets very upset if I don't take them."

I thought about the empty pill bottles. I wondered if she'd wanted him to take the prostate pills or the antidepressants. It must have been the antidepressants, since the other ones were out. I wondered again where she was. I thought about old Bill at Dad's retirement facility, how his wife had finally come back to him. Someone could intend to leave forever and still come back. These things happened. They could happen to anyone. Bill. Sal. Me.

"We're here because we're hoping you might be able to help us," I said. "You've had a lot of years to think about this. Do you have any idea why he does it? Or why he chooses his victims?"

At first, I wasn't sure he'd heard me. He stood staring into space, his arm still partially raised from when he'd wiped his mouth.

"They're good," he said.

"What?"

He looked at me as if I had just come into the room. "I thought you left the force," he said.

"I did."

"I heard you were a PI."

"I am."

"So why you getting mixed up in this business, then? For your dad?"

"Something like that."

"I need to go out and see him again. It's been a few years."

"He'd probably like that. Sal, you said, 'They're good.' What did you mean?"

He removed the still-percolating coffee, a few stray drops hissing on the warmer plate, and filled his mug. When he filled each of our mugs in turn, Tim again said he didn't drink coffee, and again Sal ignored him. He joined us at the table. He was looking at us, but his eyes had that dull quality that glass gets when the light is flat.

I sipped the coffee. It tasted like lukewarm motor oil, but I tried not to show it. Alesha sipped it too and made no attempt to hide her wince.

"Seventeen of them," Sal said. "Seventeen in five years."

"I know," I said.

"And now eighteen."

"That's right."

"There will be others."

Alesha pushed her coffee cup aside as if she were afraid she might be tempted to drink it again. "Why do you think that?" she asked.

"Because I know him," Sal said. "Now that he's started up again, one won't be enough."

"Sal," I said, "you just said, 'They're good.' Why?"

He appraised me the way a father might appraise a son who'd just asked a question a little beyond his years, as if trying to decide whether I was capable of understanding the answer he was about to give.

"Good people," he said. "All of them. I knew back then, had a sense of it, but after I turned in my badge I did a little more digging. Asked around, talked to folks. They're good people. The best kind. I don't mean like goody two-shoes. They weren't perfect. A lot of them didn't even go to church. But they were just … *good*, you know? Good to their friends, good to their co-workers, good to their spouses. Solid. Like they were just made that way."

Sal tapped his fingers on the table. I was brave and tried the coffee again. Alas, its quality hadn't changed.

"I know how it sounds," Sal said. "You're thinking, so what? Lots of good people in the world. And that's true. But I didn't know how rare these types of people are until this case. You meet one of them, you think, okay, nice person. You get that sense right away. This gal, Carmen, she worked at Denny's over there off I-5. She'd take leftovers from the restaurant to homeless people. Another woman, her name was Betty, one of the last victims, she was a first-grade teacher over in Tigard. Her kids would have walked on fire for her. Sometimes it wasn't anything like that. It was just this feeling you get when you look people in the eye."

"I will take you to a better place," Tim said.

We all looked at him. He smiled and fidgeted with his coffee cup.

"Sorry," he said. "I was just thinking about the killer's message."

"Don't apologize," Sal said. "Speak up anytime. I kind of forgot you were here."

"Yeah," Tim said. "I sort of have that effect on people."

"Not a bad trait to have," Sal said. "Blend in, go unnoticed."

"Like an Irish ninja," I said.

"Or wallpaper," Alesha said.

"Tsk, tsk," I said.

"It's okay," Tim said, "that's the nicest thing she's said about me."

"That's not true," Alesha said. "I believe I told Chief Branson you were the best partner I've ever had."

"Really?" I said.

"I think the full line," Tim said, "was that I was the best partner you've had if it was a one-person race and you ignored all of my negative qualities and focused on my only good one: I dress well."

"Ouch," I said.

"See, there's another negative quality," Alesha said to Tim. "You always see the glass as half-empty."

"Maybe we should get back to Sal here," I said.

"Oh, no," Sal said, "I'm enjoying this. Reminds me of me and Hank."

That changed the mood in a hurry. Sal seemed to realize it, because he chuckled.

"Sorry," he said. "I didn't mean that as a downer. Hank and I had a lot of fun, even though we were always giving each other a hard time."

"I'd like to give *this* guy a hard time again," Alesha said, jerking her thumb in my direction, "but no matter what I do, he won't do the sensible thing and become a cop again."

"And give up the great benefit package I have working as a private investigator?" I said.

"You have a benefit package?" Tim said.

"A joke, Tim," I said.

"Oh. Right."

"Don't be too hard on old Myron," Sal said. "What he went

through, with the shooting, the coma—it's amazing he's anywhere close to law enforcement. Me, I couldn't go back to the old life now. I mean, you can see that. I'm dealing with mayonnaise and rye bread all day instead of meth heads and hookers. I didn't even get shot. So I tip my hat to Myron. I really do." His eyes misted a little, and he took a long sip from his coffee cup as if trying to hide his face.

"What do you think of Chief Branson?" I asked him.

Sal choked on his coffee, barely managing to set it back on the table without spilling it. He wiped his lips on the sleeve of his bathrobe.

"What's the little guy, the French one with the complex?" he asked.

"Napoleon?" I said.

"Right. Napoleon complex. Clive's definitely got that. He always had it, even in the beginning, but it got worse the more he got promoted. He really looked up to your dad. I think having Hank around helped keep his worst qualities in line … Wait a minute. You don't think *he's* involved in this, do you?"

It wasn't just Sal who was looking at me like I was nuts. Alesha and Tim wore the same expression.

"I just got a weird feeling about him, that's all," I said.

"Well, we *all* get that," Sal said.

"Yeah," Alesha said. "I hear he sacrifices goats in his basement."

"Really?" Tim said.

"No, Tim," Alesha said.

"Oh."

"He's definitely a grade-A asshole," Sal said. "Always been one, just wasn't as bad."

"How about his personal life?" I asked.

"*What* personal life?"

"Yeah," I said. "He always seemed to be pretty private. I just wondered if you knew anything about him. Wife, kids, hobbies, that sort of thing."

"Nope," Sal said. "If he had a life outside of being a cop, he always kept it locked down pretty tight. How about you two? Things changed with Clive since I left?" He nodded toward Alesha and Tim.

"It never occurred to me to even wonder about it," Alesha said. "As a general rule, I don't pry into people's personal lives."

"With at least one exception," I said.

She glared at me.

"He's always seemed pretty nice to me," Tim said.

"He could shoot you in the gut and you'd say the same thing," Alesha said.

"Well," Tim said, "there's no way he would do something like that on purpose."

"See?" Alesha said. "Always rainbows and butterflies, wherever you look."

Tim shrugged. "I do try to see the positive side of things."

"You're a cop. You're *supposed* to see the negative side of things."

"Hey," Sal said, "that's not always true. Tim, don't let her ragging on you bother you too much. That sunny disposition of yours can carry you through a lot of stormy days. I … I had it myself once. You're just good, all the way through. Nothing wrong with that." Poor Sal looked like he was going to cry.

"Well, we *do* plan to catch him," I said, hoping to change the direction of the conversation. "I don't want him hurting any more people."

"I don't know if he can be stopped," Sal said, nodding to himself. "Like I said before, he's not human. I kept denying this to myself, but I believe it now. He's something else, like a … a ghost, maybe. How do you stop something like that? I just—I used to think so. I used to think he could be stopped. But now, maybe it's up to God. Only God can stop him."

"Careful," Alesha said. "You're talking to a confirmed atheist here in Myron. I remember him telling me quite clearly that he doesn't believe in ghosts. Isn't that right, buddy?"

"I'm definitely an atheist," I said. In a way, I was even more an atheist than before. I couldn't believe that if there really was a supreme being, *this* was the kind of afterlife he would have created. When people die, they just go on walking the earth forever? No eternal sleep? No chance for redemption? "I'll tell you one thing," I added, not quite able to restrain myself from saying a bit more. "If God does exist, he has a heck of a sense of humor."

"I'm—I'm not feeling well," Sal said.

"Oh," Tim said, "would you like us to get you—"

"I'm tired," Sal said. "I think you should go. Sorry."

"It's all right," I said.

Sal rubbed his forehead so firmly that his fingers left red marks on the skin. "Don't mean to be rude. Just need to lie down a while. I wish I could help you more. Look into the victims. They were all good, good in that special way. Maybe you'll find something Hank and I couldn't. Who knows. Who knows."

He stared at a place between us, not quite at the window. *Where did you go, Sal?* I rose from the table. Alesha and Tim joined me.

"Sal, we appreciate your time," I said.

"Call if you think of anything else that can help," Alesha added. She chewed on her bottom lip. "Do you have a … some kind of protection?"

"What, for the ladies?"

"Very funny."

"Of course I got a gun," he said.

"Good," Alesha said.

"He'll be sorry if he comes back."

"I don't know what I saw."

"Sure you do."

She laughed, but he barely even lifted his eyebrows. Even with his banter, his voice had been flat and unfeeling, like a bad actor reading a script.

Alesha and Tim headed for the door. I lingered. She gave me a look as she passed, as if to say, *Are you sure he's okay?* I nodded at her, even though I didn't know he was okay at all. I also didn't like that the Goodbye Killer had been in this room only minutes ago, and my gut told me there was a good chance he would come back. Sure, Sal had a gun, but I doubted it would do much good. I had a sense that Sal knew this, too. But what were we supposed to do? The man wanted to be alone. I patted Sal on the shoulder. The terrycloth robe felt crusty, as if it had been coated with one too many layers of hairspray. I wondered again about Maria. I wondered where she was and why she wasn't here to watch over him when her husband was so obviously circling the drain. I wondered if I had answered my own question.

I started after the others, but Sal grabbed the sleeve of my jacket. He pulled me close enough that my face was next to his.

"I meant what I said earlier," he said.

His awful breath made me wince. "What's that?"

"About tipping my hat to you. How you handled everything after the shooting. Got on with your life. I'm impressed."

"Don't be," I said. "It hasn't been all that easy."

"It never is. Listen, you have nightmares too?"

"Oh, I don't know. After the shooting, yeah. For a while."

He swallowed. "I have nightmares. A lot of them."

"Yeah, you said that. I'm sorry. You should see someone. It would probably help, talking to someone about it."

He pulled me even closer, dropping his voice so it was mostly a whisper. "It's like ... all the people he killed. They come to me, you know? They come to me at night and want to know why I didn't help them. Why I didn't stop him. But how can I? I mean, if he's some kind of ghost, right? I can't stop him. There's nothing I can do."

It might have been better if he'd been staring at me with the eyes of a madman, because at least then I could brush off his comment as only something a madman wearing a woman's bathrobe would say, but there was just ... *nothing*. He was dead inside. The fire had gone out, and even the embers had flickered and faded. Just when I started to rethink my decision to leave Sal alone, the life returned to his face. He gave my arm a squeeze, then let go.

"I'll go see your dad," he said.

"He'd like that," I said.

"You take care of yourself, Myron."

"You too. Okay if I maybe swing by here, check on you once in a while?"

"Sure, if it'd make you feel better. One thing, though. Make sure you knock. Someone else barges through that door, I'm shooting first and asking questions later."

He winked at me, and it was a relief. It meant that there was some part of Sal Belleni that still wanted to live.

Chapter 9

I WOULD HAVE CANCELED my date with Jak, but I didn't have her phone number. At least, that's what I told myself.

The truth is, after making plans with Alesha and Tim to meet Monday morning and start looking into the Goodbye Killer's victims, I spent the rest of Sunday in a state of nervous anticipation. The scattered mind, the crazy butterflies in the stomach, the random bursts of heart racing—all the traits of a lovesick teenager were fully present, but I kept denying that they had anything to do with Jak. I was just anxious about the case. About Dad. About Alesha, maybe. I am not a romantic man. It was one of Billie's constant complaints. I am too literal, too rational, too wedded to my need for facts and evidence to ever believe in something as silly as love at first sight. Lust? Maybe lust. Evolution designed us for procreation, so lust is written into our DNA. But whatever I was feeling for Jak, some part of me knew from the very beginning that it was more than simple lust. It was too specific, too overwhelming. I knew this because I had experienced the same feelings exactly one other time in my life.

When I met Billie.

I had all the same symptoms. I had all the same arguments against them. We didn't make sense. Our personalities were too different. We didn't really click. On top of that, with Jak there was also the age difference. And the breaking and entering. And I barely knew her. And yet ... the attraction was so powerful that we both felt at the mercy of some unseen force outside our control.

Somewhere around seven o'clock, when I was in my bedroom reading Eddie Quincy's e-book on the Goodbye Killer on my laptop, I found myself making occasional forays to the front of the house. By this time, the daylight had faded, so the house was dark. Each time, I peeked through the closed curtains, trying not to be seen by the few stalwart members of the Fourth Estate who would not be deterred despite my total refusal to engage with them. There was always another reason, of course. I wanted to stretch my legs. I needed a drink of water. I wanted a pencil from the little desk by the door. But the closer it got to eight o'clock, the more frequent these forays became. Twenty till, I added in stops in the bathroom to check my appearance in the mirror. Ten till, I changed my shirt three times, settling on a charcoal gray golf shirt with faint blue pinstripes that had been one of Billie's favorites.

Jak arrived five minutes early. I had been about to peer through the curtains again, and the abrupt loudness of her knock actually made me jerk back in surprise. I took a couple of deep breaths and told myself I was being stupid, that I should cancel this date as soon as I opened the door. Yet as soon as I *did* open the door, I knew right away there was no chance I was going to cancel.

She wore a stylish black leather jacket over a low, V-cut gray shirt, hip-hugging designer jeans, and toeless leather sandals that showed off her silver-painted nails. The emerald pendant hanging between her breasts brought out the green in her eyes—eyes that showed the same mixture of nervousness and vulnerability that I'd seen earlier. Her blond hair hung loose like before, but this time there were no clips holding it in place, and the evening breeze stirred the hair across her face and neck. I also thought I detected a shade of red mixed in with the blonde. Had she dyed her hair? It was her third transformation in less than two days. If she'd been the grunge girl the first time I saw her and the country-club socialite the second, then this time she was the hip Portland professional out for a night on the town. With *me.*

"Hi," she said.

"Hello," I said.

"You look nice."

"So do you," I said. "Different, but, um, good."

She smiled. It was a conversation fit for two giddy teenagers, and that's exactly how I felt. Stupid and young and driven by hormones instead of brains. Why was I doing this? I looked past her and saw that only one news van remained at the curb, parked in the cone of light under the streetlamp. Across the street, a hospital orderly in a green uniform pushed a rattling empty gurney along the sidewalk. Good bet he was a ghost. A young man in a dark suit, holding a pen and notebook, got out of the passenger seat of the van. Good bet he was real. I stepped aside and let Jak into the house, closing the door behind her just as the reporter shouted my name.

The two of us stood there staring at each other.

"Looks like they're mostly gone," I said. My voice sounded strange to me.

"Yep," she said. "Even Betty Big Boobs called it a night. That guy works for a local station. He's real new and desperate for a story."

"I don't plan to give him one," I said.

"Good. I want your story all to myself."

"Hmm. Still determined on that front, huh?"

"Big-time. When I'm into a story, I'm obsessed with it."

"That's what I am to you, then? A story?"

"Oh, I'm obsessed in another way, too. I admit it. And I'm not the only one."

"What do you mean? I just said yes to this date because I knew you would never give up until we actually went out and you saw we were incompatible."

She smirked. "Oh yeah? Then why were you watching for me from the window?"

"I wasn't."

"I saw you. You kept looking out every couple of minutes."

"Every couple of minutes? How long have you been out there? I didn't even see your car."

"I parked around the corner. Figured I would attract less attention from the press that way. I didn't realize so many of them would leave in the last hour."

"So what, you were just standing out there watching my house?"

"Don't change the subject," she said. "You were the one who kept coming to the window every two minutes looking nervous."

"I'm not nervous."

She stepped closer to me, close enough that I caught a whiff of her lavender scent, close enough that I saw the different shades of green in her eyes. "Say that again."

"I'm not … nervous."

Another step. When she spoke, this time I felt her breath on my chin. "Again," she said.

"Um."

"God, I want you to kiss me," she said.

"Wow. You really are forward."

"Life is too short not to go for what you want. And right now, I want you."

We were like two magnets. The pull was so strong that it took every ounce of my willpower to turn away from her. I got my leather jacket and asked her where she wanted to eat. She replied that we should eat in so we were closer to the bedroom. I ignored this and asked if she liked Italian. She said she didn't usually go for Italian men, but if I was part Italian, she would happily make an exception. Grabbing my keys and wallet, I asked if she would be making cracks like this all night. She said yes, without a doubt, though she also assumed much of the night wouldn't be spent talking at all.

So it went. We took my Prius, gliding through a few side streets to lose the news van before heading over the Ross Island Bridge. *Sorry, fella. You'll have to get your story another day.* It had not rained in a week, but the way the air hung like a veil over the lighted buildings downtown and the way the yellow lines glowed electric on the glistening asphalt resembled a city that had just endured a thunderstorm. Even the air, as we got out of the car near Pioneer Square, felt heavy and damp on my face.

On our way to La Bella Pera a block up the street, Jak took my arm. A pleasant warmth spread up my arm and my neck. I hadn't realized how much I had missed the simple things a woman can offer a man—a gentle touch, an affectionate smile, a laugh at a joke that didn't deserve a laugh. All my objections to her attraction (to *my* attraction) seemed pointless. Why was I fighting this? Yes, there was Alesha, there would always be Alesha, but this thing with Jak was simple and straightforward in a way a relationship with Alesha never would be. No doubt I could use some simple and straightforward in my life right about now.

We walked in comfortable silence until we reached La Bella Pera, where the maître d' wrote our names in a little black book and yet seated us immediately at a back table, a candle burning low in a ribbed green glass vase. Similar candles in similar vases burned low at other tables. The red tablecloth matched the red walls. Opera music played low. A few other couples occupied tables around us, and though I had not eaten there in over a year, the place did feel much more deserted than I remembered. I also realized something else.

No ghosts.

There were no ghosts in the restaurant, not judging from the way the waiter interacted with the other couples. He knew they were there. There were no ghosts on the walk here, either, at least as far as I could tell. This absence was certainly not unheard of for me, but it was unusual. In fact, if I had been thinking a bit more clearly, I probably wouldn't have chosen La Bella Pera at all, since Italian restaurants, in my experience, were often haunted by more ghosts than other places were. It had something to do with their intense sense of family and culture.

"A million miles away," Jak said.

"What's that?"

She folded her hands and rested her chin on them. "You. You're a million miles away. Where did you go, Myron Vale?"

"I'm still here."

"Now you are. But a second ago, not so much."

"I was just thinking."

"Hmm. About what?"

"Um … about serial killers."

"Nice. And here I was hoping you were dreaming about what I would look like naked."

"Maybe I'm dreaming about that, too."

"Ah!" she said, sitting up straight.

"What?"

"You flirted back! That's the first time. Progress. It's good."

Her smile was wide and authentic, a real sparkle to it. The music finished, leaving a gap between songs, and the room filled with the murmur of conversations and the clink of silverware. I took a drink of water and found the glass much colder to the touch than it ought to be. Why was I so warm? I couldn't be that nervous, not with her, this silly forward girl who was way too young for me. Too bold. Too beautiful. Too much.

"I … read some of your blog," I said.

"Oh yeah?"

"Yeah. Just a few articles." That was a lie. Before I'd delved into Quincy's book, I'd spent hours devouring her blog, her Twitter feed, and all the other dozen places she showed up online—at least that I could find. She seemed pretty ubiquitous, one of those people who seem even more real through social media than they do in real life. "It was interesting."

"Interesting? That's what my neighbor says about my writing. Well, that's very *interesting*. Like it was the closest she could come to a compliment without lying."

"I didn't mean it that way. It was very good."

"Now you're just saying that."

"No, you write very well. You're amazing, okay? Geez."

She rested her chin on her folded hands again, blinking her eyes at me. "Say that again."

"What?"

"I'm amazing."

"You're an amazing writer."

"Leave off the writer part."

"Okay, this is getting silly."

"Just say it. Please?"

I sighed. "You're amazing."

"Without the sigh."

"You're amazing."

"Much better," she said, grinning wryly. "Would you mind saying it one more time so I can record it with my iPhone? I want to be able to play it back late at night to myself."

"Absolutely not."

"Aw…"

I was rescued by one of the waiters, a middle-aged man with oily black hair slicked straight back and a pencil-thin mustache that looked askew, as if affixed to his lip by old tape. His clothes looked as if they had started the day in fine shape but lost the battle as the hours progressed, the red tie loose, the white shirt untucked in the back and spotted with red sauce, the pants sagging and wrinkled. He walked like a much older man, shuffling his feet, his shoulders stooped. When he spoke, he mumbled.

"*Benvenuto a case mia,*" he said, with the kind of raspy voice that reminded me of Marlon Brando in *The Godfather*. "I am the owner of La Bella Pera, Carlos Collani. I always check, is everything good? Is there nothing I can do for you?

"Everything's great," I said to him. Then I added, with a laugh, "Except my date here. I think I'm in *way* over my head."

He stared at me, unblinking. So much for humor. Maybe his English wasn't quite as strong as it had seemed.

"Well, I guess we're ready to order," I said.

When he went on staring, that's when it finally dawned on me what was going on here—what should have been obvious from the beginning. You'd think, at some point, I would finally learn. The waiter wasn't just staring. He was *gaping*. He was gaping because he was a ghost and I wasn't. He was gaping because I talked back to him when none of his other customers ever did.

He also wasn't the only one staring. All of Jak's easygoing, flirtatious demeanor had passed behind a cloud of confusion.

"*You*," Carlos rasped.

"Are you making a joke?" Jak said.

"Huh?"

"Who are you talking to?"

"You," Carlos said again. His voice rose, even as he took a step away from the table. "The Ghost Detective. You are he, yes?"

"No one," I said to Jak. I laughed. "I was just messing around."

"You were messing around by pretending there was a waiter standing at our table?"

"*Signora,* I am *no* waiter," Carlos said indignantly, patting his chest. "I am *owner*. This restaurant, it is in my family for thirty-five years."

But of course, Jak didn't hear him. She couldn't. Most ghosts were either intimidated or terrified of me, but that wasn't exactly the vibe I was getting from Carlos. It was more like he'd just witnessed the divine appearance of the Virgin Mary in his Alfredo sauce.

"You must do something," he said. "If you are truly Ghost Detective, you must stop this—this *mostro* from ruining our city."

"Well?" Jak said to me. "I'm still waiting for your answer."

"I'm an actor in my spare time," I said. "Community theater, that sort of thing. I was practicing a scene."

"Oh yeah? Which play?"

"I forget."

"Maybe you forgot because it's not true."

"Actually, I was just performing a little experiment. It's called Confuse Your Date. I read about it in *Vogue*. It's supposed to be a way to spice up the evening."

"Keep trying," Jak said.

"*Signor,*" Carlos said. "*Per favore* ... speak to me on this matter. My business, the customers, they do not come. I fear it will be this way always if something does not change."

"I tell you what," I said, still concentrating on Jak, "you come up with a reason for my behavior there. Let's make it a game."

"Oh no," Jak said, "I'm not letting you off the hook. There's something going on with you, Myron Vale. Something that makes you very different."

"Good to know," I said, rubbing my temples. I felt one of my really bad headaches coming on, a throbbing behind the eyelids, a pulsing at the back of my skull, spreading, working its way forward. "I appreciate the heads-up."

"*Signor—*" Carlos pleaded.

"Something happened to you when you were shot, didn't it?" Jak said.

"I don't know what you mean. I was in a coma. The recovery was a bit rough."

"More than a bit, from what I heard," Jak said.

"*Signor,*" Carlos tried again. "My business, if nothing changes—"

"Man, it's noisy in here!" I exclaimed, my frustration at the invisible vise tightening around my skull getting the better of me. "Maybe we should go somewhere else. I'd love a little more peace and quiet." It took all of my willpower not to look directly at Carlos, but I hoped he understood that my message was directed at him.

Jak squinted at me. "What are you talking about? It's dead quiet—except for you. You just got the few people in here to give us the cold eye."

"*Signor* Vale," Carlos said, "I do not wish to be a bother. I only wish you to know how important this is to me, to many of us. My family, they depend on La Bella Pera."

"I'm doing everything I can," I said.

"Huh?" Jak said.

"Sì, sì," Carlos said, bowing his head. "I will leave you now. But if you need anything, *anything*, please say. Money? I can get you money. Many of us can. Or some help? People are afraid, but there are some who would help on both sides. People in the family will do what they can. Please know. We will—"

"Myron," Jak said, "do you see ghosts?"

This was such a bull's-eye that both Carlos and I stared dumbfounded at Jak. My headache, which had been grinding slowly across my brain, accelerated its pace, the pressure so significant that I saw bursts of white at the edge of my vision. Nausea took hold; even the sweet aroma of tomato sauce wafting out of the kitchen was enough to make my stomach do flip-flops. Carlos, who'd been able to overcome his fear of me because of the urgency of his need, must have found Jak's question unnerving enough to push him over the edge, because he scooted away from the table with hands raised as if someone were pointing a gun at him.

I reached for my cup, but even the thought of trying to swallow water was enough to kick in my gag reflex, so I just let my hand rest on the cool glass instead. "What—what would give you that crazy idea?" I asked.

"It's what people said when you were, um, institutionalized. I looked at some of your files. The doctors wrote that you talked about ghosts who came to see you. They said you were quite convinced."

"You talked to my doctors?"

"Now, don't get mad."

"Why would I be mad? I mean, Jesus. You're looking into my damn files!"

"Myron—"

"I thought we were on a date? I didn't know I was going to get the Spanish Inquisition."

"I'm not—"

"I'm leaving."

I rose, bumping the table hard enough that the water in my glass splashed onto the tablecloth. In my blurry vision, the now full-on migraine making my eyes cloudier by the second, the spots on the red cloth looked like blood. Everybody in the room stared at us—a lot more people than before, old men in dark suits gathered around Carlos, gawking and pointing at me, young women in veils, kids with chalky white faces, a black man in an oil-stained mechanic's uniform whose head was severed right down the middle. Now even the weird ghosts were coming out of the woodwork. Or was I just imagining them? When the headaches got really bad, sometimes I really did start hallucinating. I took a ride on the Myron merry-go-round and where it stopped, nobody knew.

Somehow I staggered toward the exit. The heavy night air helped calm my queasy stomach, but it did nothing for my headache. I headed for the Prius, Jak calling my name behind me. The yellow halos surrounding the streetlamps pulsed in time to the throbbing behind my eyelids. Jak caught up with me and grabbed my arm.

"Hey," she said.

"You should call a cab," I said. "I'll—I'll give you some money if you need some."

"Come on, Myron. Don't do this."

"I'm not doing anything. You are."

"I don't know what—"

"I'm not going to be your story, Jak. If that's what I am to you, then this—whatever this is—it has to end now."

"Myron—"

"Now, Jak."

"If you'll just—"

"Choose. Me or your story."

I could barely see her face because the pounding behind my eyelids was so bad it blurred my vision, but her silence was enough. I ripped my arm away from her and hightailed it toward my Prius. For once, I was glad my car was that lovely shade of lime green; it stood out among all the other cars like a radioactive lily pad.

I hadn't gone more than a dozen steps when she grabbed my arm, spun me around, and kissed me.

I got a brief flash of wide green eyes before her lips met my own. She stood on tiptoe and pressed her whole body against mine, leather jackets rustling against one another. She tasted like cinnamon-flavored espresso. I was no connoisseur of first kisses, but in my limited experience of maybe a dozen first kisses in my whole life, this one was right up near the top. There was fierceness but not pushiness.

For the first second or two, my participation ranked somewhere between passive observer and helpless victim. Then I felt myself kissing her back. My hands found their way to her hips, found the warmth of her body, the coarseness of her jeans. After a minute or an hour or a year, she finally pulled away—but only inches, her breath warm on my chin, her eyes shiny and alert.

"Don't," I said.

She kissed me again, a quick one, like the brush of a butterfly's wings. Mercifully, I felt the pounding in my head begin to subside. Maybe she was like an elixir for my migraines. Maybe she would be good for me. Maybe.

"Don't," I said again.

"Don't," she said, mockingly.

"This—this is a bit too fast," I said.

"So learn to go faster."

"I'm not into one-night stands."

"Who said this had to be for one night?"

She leaned in, moving her head under my chin. Her hair smelled like apricots or some other sweet fruit. She slipped her arms under my jacket and pulled me closer. I didn't understand how this could feel so right and so wrong at the same time. I glanced up and saw, across the street and standing under a street light by a closed doughnut shop, a Native American man dressed in cowhide and beads, a feather in his braided jet-black hair. He stared at me for a long moment. I stared back. He bowed his head and strode on, revealing the feathered arrow embedded in his shoulder before he passed into the shadows. If most ghosts were hunkering down in fear of the Ghost Reaper, it was no surprise that the weird ones were still out in force.

Even this didn't kill the mood. That's how enthralled I was with the warmth of the young woman in my arms.

"I want you to trust me," she said.

"I know so little about you," I said.

She sighed, and I felt her breath on my neck. "Myron?"

"Yes?"

"Let's go to your place."

"Jak …"

"Or at least the car. It's—it's pretty small, but it will do."

"Jak, come on."

Her hands, cupped in the small of my back, moved. They slid lower, over my hips, other places. I started to protest, but the words died in my throat. Just like that, all my resistance dissolved like a dam made of snow.

We barely made it back to my house, leather jackets discarded in the Prius, shirts flying free on the way to the bedroom and a few buttons popping to the hardwood floor along the way. Lips probing, we moved in concert through the shadows. Somewhere distant, maybe in a house next door, I heard a man belting out some kind of Irish drinking song and I wondered, perhaps for the thousandth time, whether this sound reaching my ears was real or from a ghost—but then Jak stopped me in the doorway to my room with a hand on my bare chest, and all I could think about was her.

With a sly smile, she unhooked her bra and slipped off her pants and tiny lace panties, standing before me as God intended—if there was a God around to do the intending. Looking at her was almost enough to make me a believer just on the proof before me: all that smooth, pliant flesh in and out of darkness, all those wonderful slopes and curves packed into such a small frame. How could there *not* be a God if something so perfect could exist?

She wanted me to see her. That much was obvious, the reason she'd stopped me in the doorway. But there was something vulnerable behind the brash facade, and it was that hint of insecurity, not the cocky exterior, that made her so irresistible. She wanted me to see her naked but she was also afraid of me seeing her naked, as if it was the fear itself that prompted her to do these crazy things, like she had to prove that fear could never stop her. But the real Jak, the *Jacqueline* behind the mask, she needed something from me. She needed it desperately and didn't want to show the desperation. If I had said something cutting in that moment, some kind of insult about how she looked, no matter how small, it would have destroyed her.

But I didn't want to destroy her. I wanted *her.* It had been so long since I'd been with a woman—even longer if you didn't count the special kind of intimacy that Billie and I had shared, infrequently as it was, when she'd been a ghost—that I'd been wondering lately if I was even capable anymore, so it was good that the animal part of my brain had fully taken control. I kissed her hungrily, all my doubts vanquished, edging her toward the bed. A moan escaped her throat. Even as our lips remained locked, her fingers worked on my pants.

Then we were both naked. Then we were on the bed. Then we were moving in concert once again, hands groping over flesh, warm bodies pressing together, all the world falling away, ghosts and all, as we lost ourselves completely in one another.

LATER, MUCH LATER, we lay entwined on the bed, sweat cooling on our bodies, our legs and arms so draped and crisscrossed over one another that looking down at us through droopy eyes, I wasn't sure what was me and what was her. It may have been an hour since our last go-round—there had been a few—but we hadn't made any attempt to get under the covers. Her nose nuzzled against my neck, her breath warm on my throat, her hair on my shoulder. Her lovely nose. Her lovely throat. Her lovely hair.

"I can't believe I did that," I said.

"More than once," she said.

"More than once."

"Hmm. You can't believe you did it at all, or you can't believe it was more than once?"

"Both," I said.

She was quiet a long time, and when she spoke, there was that note of vulnerability again. "Do you regret it?"

"No," I said.

I replied quickly to assuage her fears, but I also meant it. I didn't regret it. She might have been a decade too young for me, but what was age now that I knew that death no longer had any real meaning? The physical intimacy might have been fast, way too fast by my normal standards (I was usually borderline puritanical in my dating pace), but I couldn't regret some of the best sex of my life, especially since I had just come out of dry spell long enough that it might have even impressed the monks who lived in Mount Angel Abbey.

Jak, purring like a kitten, slid her hand down my belly. I caught it before it reached its intended destination.

"Aw," she said.

"You've got to give me a little break here."

"We've had a break."

"A little longer break."

"Hmm. All right. Only this once. But I warn you, I'm pretty insatiable. If you have to pop some Viagra to keep up, I don't mind."

"Um … I don't think that will be necessary."

"Care to prove it?"

"In a minute, in a minute."

"Don't get me wrong, you're pretty damn good. Real good. So it's not a question of performance. Endurance is an entirely different—"

"Jak?"

"Yes?"

"Shut up."

She laughed, then snuggled even closer to me, falling silent for a while. I felt a heartbeat and wasn't sure if it was hers or mine. Through the cracks in my curtains, I saw the first blush of dawn, a mix of rose and amber hues. I closed my eyes. I might have dozed, because I woke to Jak's whisper.

"Myron?" she said.

"Yes?" I said.

"I choose you, okay?" she said.

"Okay," I said.

"I won't write anything about you, or us, unless you see it first."

"I appreciate that."

"Do you want me to stop completely? Writing about you? I can if you want. I've—I've never done it before, stopped a story for someone. But I will. I will if you want me to."

"No," I said. "No, you don't have to do that. But a heads-up about what you're writing before you put it out there for the world to see would be nice."

"I can do that."

"And no more digging into my medical files, okay?"

"I'm sorry."

"It's all right. It should be pretty obvious I forgave you."

She laughed. I laughed, too. I knew in that moment I could spend the rest of my life trying to make her laugh. Boy, was that different from Billie—she'd never been a big fan of laughter. Brooding? Sure, she could brood with the best of them, an Olympic brooder she was. But hearing Jak laugh, so rich and genuine and completely her, was tonic for my soul. Then I said something that completely surprised me, something I had not said to anyone in the past six years, at least no one living—not unless you counted the doctors at the facility when I was still trying to put my fragile mind back together. Since I was not myself then and have only fragments of memories of that time, I don't.

"I see ghosts," I said.

Her breath caught in her throat, her body suddenly a bit stiffer. In the silence, I heard the drip of the faucet in the kitchen. Somewhere distant, the muted screech of a bus's brakes bounced over the rooftops, but otherwise the city slumbered.

"Not just one," I said, "but all of them. And not just some of the time, but *all* of the time."

Finally, she expelled her breath. When she spoke, I heard relief.

"I believe you," she said.

"Remember your promise. Not to write anything without showing me first."

"I remember."

"I don't want anyone to know," I explained. "My life is hard enough as it is. You see, I—I have a hard time telling them apart. That's why, at the restaurant, that's why I seemed to be acting so strangely. The owner, I thought he was real."

"You can't tell them apart at all?"

"Not without touching them."

"Wow. How many are there?"

"Billions."

"You mean," she said, "when people die—

"They don't go anywhere."

"Oh wow," she said.

I'd been so worried that she would treat me differently once she found out, it hadn't occurred to me how she might grasp her whole concept of life and death being thrown into the blender. Not everyone would be able to handle such a leap.

"So," she said, "like my father? He died when I was little. At least that's what Mom always told me. You're saying, you're saying he's out there somewhere? You're saying—"

"Yes," I said.

"Sometimes I think, I don't know, I think I've heard him talking to me. Telling me he's proud of me, my writing. Is that crazy?"

"It's not crazy at all," I said. "A lot of people have *some* connection to ghosts, even if they're not totally aware of it."

"I kept telling myself I was nuts for believing it, but I always wanted … hey, can you get in touch with ghosts? You know, if you want to talk to one in particular? Like, if I really wanted to talk to my dad, could you act as a medium?"

"It's not easy," I said. "It's not like they use the postal service. They have their own way of doing things. I'm still trying to make sense of it all. Some of it probably never *will* make sense."

"Are there ghosts in here now?"

"No."

"Well, that's good. So ... how about your, um, wife? Is she still around?"

"No," I said. "No, she left me."

Then it all spilled out, starting with the shooting, all the crazy things that led to my being the way I am. Billie's death. The investigation that revealed all those buried secrets. I told her about Elvis. I told her about the Department of Souls. I told her about the Assistant Director, the priest who wouldn't tell me his name, and lots of other details about the world she couldn't see. I told her about the headaches, the little embarrassments, the struggle to make ends meet when I had a hard enough time just keeping myself sane. I even told her about the Ghost Reaper, about why he was such a threat to both the world of the living and the world of the dead. I told her that everyone was sure he was going to strike again, and soon.

When I finished, Jak said nothing. Rimming the curtains, the light of dawn continued brightening, creeping into the room, sending rosy tentacles along the wall. I heard a school bus pass by my house. School. Monday morning. People putting on nice clothes and going to work in cubicles. The MAX whipping thousands of people back and forth between homes and office buildings. The roads clogged with cars, the air filled with carbon monoxide, the Internet buzzing with emails. I lay in bed with a pretty girl and the world went on rotating. A serial killer still lurked and life shrugged and continued shuffling along in spite of it all.

"Thank you for trusting me," Jak said.

"It's a relief, really."

"I'm—I'm still trying to take it all in."

"I bet," I said, holding her a little tighter. "But I've talked so much about me. I want to know all about you now."

"Oh, I don't know," she said. "It's really not that interesting."

"Come on, Jak. That can't be true. You told me your dad left when you were little."

"Yeah."

"That must have been hard."

She didn't pull away, but I felt her muscles tighten, her body grow taut. I wondered if I'd gone too far. Reading her blog, it had been obvious that she was more than happy to share her life in the present— overshare might be a more apt description—but her past was a bit vague. That tidbit about her dad leaving when she was little was the first glimpse into her childhood I'd seen.

"I really don't like talking about that stuff," she said.

"Okay," I said. "I thought we were trusting each other here."

"It's not about trust. It's just … I'd rather not think about it. It's not like it matters."

"Fine," I said.

"Don't be mad."

"Why would I be mad? It's your past. I get it. You don't have to talk about it if you don't want to."

"Myron, please. I don't want any coldness between us right now. It feels so right. I don't want to ruin it by bringing up a lot of crap from my childhood. That stuff ruined enough of my life as it is."

"I said it's fine."

She rolled partly on top of me, her naked breasts pressed against my chest, her blond hair framing her face. Those green eyes, so big and bright, shimmered as if she was holding back tears. When she spoke, it became obvious she *was* trying not to cry; her voice sounded hoarse and strained.

"Look," she said, "look, I'll tell you some stuff, okay? I just—I just don't like to talk about this. But I'll tell you. I don't want to lose you. I don't know what's happening here. I don't understand it. It's not like it's been with other guys. I feel … I don't know what I feel. But I can't have you mad at me. Not that. So I'll tell you, okay? It's not that big of a deal, really. I just … Dad left when I was just a baby. Mom said he died in some kind of accident, but who knows. By the time—by the time I was old enough to really ask the question, she was already pretty heavy into drugs. Meth, mostly. Totally ruined her life."

"Jak—" I began.

"She was in and out of jail a bunch," Jak went on, her voice rat-tling worse the more she talked, like a freight train breaking apart as it rumbled along the tracks. "I went into foster care. She died of an overdose, but I don't care. She doesn't mean anything to me. Get it? Nothing."

"Jak, you don't have to do this," I said.

"No, you wanted to hear it," she said, sniffling and blinking rap-idly. "You asked. And I'm telling you. No secrets, okay? That's got to be our promise to one another. I just, I always wondered about my dad, you know? I'd like to talk to him. Mom got into drugs, but what was his excuse for checking out on me? That's what I want to know. That's all I want to know, Myron. Myron. There's—there's more. I just. I want. I want to tell you …"

Whatever was keeping that freight train together, it finally lost its battle to forces trying to tear it apart. She cried, her whole body convulsing. I wiped my thumb across the tears on her face. She again tried to speak, but I shook my head and pulled her closer. With one hand on her hair, I used the other to stroke her bare back, whispering to her that it would be all right, there was no need to talk, just to let it out, let it pass. She cried it out for a while, a good long while, then finally the tremors subsided and the breathing came easier.

"I'm sorry," she said finally.

"Don't apologize," I said.

"I just—I don't go there much. Not even in my own head."

"I get it."

"Myron—"

"Just lie here for a while. No need to talk."

And that's what we did, warm bodies entwined, me stroking her back soothingly. We lay like that until she began tracing circles in my chest hair with her finger. This stirred something below, the old in-voluntary male response, and our physical closeness meant Jak felt it too. She raised up, smiling with her tear-streaked face, and leaned in close to kiss me. Our lips were about to meet when someone in the room spoke.

"Vinnie?"

I froze. A bucket of cold water would have had the same effect on my amorous state of mind. Only one person in the world called me by the shortened version of my middle name, but I would have recognized her even if she had only sighed disapprovingly.

"Mom?" I said.

Jak, so close I felt her breath on my lips, stopped and blinked at me, eyes questioning. There was a moment's pause, just long enough for me to wonder if I had imagined the whole thing, before Mom spoke again in an anguished voice.

"Vinnie," she said, "it's—it's your father. I can't find him anywhere."

Chapter 10

OF ALL THE PEOPLE living or dead I did *not* want to see when I was in bed with a woman, my mother topped the list. In fact, she would be on a list all by herself, since she was so far ahead of anyone else that it wouldn't even make sense to put her in the same category. Yet any anger I felt at her violating my privacy—something we had been at odds over even when I'd been a boy and she felt the need to snoop through my things while I was at school—was forgotten the moment I grasped the meaning of what she had just said.

I bolted upright fast enough that Jak, spinning off me, actually yelped. Mom stood in the open doorway to the bedroom decked out in a black dress and black shawl as if she had just come from a funeral, slightly hunched, supporting herself with one hand on the door frame. The bright morning light, slipping through the cracks in the curtains, filled the room with a gauzy warm glow that made Mom's attire look all the more out of place.

"He's *what*?" I said.

Mom started to speak, then covered her mouth with her hand. Jak, her nakedness exposed from the waist up, grabbed my arm.

"What is it?" she said.

"My—my mother—" I began.

"She's *here?*"

Before I even nodded, Jak yanked the sheet over her breasts, glancing furtively around the room as if was possible to detect some sign of her.

"Yes," I said. "In the doorway, there."

Jak scooted a little closer to me. Mom, as if finally realizing there was someone else in the room with us, lifted her head and stared defiantly at Jak. The lines in her face appeared even more severe than usual, the chalky white skin pulled taught over cheekbones so sharp, the TSA would have classified them as weapons. She wore no makeup, an aberration I had witnessed only a half-dozen times in my life. Red veins webbed the whites of her eyes.

"Who's this little tart?" Mom said.

"Forget that," I said. "What do you mean, you can't find Dad?"

"Your dad's missing?" Jak said.

"For God's sake, Myron," Mom said. "You're married! And you're—you're in bed with a tramp half your age!"

"Mom! Tell me about Dad."

Mom burst into tears. These weren't just a few symbolic tears, either. This was a full-out sobfest, waterworks aplenty, her chest shuddering like an old rusty engine that hadn't been used in years and was now pushed to the max. I groped around until I found my boxers on the floor, slipped them on, and rose out of bed. Jak wrapped the sheet even tighter around herself. I approached Mom, raising my arms to touch her shoulders, then remembered that there could be no touching, which was just as well because I wasn't sure what would have happened even if I could have touched her. She had not been the touching sort, even when alive. I think once, when I'd been three or four years old and presented a drawing of a tree I'd made for her at school, she'd patted my head.

"Mom, please calm down," I said.

"I was—I was just down the hall for a moment—"

"What?"

"And when I came back, when I came back—oh, oh my ..." She

took big, gulping breaths. It would have been comical if the news she was keeping from me weren't so urgent. "I—I came back, and he was gone."

"What do you mean gone?" I said.

"Gone!" she shouted. "He's gone! He left, or—or someone *took* him!"

"That's crazy! No one's called me from the Mistwood. They would call if he was missing."

"I looked for him everywhere!"

"You've got to be mistaken," I said. "He—he can't go anywhere. He wouldn't even, he wouldn't even know what to do."

Even as I spoke, though, I could see that the truth was written plainly on Mom's face. Eleanor Vale was many things, but she was no kidder. It may have been the challenge in my voice, but it doused her hysteria a bit and allowed her to reclaim some of her cold precision. She leveled her gaze at me, her face—at least for the moment—as still as concrete.

"Myron," she said, "he's gone."

WE TOOK THE PRIUS, ending up square in the middle of Monday-morning rush-hour traffic. On the way, I called the Mistwood from my cell and asked them to check on Dad. They put me on hold, forcing me to listen to flutes and harps accompanied by a babbling brook. The music—if it could be called that—was probably intended to be soothing, but it actually made me want to slam the phone into the dashboard. The only reason I didn't was because I didn't have any money to replace it. If Dad was truly missing, being phoneless was not the smartest option.

"I just don't understand why I have to sit in the backseat," Mom said. "Why does that little tart get to sit up front?"

I ignored her. Jak, conscious that Mom was sitting back there, glanced behind her often enough that I didn't want to make her even more anxious. Going for a ride with the mother of the man you'd just slept with would be awkward enough. Going for a ride with the *ghost* of the mother took the awkwardness to a whole new level.

I'd told Jak she didn't have to come, but she refused to listen, and I couldn't quite bring myself to leave her behind. Dressing in a hurry, Jak had donned my black Blazers baseball cap, her now somewhat ratty blonde hair pulled out the back. She also wore one of my T-shirts, a plain white one she'd tucked into her designer jeans. We crawled bumper to bumper over the Ross Island Bridge, breathing in the diesel fumes of a Schwann truck in front of us. Some kind of accident clogged the traffic, forcing us to inch along. I saw two old men in tuxedos and top hats sitting on the edge of the bridge, as if readying themselves to jump. I saw a girl, her face so melted by fire that her cheekbones poked through her blackened skin, staring at us from the back of a city bus. I saw a sheikh in a tattered red robe—it may have been covered in blood, or it may have just been red—riding an emaciated camel along the sidewalk.

A hundred years passed before the woman from the Mistwood returned, panic in her voice, to say that they couldn't find my father anywhere.

I hung up and called Alesha. She answered on the first ring.

"Dad's missing," I said even before she managed a hello.

"Myron?"

"Can you contact the Forest Grove police? Have them start a search?"

"Your dad—" Alesha began.

"Maybe a perimeter of five miles," I said. "Work inward. He's probably just wandering, confused. He wouldn't go far. I know they'll balk at committing many resources to it when he hasn't been missing long, but we have to act fast."

"Myron, slow down," Alesha said. "Start over. Your dad is missing?"

"We don't have time for this! I'm on my way there now."

"I'll make some calls."

"Thank you."

"And I'll meet you there. I'm actually over at the station with Tim, going over the old files, so I'll probably be there before you."

It took us ten years to get to the Mistwood, give or take. Mom complained most of the way about being relegated to the back and Jak kept glancing back there, which only made Mom more irritable, spitting out a variety of insults. I would have put a stop to it, but all I could think about was Dad. On his own. Wandering the streets.

Or worse.

Maybe the Goodbye Killer …

No, I wouldn't let my mind go there. That's not the way Portland's favorite serial killer liked to operate. As far as we knew, he only targeted random people. If he had wanted to take out Dad, he would have done it long ago.

But if I was right, he *had* visited Sal's apartment only yesterday. Why?

A breeze stirred the cherry-blossom trees lining the street near the facility, dappling the sidewalk with pink shadows. When I parked the Prius in a handicap spot near the door, the only spot available, Alesha and Tim exited the building to greet us—Alesha in her black pantsuit and leather jacket, Tim in a crisp white shirt and a thin red tie roughly the same color as his hair. Not only that, but Eddie Quincy followed right behind, rumpled as always, jotting notes on a pad of paper. The way his few strands of hair rippled in the wind reminded me of a propeller on a beanie cap.

Seeing me, they all looked concerned. Seeing Jak emerge next to me, their expressions all changed instantly, ranging from mild surprise (Tim) to outright hostility (Alesha) to a weird, googly-eyed shock that I assumed was a mixture of lust and envy (Eddie). Behind them, under the atrium that covered the wide sidewalk leading to the tinted-glass front doors, a man in overalls painted the stucco walls. Since his outfit appeared fifty years out of date, I knew it was a good bet was no longer among the living.

"Hey," Jak said, nodding.

"Nice hat," Alesha said.

"Thanks," Jak said.

"I'm pretty sure I'm the one who bought it for Myron." She looked at me. "Remember that, Myron? I won a couple of Blazer tickets at that charity thing. You bought me one of those silly giant fingers. I got you the hat."

The hurt in Alesha's eyes cut into me with the precision of a surgeon's scalpel. Jak fiddled with the hat self-consciously, the shadow of the brim hiding her eyes. I had been expecting some awkwardness with Alesha when the state of my relationship with Jak became known, of course, but I hadn't meant to shove it in her face. But what of it? How many men had she slept with in the years since we'd known each other? A couple dozen? I might have snapped at her, but we didn't have time for petty nonsense.

"I need to talk to the staff," I said, heading past them to the doors.

"Already did," Alesha said, falling in step next to me. "Myron, he's gone."

"I want to search his room."

"Did that, too. Just a second ago."

"Well, I'm doing it again!"

She snapped her mouth shut. Eddie, his legs planted in place as firmly as the trunk of a tree, gaped at Jak as she passed only inches from him. When I got to the door, I realized that Mom hadn't made a peep either, which was a far more unusual state of affairs. I glanced behind me and found that she wasn't there. Not on the sidewalk. Not sitting in the backseat of the car. What the heck was going on here?

Assuming she'd slipped past and gone in ahead of us, I entered the building. The commotion inside made it obvious that something bad had happened—two people behind the counter on the phone, faces harried, loud voices down the hall, people wearing name badges hustling about. One of those people in name badges, a silver-haired man with saggy jowls and an even saggier gut, rushed up to me.

"Mr. Vale," he said. "I'm Jim Thorndike, the manager here at the Mistwood. I want you to know we're doing everything—"

"You can't find him?" I said.

"We have people—"

"How can you lose someone who gets lost on the way to the bathroom?"

"Well—"

"I want to see his room," I said, pushing past him.

Even the residents wandered about the reception area and the hall, looking worried and perplexed. Some gaped at me. Most ignored me. I ignored them all, living and dead alike. Thorndike said something about Dad being there when the night staff did their count at the end of their shift, which would have been about seven in the morning, but he was gone an hour later when the morning staff went to see if he was awake for breakfast.

His room was empty, of course. Just the same, I searched the closet, the bathroom, under the bed. A pale Thorndike watched, probably wondering, like me, just how this was all going to play out when I sued their asses for negligence. Nothing was missing except his shoes. Well, that was good. At least he wasn't walking around town barefoot. Dad's favorite blue blazer was also missing, which was interesting, because he never remembered to put on the blazer these days unless someone asked him if he wanted to wear it. Did someone lead him out of this room?

Alesha told me she had a couple of Forest Grove uniforms crawling the streets this very minute. She said this while looking at Jak, as if challenging her to come up with something equally helpful. Tim watched from the hall, along with Eddie, who was *still* staring stupidly at Jak. It made me want to punch him, not out of jealousy but because Eddie was so craven that he could actually feel something like lust at a time like this. Mom still hadn't shown her face. What was happening here? Was everybody insane?

Crestfallen, I sank onto the bed. Then it occurred to me that the bed was *made*—and not just made, but neat and tidy, the sheets smartly tucked, the bedspread so tight I could have bounced a quarter on it.

"Did someone make the bed?" I asked Thorndike.

"Um, no," he said. "No, I don't think so."

"You don't think so?"

"I mean no, no one made the bed, Mr. Vale."

"Dad wouldn't make the bed. He can barely dress himself these days."

I didn't need to say it. The implication hung in the air, and by the look in everyone's eyes, they understood it, too.

Dad didn't just leave.

Someone took him.

THERE WERE LOTS of assurances from all involved that Dad would be found in the shortest order, none of which proved to be true. A thorough search of the facility turned up nothing. The cops combing the streets also turned up no sign. Alesha and Tim interviewed some of the staff, asking them if Dad had displayed any unusual behavior. I asked Jak to talk to some of the living residents while I surreptitiously tried to get information from the other kind.

On my way upstairs, Eddie Quincy hustled to catch up with me, his face puffy and red, sweat stains around his armpits. His garlic-and-coffee smell was strong enough to even mask the ever present odor of disinfectant that seemed to pervade the halls of the facility.

"Hey, Myron, pal," he said. "Hey, sorry about your dad."

"What do you want?"

"Nothing. Just want to help, right? Hey, that girl down there—she your girlfriend now, huh?"

I leveled my gaze at him. "What does that have to do with any-thing?"

"She just, uh, looks familiar. I was just curious about her, is all."

"Don't be. Didn't you hear? Curiosity killed the cat."

"Well, um, I'm already dead."

He stared stupidly. It would have been funny if I had been in the mood to laugh. I continued upstairs. Eddie hung back, far behind. For the most part, the ghosts at the Mistwood knew me, so at least I had a more receptive audience than usual. I talked to a young woman dressed like a flapper from the twenties. She smiled and flirted with me, asking me if I wanted to go with her to the local speakeasy, but stared blankly when I asked about my father. I talked to two men in gritty miner's overalls playing poker, the headlamps mounted on their helmets faintly aglow. They knew Hank Vale but said they seldom saw him outside his room. I talked to a woman wearing a nun's habit riddled with bullet holes. Before I'd even finished my question, she snapped her Bible closed in a cloud of dust and marched away from me without saying a word.

No one could remember seeing anyone who didn't belong on the premises, though it was hard to be certain with all the comings and goings. No one saw Dad acting strangely. I talked to the living, too, but the picture that emerged from them was the same: Hank Vale, who was not a ghost all, was very much a ghost to all the inhabitants of the Mistwood. Now, mixed in with all my anxiety at his disappearance, I also felt a growing sadness that a man who was once larger than life, a man who could make both women and men stand a little straighter at his mere presence, had been reduced to nothing more than a shadow. I had known that he had been fading, of course, known it on a deep, emotional level, so it should not have come as a surprise to have this truth confirmed to me by others, but somehow I had convinced myself that I was the only one aware that my father was a shell of his former self.

I made a few mistakes, talking to a ghost who was in the presence of someone living, and got a few shocked stares, but most of the folks of the Mistwood were used to strange behavior, so their surprise didn't usually last more than a moment. Still, my carelessness could come back to bite me if word made its way among the living residents that I showed an unnerving tendency to talk to people who weren't there. I was about to give up trying to get information from the residents when I stopped to talk to a young man reading in a wingback armchair in one of the window alcoves, his checkered gray morning coat draped over the side of the chair, his two-tone saddle shoes so shiny, they reflected the morning sun coming through the window.

He could have been living or dead, but what did it matter? There was no one around to hear us. When I spoke to him, there was panic just for a second before it vanished. He rubbed his fingers over a mustache so thin, I hadn't even seen it until he made that gesture.

"The Ghost Detective," he said.

"I prefer to go by Myron," I replied. "Do you know Hank Vale?"

"No," he said. "I'm afraid not. This is your father?"

I explained who he was, that he had been a resident for some time, though he was suffering from Alzheimer's. It still didn't jog his memory.

"Notice any kind of strange activity around here lately?" I asked.

"No. But I spend most of my time reading. Have you … have you had much luck with that awful fellow who killed that poor college girl?"

"I'm working on it."

"People are quite nervous about him."

I thanked him and turned to go.

"Oh, wait," he said.

"Yes?" I said.

"I don't know Hank," he said, "but I know Eleanor a bit. Nice woman. Would sometimes sit right where you're sitting and chat with me."

"Really? We are talking about Eleanor Vale, right?"

"Of course."

"What's your name?"

He sat a bit straighter in his chair. "I'm Matthew Monahan Gunn. I was an actor of some renown in the thirties on Broadway. Perhaps you've heard—"

"What did you talk about?"

"With Eleanor?"

"No, with Laurence Olivier. Yes, of course, with my mother."

"Oh, this and that. She's quite into literature, as I am. Graham Greene, Willa Cather, the good stuff. A little about all the travails of the Middle East. Other current events if it piqued our interest. About you, sometimes. She was quite proud of you, about this new role you had."

"Really?"

"Yes, truly. She was a bit uncomfortable with your ... celebrity, at least among people on our side. But she was quite proud. Mostly we reminisced about life before the, um, the big change."

"The big change?"

"You know," he said. "Before we *crossed over.*"

"Oh, right. Did she ever talk about my father?"

"No," Matthew said. "In fact, from the way she talked, I had the feeling her husband had died many years ago and, like many spouses, had decided to go his own way in the non-corporeal life. Now that I think about it, she didn't say so explicitly, but that was the impression she gave me. I had no idea he was just downstairs."

"Apparently hardly anybody else did either," I said.

"Yes, I'm sorry to hear that. I'm sure he was a fine man in his prime."

"He's *still* a good man."

"Right," Matthew said. "I did not mean to offend. Your mother, I think she was just lonely. I don't think she talked to many people, which makes sense now. She was probably at your father's side a great majority of the time." Though it was barely detectable, I caught a bit of a wince.

"What is it?" I asked.

"Well ... I do have some other information, but I'm not sure it's my place to say. It seems a little ... salacious."

"What?"

He swallowed. "Perhaps you should talk to her."

"Tell me."

Still, he hesitated. Impulsively, I reached out and placed my hand on his jacket shoulder, letting my fingers sink a few inches into his form. The buzz surprised him more than it did me. His face paled, and all that mannequin-perfect composure began to crumple.

"That—that was *not* necessary!" he protested.

"Tell me," I said.

"Fine! It's none of my business, but—well, I got the sense from your mother that she was not … how shall I say it? One-hundred-percent faithful to her husband."

"What?"

"She spoke once of an indiscretion that she regretted. It was not my place to press that matter, and she did not elaborate."

"You must have misunderstood."

"Perhaps. But if you had seen the look on her face … Well, the remorse was quite palpable."

I stood there processing it all, trying to convince myself that what he was saying was even possible. An affair? *My* mother? "I want to know who this guy is," I said.

"I wish I could help."

"Who might know?"

"I'm afraid I don't really know that either," Matthew said. "Ever since I passed away in my sleep, two decades ago in this very establishment, I have mostly kept to myself."

"You've got to know—"

"Myron?"

It was Alesha, just behind me. I turned and saw her there, a dozen paces away but still more than close enough to have heard me talking to what appeared to be an empty chair. Her expression appeared both confused and concerned.

"Oh, hi," I said.

"Um, who were you talking to?"

"No one," I said.

"Well, *really*," Matthew said huffily, "I certainly *am* someone. At least I was, once."

"I heard you," Alesha said. "You said, 'Who might know?'"

"I was thinking out loud."

"It looked like you were talking to someone in the chair."

I couldn't think of a good response to this, so I merely shrugged and walked past her. There was no time to try to come up with an explanation that would satisfy her. I needed to find Mom. I swept through the floor, glancing in open doors, searching every corner and alcove. Alesha, trailing behind me, asked what I was doing, but I didn't stop for her. How could I explain that I was looking for my dead mother? On the first floor, I stopped by Dad's room again, but it was still empty. I picked up Jak and Tim along the way, and they seemed equally confused by my frantic behavior as I doubled back over areas they insisted they had just searched. Soon all the residents, living and dead, lined up to gawk at me, since word had now spread that Dad was missing. The Ghost Detective's dad. With that strange serial killer on the prowl. That poor boy.

Now I had two parents missing. In the lobby, with dozens of them staring at me, I jumped up on the brick fireplace, the bluish flames burning low behind the arrangement of fake wood that wouldn't fool even the most casual observer. With all of them gathered in the spacious room with the high ceiling, I felt like a vaudeville performer on a makeshift stage in front of a campfire. The heat from the gas fireplace, weak as it was, warmed the back of my legs.

"Hey!" I shouted to the sea of faces. "You know who I am—Myron Vale. You know my father is Hank Vale. If someone here knows something that can help, say something!"

Feet shuffled, voices murmured, and most of the faces wilted away from me. Alesha, alarmed, reached for me.

"Myron," Alesha said.

"Anything at all!"

Alesha clamped down on my arm, and I jerked myself free. Surveying my audience, looking for any clue at all, I spotted Eddie Quincy at the rear of the crowd, leaning against the opening to the hall that led to the rooms. Something about his sweaty, twitchy face, waxen in the bright shaft of morning light streaming from the windows in the arched ceiling, didn't sit right with me. Why did he look so nervous?

He knew something.

Eddie must have seen something in my expression that alarmed him, because he turned and fled. I leaped from the fireplace in pursuit. I wove past the residents, buzzing the shoulder of the ghost of an old man in a gray turtleneck sweater and bumping the walker of a hunched old woman who was obviously real. The old man yelped, and the old woman cursed at me in Italian. Both Alesha and Jak shouted my name.

With a good head start on me, Eddie had already crossed half the hall. In the clear now, I sprinted after him, quickly closing the gap between us. He ran—if it could even be called running—like a drunk in ski boots, on the verge of falling with each step. I caught up to him where the hall angled ninety degrees to the left, reaching my hand straight into his back. Whether it was from his fear or my rage, the electric shock our contact elicited was powerful enough to rip up my arm and set my hair on end.

He felt it, too, screaming and toppling on his hands and knees. He scrambled onto his back, edging away from me. His loose strands of hair looked like they belonged to someone else, the clippings from the floor of a barbershop that had been glued to his sweaty scalp.

"Tell me what you know!" I said.

"I'm—I'm just here because I'm writing—writing a—"

"Don't give me that! You know something—something you're not telling me!"

He backed his way to the wall, pressing himself against the peach wallpaper. I reached for him, prepared to give him another unpleasant shock. I thought I had him cornered—forgot, for a moment, who exactly I was dealing with—and was therefore surprised when he sank right into the wall, vanishing before my eyes.

I stared stupidly for only a moment, then hurried to the window off to the right. I saw him lumbering across wet grass, sprinklers whirring all around him. He glanced over his shoulder and we made eye contact, prompting him to lumber even faster.

Cursing, I bolted past the window to the far end of the hall, where I found an exit. I sprinted around the building, crashing right through a pair of young men marching side by side in crisp green World War II uniforms, giving us all a jolt, and yelled my apologies over my shoulder without breaking stride. It couldn't have been more than ten seconds before I reached the front of the building, but it didn't matter.

Eddie was gone.

Now what? He could have gone anywhere. Feeling a shroud of hopelessness settle over me, I stood in the wet grass trying to decide my next move, barely conscious of the inground sprinklers wetting my pant legs, when Mom spoke from behind me.

"Myron," she said.

I turned and saw her on the sidewalk near the building. With her shiny black dress and pale gaunt face, she could have been the Grim Reaper's sister. Off to her right, I saw Jak, Alesha, and Tim all spilling outside from the same door I had used. The way they looked at me, with that particular blend of concern and bafflement I had seen on people's faces more than a few times in the past six years, I half expected one of them to be holding a straitjacket just my size.

They couldn't see Mom, but she saw them, affording them a quick disapproving glance before fixing her gaze back on me.

"Myron," she said, "we need to talk—*in private.*"

Chapter 11

WE CRUISED the surrounding neighborhoods at slow speeds, just me and Mom, with the electric engine barely making a sound. The Prius was so silent, it could have been a panther on the prowl, if panthers were big and boxy and lime green.

It had been Mom's idea to look for Dad while we talked, but it had been ten minutes and she still hadn't said a word. Around us, there was very little activity, the tidy, one-story houses with well-kept yards waiting silently for their owners to return from work and school and play on this March Monday. Several cats crossed the road. On one corner, a big bull of man in a dirty overalls chopped wood. The way he swung his ax, he looked like he could have cleaved my head clean off with one stroke, but when he made eye contact with me, he turned and fled behind the maple tree that shadowed the corner.

"Why did he do that?" Mom asked.

"Some ghosts are afraid of me," I said.

"He was a ghost?"

"Mom, come on. Let's not do this now."

"I just don't understand why he would be afraid of you. You're a nice boy. You wouldn't hurt anyone."

I thought of the Glock underneath my jacket, the holster an ever-present reminder that I *would* hurt someone if it came to it.

"Mom," I said, "this was your idea. You said you wanted to talk to me."

"She could have come with us, I guess."

It took me a moment to realize she was referring to Jak. When I'd recommended that everybody split up and search the neighborhoods, I'd asked Jak to do some searching on foot while I took the Prius. Everybody had agreed, but I could tell by Jak's icy tone that she hadn't been happy about it.

"She'll be all right," I said.

"She seemed quite hurt."

"I'll make it up to her later."

"Myron, please. I am your mother. One image in my head of you in a … compromising situation with that girl is more than enough."

"I only meant I'd buy her an ice cream cone."

"That would be more appropriate. She is young enough to be your daughter."

"No. She's not."

"Well—"

"Mom, what did you want to talk to me about?" When she continued to stare out the passenger-side window, I pressed ahead, hoping to come at the subject a little more obliquely. "Why did you disappear on me when we got to the Mistwood? One minute you're in the car with me, then you're gone."

She sighed, a real doozy. Mom had always been a master practitioner of the sigh, imbuing the sound with all kinds of meaning and nuance that ordinary people simply could not do, and this one carried years of angst. It even allowed a ripple of emotion to pass through her stern features, the hard lines and angles softening, if only for a moment. "It was that man," she said. "Eddie Quincy. I—I did not want to see him. Not right then."

When I put this comment together with what I'd learned from Matthew, I suddenly felt the urge to pull the Prius over so I could vomit into the gutter. "Oh no," I said. "You—you had an affair with *him*?"

Based on Mom's reaction, I might as well have set off a grenade. She whirled around in her seat, aghast. "What?"

"I talked to the guy upstairs," I said. "The actor. He told me—"

"I would *never* have an affair with that slimy little man. How could you even think that?"

"You just said—"

"I said I did not want to *see* him. Oh my. Oh my, I can't believe you thought I and—and that little urchin … Do you really think I'm— I'm so undesirable that—"

"Mom, stop."

"—that I could only appeal to such a vile, repulsive, repugnant, smelly and … and *short* man?"

"Short?"

"Don't make jokes! This is not funny. I can't believe you think so little of me."

"Mom, don't get all huffy. You just said you didn't want to see him."

"See him, yes!"

"Well, then, why?"

She started to answer, then shook her head in disgust and went back to staring out the window. Her black dress could not have been more solid and stark in the bright morning light, the grooves in her face as real to me as the steering wheel beneath my fingers or the floor mat beneath my feet … and yet just for a second, as the glare of the sun flashed over her pale face, I had one of those fleeting moments where I got glimpse of the world beyond her. Of her transparency. Of her *ghostness.* Those moments were so powerful that they always made my breath catch in my throat, powerful because for just that one instant, I could actually *tell.* I could tell the difference between the living and the dead. I didn't know why they happened, but when they did, they rekindled what little hope I still had that someday my affliction would finally end.

Mom must have sensed something was wrong, because she

turned back to me, and just like that, the moment was gone. She was just as real and solid as always. We'd passed through the neighborhoods, arriving at a stop sign before a main thoroughfare with steady traffic.

"What?" she said.

"Um, nothing. Tell me why you didn't want to talk to that short, repugnant man."

"I said no jokes."

"I was using your words."

"Fine. Park over there. I don't want you driving."

"It's that bad?"

"Please," she said.

She pointed across the road at the Safeway. I parked in the rear of the lot, near an empty shopping-cart rack, and killed the engine. Mom took her time, running her hands over the dark, sheer material of her dress, straightening the wrinkles. Her hands were trembling.

"He's writing a book," she said. "He's writing another book about all this business with the—with that serial killer your father tried to catch."

"The Goodbye Killer."

"Yes. That one. Or the other name he goes by."

"The Ghost Reaper."

"Eddie—*Mr. Quincy,* he's been working on this book, this sequel even before he ... before he ..."

"Died?"

"Yes. He wanted my help. He wanted my help back then, too, but I wouldn't give it to him. But, well, he found out about my, my *indiscretion.*"

"Your affair?"

"Please don't use that word," she said. "He found out about my indiscretion and said if I didn't cooperate, if I didn't let him interview me about anything I knew about your father, he would put it all in the book. And, well, what could I do? I didn't want it all getting out. So I told him. I didn't know a lot about the case, really. It's not like Hank said all that much about it. And Sal didn't say much either."

Her voice trailed off quickly, and she flicked a glance at me, a glance filled with all her pent-up nervousness, and then I knew. The heaviness in my stomach wasn't quite as bad as when I'd thought she'd had an affair with that slimy little man, but it didn't feel much better.

"Oh," I said.

"Please, Myron. Don't be angry with him."

"Him?" I said. "I barely even know Sal. I'm not angry with *him*."

In the confined space, the brittleness of my voice echoed back at me. I didn't sound like myself. She looked at her lap, the barest hint of a blush blooming in her face, like thousands of tiny specks of red dust on her alabaster skin. Outside, a man dressed in a deerskin cap and grungy cowhide, a musket slung over his shoulder, pushed a rattling shopping cart past the Prius. He glanced inside. I glared at him. He swallowed and hurried away.

"Please don't be angry with me either," Mom said finally. "It didn't …" She started to say something, then trailed off into silence.

"It didn't what?"

"Nothing."

"Mean anything?"

"No. That's not what I—"

"Last long?"

"I can see that you're angry."

"Your powers of deduction never cease to amaze me. You should be a detective."

"Myron—"

"I love it when you call me Myron. It's almost like you remember that's my real name. How did it start?"

"I don't know, really," she said. "He was over a lot, of course. A lot of dinners. You must remember. And then there were a few times when he stopped by and your father was out doing something. Running an errand. Or maybe doing something with you. He was always—he was always just dropping something off, you know, a sweatshirt he'd borrowed, a tool, but I wondered later if it was just an excuse. Then it just … it turned into more. Your father and I, well, we were having a very hard time. And—"

"Don't blame him."

"I'm not!" she insisted. "I'm not blaming him at all. Don't you see? That's—that's what I was going to say. It didn't mean I ever stopped loving your father. I didn't. Not for one second. It was just, for a while, I wasn't sure if I—if we were going to last, even though we loved each other. Sometimes, sometimes you can love someone, and it still doesn't work. For a while there, I just didn't know."

It may not have hit me so hard if I hadn't been wronged by a woman in the same way, a wrong that led directly to the shooting that made me the way I am. I was surrounded on all sides by betrayal. "Did you love him?" I asked.

She turned her attention to the parking lot, her gaze falling on the man in the deerskin cap. "Not like your father," she said.

"But you did?"

"It would be unfair if I said I didn't. But it wasn't—it didn't change how I felt about your father. In fact, and I know this sounds strange, but it made me love Hank even more. It made me realize how good a man he is, how … how strong. He was always there for me. For us. No matter how bad it got, he never left."

"Unlike you," I said.

"I didn't leave."

"Yes, you did. In the most important way."

The glass shattered. The vase broke. The fault lines in her face revealed themselves in a violent tremor. There it was, a flare of red on alabaster skin, a welling in the eyes, a couple of tears cascading down white slopes. There was no melodramatic display, no wailing and sobbing, no sniffling and shuddery breathing—just this, the barest hint of anguish, but it was enough to know how much more pain lay underneath. If I'd wanted to cut her deeply, to really hit her hard in that emotional core that Mom kept buried so deep within herself, I'd succeeded. Score one for Myron Vale.

"All right," she said softly. "All right, then. Yes. Yes, I did leave him that way. It's fair. It's fair to say that."

"How long did it last?"

"Not long. A couple months."

"And Dad never knew?"

"No."

I caught the hesitation in her voice. "You're sure?"

"I don't know. I don't think he did, not back then."

"Do you think he found out now, and that's why he ran away?"

She started to answer, then merely shook her head.

"Mom?"

"I don't know," she said. "Sometimes, I think he can really hear me. Just for a second, you know, now and then. Maybe he overheard me talking to Matthew. I needed someone to talk to, when that—that little man came around. I needed advice."

"I don't know how Quincy could even publish another book."

"He said he had a way, a way of giving it to someone. Someone who was, um …"

"Alive?"

"Whatever. Yes, alive. He said he had a connection with this person. He said he could use this connection to get the book in print."

"Hmm."

"I don't want—I don't want to talk about him," Mom said. "I don't care about him. He's, he's just out to make a buck. I just needed you to know. Because of your father running away, I thought you needed to know."

WE LOOKED EVERYWHERE. We looked through the morning, the afternoon, the night. We looked in grocery-store aisles and under bridges and in all the back alleys of Forest Grove. We looked until our eyes turned bleary, until our feet throbbed from walking and our backs ached from driving and every last bit of adrenaline was spent. We looked until there was barely a *we*, until the Mistwood staff turned to the needs of residents who hadn't fled the coop, the uniformed police were called away to burglar alarms and domestic disturbances, and Alesha and Tim were scolded back to the Goodbye Killer investigation by Chief Branson. Mom decided to do some exploring on her own. I picked up Jak and we kept searching, trying the Greyhound terminals, the MAX stations, and the taxi companies, all of them turning up nothing.

As the first hint of dawn brightened the eastern sky, I took Jak back to her car—a seven-year-old gray Ford Taurus that wasn't exactly what I imagined someone who made big bucks from blogging would drive—and told her it was time for both of us to get some rest. When she pleaded to stay with me, I told her we both knew that if we slept in the same bed, there wouldn't be a whole lot of sleeping going on.

Then the *we* was an *I*, and after stopping home long enough only to take a scalding shower and scarf down some cold leftover pizza, I went out looking some more.

When the Tuesday-morning traffic picked up steam, I headed to the office, still having found no sign of Dad. No press currently staked out my building, thankfully. An orange haze hung low in the sky. In the distance, beyond the jagged rooftops, the snow-capped Mount Hood towered over the city like an elephant over an ant colony. Always impressive. Always indifferent to our troubles. One glance at the mountain usually helped me gain a little perspective, but it wasn't happening today. Dad was missing. Dad was missing, and some weird, freakish killer may have already killed him.

Killed him.

I made it up the stairs before this thought, rebounding in my brittle psyche, got the best of me. I plunged into the bathroom and over the toilet bowl before what was in my stomach made a return visit. Kneeling on the gritty tile, I heaved a while longer, the stomach acid burning in my throat and in my nose. I flushed the toilet a few times but stayed on the floor, focusing on what remained of the peeling sunflower wallpaper behind the toilet, reminding myself to breathe. Just breathe, Myron. You're no good to your dad if you let this crap take you down.

I was still on the floor when a voice I recognized spoke behind me.

"Are you all right?" the priest asked.

From the corner of my eye, I saw the black robes looming before me. I rose and turned on the faucet, splashing cold water on my face. I took a wad of paper towels and dabbed away the moisture, only then squinting at him in the cracked mirror. The concern etched into his deeply grooved face matched the concern in his voice. I wanted to punch him. I wanted to take the obscenely large cross around his neck and beat him with it.

"Where's my dad?" I said.

"I don't know," he said.

"Stop lying."

"Myron, I really don't know. I wish I did."

"Is there anything you *do* know? Forget it. Even if you did, you probably wouldn't tell me."

"Myron—"

"Save it."

I stepped through the doorway, making no effort to move around him. I knew he had some remarkable telekinetic ability—he'd demonstrated it to me before by touching me in the most solid way a ghost could touch a person—but I was prepared to go through him anyway to see what he would do. At the last second, he leaned away and my shoulder only grazed his chest. The mild buzz barely penetrated my nausea. We'd played a game of chicken and I'd won, a pettiness I was happy to embrace in the moment.

He followed me into the office, the rustle of his robes breaking the stillness. No chanting from the Higher Plane Church of Spiritual Transcendence filled the hall. A good thing. If I'd been subjected to that auditory torture in my present state of mind, I may have convinced myself that it was time to demonstrate to my neighbors just how fast a Glock could redecorate a room.

Approaching my desk, I saw Patch perched on the windowsill

outside. The morning light cast an orange hue on the white starburst over his left eye. I opened the window and he stepped inside, watching the priest warily. I left the window open. I caught the scent of hot dogs on the breeze—Elvis already hard at work.

"No hiss from your companion," the priest said. "That's progress, I guess."

Patch hissed at him.

"You were saying?" I said, settling into my chair.

"Mmm. I think he likes me even less than you do."

"What do you want? If you're not here to help me, you must want something."

"I *do* want to help you," he insisted.

"Prove it. Tell me where my father is."

"I told you, I don't know that. But I sensed you might let this sidetrack you, which is why I am here."

"Sidetrack me?"

"The best way to find your father is to find the Ghost Reaper. You must stay focused on that. And you must also—"

"You're saying he has Dad?"

"No. I am fairly certain he doesn't, actually."

"How do you know that?"

"Rumblings," the priest said. "Rumors. Nothing definitive, but my feeling is that he left on his own accord. Myron, there are many factions within the Department, few of them working in concert with one another. My own division's influence has waned considerably as of late. I'm more … in the dark than usual. It's left me feeling a bit off balance. But let me finish what I was going to say. You must stay focused on finding the Ghost Reaper. Your father is either looking for him himself, or he is in hiding from him."

"Dad wouldn't hide," I said.

The priest regarded me sympathetically. Feeling the urge to punch him again, I instead took out my Glock and placed it on the desk. The priest raised his eyebrows.

"You *do* remember," he said, "my non-corporeal status, correct?"

"Dad wouldn't hide," I repeated.

"All right then. But let me finish. If you want to find your father, you must stay focused on the Ghost Reaper, *but*—and this is important—you must also be extremely careful. Not just because the Ghost Reaper, whatever he or it is, is very dangerous. No, you must also be careful because you were not chosen to help just because of your unique abilities. Or rather, I should say you were."

I sighed. "Riddles again?"

"Myron, I now have information that there are powerful people within the Department that have actually been holding back in the pursuit of the Ghost Reaper. Not deploying all the resources we could to find him. It's as if the Department doesn't really want to find him."

"That doesn't make any sense. The Associate Director came to me himself. And even the Director—"

"Yes, I know."

"But why would they hire me if they didn't want to find him? They seemed desperate for my help."

"Yes. Desperate for *your* help. If it's true that the Ghost Reaper can kill both the physical body and the ghost inside, think about what that means for you. Then think about why there are those within the Department, those who fear what you are now and what you would become as a non-corporeal being, who would want you to find him first."

I didn't need to think long. The priest had connected the dots, and the picture they formed was pretty clear, a picture of our serial killer doing to me what he had done to all his other victims—not just killing them, but making them disappear. Erasing them from existence. Was I just a pawn? Not just a pawn. *Bait.* I felt something cold slide into the pit of my stomach, not fear exactly, but the queasy awareness of the mark who had been played. I looked at the Glock again. I looked at the priest.

"So we're playing a game," I said, "and I'm just a piece on the board. What can I do? I can't stop playing the game, can I?"

"No," the priest said. "Not if you want to save your father. You've just got to play the game better than everyone else."

* * *

So I DECIDED to play the game. What else could I do? After the priest left, I made a few calls to check with the police and the Mistwood, but of course Dad still hadn't turned up. I checked the computer and there was an email from W. Hopner expressing sympathy for the disappearance of my father and reassuring me that they were employing their own methods in finding him. Of course, he also implored me to "continue with all due haste in my investigation, which must take priority at the present time." I found it funny that he used Gmail. Maybe in this case, the *G* stood for *Ghost*?

I started to type something, but I deleted the email before I'd gotten far. I may have been playing his game, but I didn't have to play by his rules.

I spent the rest of Tuesday morning digging through all the various websites and forums dedicated to the Goodbye Killer, searching for even the tiniest clue. The fan fiction—mostly involving necrophilia threesomes with the Goodbye Killer, Jack the Ripper, and Ted Bundy—was enough by itself to make my skin crawl. The Goodbye Killer Will Return Fan Club site, by far the biggest and most active of the bunch, had a number of interesting discussion threads speculating on the serial killer's identity. Most of the theories were nonsensical (the Dalai Lama? The Illuminati?), but Clive Branson was also on the list. Apparently someone had staked out his house and found "a strange woman living inside who never leaves." I made a mental note to look into it. Of course, *I* was on the list, too, and that theory had picked up a lot of steam lately with my recent appearance in the news. The fact that I was barely out of diapers when the first murder was committed apparently didn't dissuade anyone.

People also speculated that Dad and Sal committed the murders, as a way to make themselves famous. I might have found this idea more compelling if I didn't still have vivid memories of that long-ago conversation while I hid under Dad's desk, when my father and Sal talked about seeing the Goodbye Killer's face for the first time.

Thinking of Sal, I headed to his sandwich shop around noon. A lonely news van, which had parked outside my office by this time, followed me for a few blocks before I lost it with a couple of quick turns. I parked the Prius across the street and watched the lunchtime traffic coming and going from Maria's—a healthy business, it seemed—but I didn't go inside. What would I say? The sun glaring on the window made it difficult to see Sal, but now and then I caught a glimpse of his white apron. Whatever happened between him and Mom, it was a long time ago.

I was sitting there when the phone rang. It was Jak. When I'd dropped her off, we'd exchanged numbers.

"Where are you?" she asked.

I told her.

"How long are you going to be there?" she asked.

"I don't know," I said.

"Where are you going next?"

"I don't know that either."

"You should get some sleep."

"Later."

"I could meet you at your place? Help relax you a bit?"

"Not in the mood, Jak."

"Okay. Can I come with you, wherever you're going?"

"Not right now."

"When?"

"I don't know, okay? Maybe later."

She said nothing, the silence filled by a faint background hum, like freeway traffic just over a rise. Across the street, a black man sitting on a silver pail shined a pair of shoes, nobody looking his way. When he saw me staring, he grabbed his pail and hurried away, giving me one last fearful glance over his shoulder before disappearing down an alley.

"Are you angry with me?" she asked.

"Of course not."

"When can I see you again?"

"I don't know. Look, I need to go."

"Okay."

"I'll call later."

"Sure. If you can fit it into your schedule."

"Jak—"

She hung up. I called her right back. She didn't answer. I thought about leaving her a message, but I didn't know what to say. Truthfully, it might have been better if we cooled it for a while. It had all happened way too fast. Strangely, I didn't regret any of it, and I *did* want to see her again, but there was just too much happening right now to fit in any kind of relationship. I also didn't want to give the Department any more leverage over me than they already had. Hopner had already threatened Alesha. The last thing I needed was for him to know there was another important woman in my life.

The rest of the week, I didn't see Jak. She didn't call either. Alesha and Tim reported back that they'd learned nothing more from digging into Jasmine Walker's life than what we already knew: everything about her was pure good, the kind of character who was so uncorrupted and morally true that it almost came off like an act. Did people this good really exist, the kind of people who never forgot to send cards to their ninety-year-old grandmother, who volunteered at the Humane Society, and who never said a cross word about anybody? Apparently they did, because when I tagged along with Alesha and Tim digging into the Goodbye Killer's past victims, it was always the same story. I kept waiting to unearth an affair, a drug addiction, even some petty theft from the office social fund, but no, all the victims shared the same spotless reputations. It was the only thing they had in common, as far as we could tell.

Dad remained missing. Mom stopped by twice, growing increasingly desperate, but all I could offer her were repeated assurances that I would keep looking—which I did, at night when I should have been sleeping, combing the streets in the Prius, catching catnaps in parking lots when I finally couldn't keep my eyes open. I wanted to talk to Eddie Quincy about this book he was writing, specifically about the supposed connection he had who could get it published in my world, but I only caught a glimpse of him once from a distance—inside the mall at Clackamas Town Center, where we'd gone to talk to a grown child of one of the Goodbye Killer's victims. He'd obviously been following me. Eddie vanished into the crowd before I managed three steps in his direction.

I swung by Chief Branson's place in the hills near Forest Park a couple of times, but I was too sure he knew my car to stake out his house for long. I never saw more than closed drapes, even when his Mercedes was parked in the driveway. I saw no woman. I saw nothing interesting at all. I didn't get that strange, queasy feeling, that coldness of the soul—not at Branson's place, not anywhere. I was beginning to wonder if the Goodbye Killer was going to sink back into the shadows where he'd been hiding the past few decades before I even got a decent lead.

And then very late Thursday night, nearly a week after Jasmine Walker had been found dead in her dorm room, I awoke to sirens in the distance—over the Willamette River, up in the hills, the sound carried to my ears like the far-off song of a mermaid beckoning a sailor to his doom on the rocks.

Chapter 12

His name was Brent Conrad. Forty-four years old, in perfect health except for a slight paunch and some typical male-pattern baldness, a season-ticket holder for the Timbers, Portland's Major League Soccer team. Half Cuban, though you could barely tell by his sandy-blond hair and pale freckled skin. Married for nineteen years to his college sweetheart, LuAnn Conrad, who co-ran their highly successful real estate agency. Father of two children: Annie, eleven, and Kort, seven. Coach of his daughter's volleyball team and his son's Little League. Volunteered at the Boys & Girls Club, the Salvation Army, and the Doernbecher Children's Hospital. The last one was because he'd had a childhood friend, Gavin, who'd died of leukemia—and he had Gavin's name tattooed on his right upper arm as a constant reminder of that friendship.

In short, he was just like all the other victims of the Goodbye Killer: a representative of the very best that humanity had to offer.

Tim relayed all this to me on our way to Conrad's house early Friday morning in the Irvington neighborhood, while I scrutinized the guy's picture on Alesha's cell. It was from the Conrad Real Estate website, and it was listed right next to his wife's picture, along with a touching story about how the two of them met when working for Habitat for Humanity in college.

I sighed and handed the phone back to her, the headlights cutting through the morning mist on NE Broadway. The thick air gave the orange sky a creamy appearance, like slightly melted sorbet. The older, Victorian-style homes were all much smaller than the massive estates found in Lake Oswego, where much of Portland's well-to-do lived, but most of these homes were actually twice as expensive. I knew this area quite well. Before Billie and I bought our house in Sellwood, we used to go for walks in the Irvington area, pretending, as we often did, that we were house shopping. That one had nice boxwood hedge lining the sidewalk. This one had a wonderful covered porch complete with a swinging wooden bench. Noting positive qualities. Cataloging flaws.

"And the goodbye message?" I asked.

"On the vinyl floor in the kitchen," Tim replied, peering at me over his seat, both his eyes and his voice far too alert and energetic for such an early hour. Clean-shaven, red hair perfectly parted, his skin so bright and glossy it looked as if it had been touched up by Photoshop—it was as if Tim was playing a part on a television show, the makeup crew close at hand. "Written in peanut butter. Apparently he'd gone down last night to make himself a late-night sandwich. It was still there on the kitchen table when his wife found him. He was sprawled on the floor."

"Only a week between victims," I said. "It used to be months. He's speeding up. Branson know you're bringing me?"

"What do you think?" Alesha said.

"You're playing with fire."

"I'd like to see him suspend me. I'm the best detective he has."

"The most modest, too," I added.

"Modesty is for chumps."

"Uh-huh. The press know about this one yet?"

Alesha snorted a laugh. I didn't know why until I looked over her shoulder and saw, a block ahead, the army of news vans flanking the narrow street—at least a dozen of them, a mixture of national and local news. That wasn't the strangest part. An exodus of people crowded the sidewalks, hurrying away from the house where all the press was gathered. Judging by their motley mixture of clothing, mostly from decades or even centuries past—a female nurse wearing a matching hat and bright white uniform, a Native American dressed in little more than a loincloth—these were mostly ghosts, maybe all of them. I'd seen a few more obvious ghosts on the streets on the way to the house, but I hadn't thought anything of them until now. Something was different.

After we parked a block away from the throng, I made sure, when we all got out of the car, to hang back from Alesha and Tim. Headed toward me was a spindly middle-aged woman dressed in a thick fur coat and enough pearls to completely hide her neck. She lugged a mammoth wooden suitcase behind her. She started to veer around me, but I stepped in front of her and made eye contact. She dropped her suitcase and raised her hands in surrender.

"Don't hurt me!" she cried.

Alesha and Tim didn't hear this, of course. She could have screamed with a megaphone and they still wouldn't have heard it. But the ghosts lining the sidewalks heard her reaction, and it started something of a stampede, all of them fleeing away from me, giving us a wide berth. I stepped closer to her, lowering my voice to a whisper.

"You know me?"

"Y-y-yes. You're the—you're the—"

"The Ghost Detective?"

"—Ghost Reaper."

"What?"

"They say—they say it has to be you." She started to cry. "Please don't hurt me. Please, I just want to escape with everyone else."

She took advantage of my dumbfounded state of mind to slip past me. I had lots more questions, but my slowness prompted Alesha and Tim to turn and look at me, their faces questioning. I pulled out my phone and pretended to check a text, moseying after them. Me, the

Ghost Reaper? Alesha asked me if everything was all right, and I told her someone thought they'd seen Dad but it turned out to be someone else.

As I approached the house, the familiar feeling took hold, starting as a prickle on the back of my neck and working its way into my stomach, then outward, until the uneasiness pervaded my entire body. My eyelids twitched in time with my pulse. Up ahead, a gnarly old oak appeared to bend toward me, stretching its limbs like claws, but when I focused on it, it was just a tree. From the corner of my eye, the ivy clinging to the white brick chimney across the street appeared to shimmer and writhe like a nest of vipers, but when I stared, it was only ivy.

Was the killer here, or was this just a residue of his presence? It didn't feel quite as strong as the past two times I'd seen him.

The disturbing feeling faded a bit, but it did not disappear entirely. The Conrad residence was a perfect representative of the older, picturesque houses on the street: powder blue with white trim, steeply angled roofs over dormered windows, large and sweeping, a two-foot-high white picket fence surrounding the whole thing. The press crowded against the fence, bowing the wood forward, shouting questions at the two uniformed police officers standing on the covered porch. No back-alley entrance let us avoid the melee this time. Someone, a young guy with perfectly coiffed brown hair, pointed to us, and within seconds, the whole mob of reporters and camera operators swarmed us like hungry piranhas. A woman's shrill voice pierced through all the other shouts.

"Myron Vale! Myron Vale!"

It was Betty Big Boobs, dressed in a sleek gray trench coat over a bright blue pantsuit, pushing through the mob with her bosom like a truck with a snowplow. She shoved an obscenely large microphone in my face.

"Myron Vale," she said, "do you think your father's recent disappearance is connected in any way to the Goodbye Killer?"

Alesha attempted to pull me through the gate, but I stopped and stared at the reporter. "How did you know about that?"

Thick layers of makeup had turned Betty's face into a hardened mask that betrayed no emotion, but she did blink at me a few times. "I'd love to have an exclusive interview with you, Myron. We want to know all about your personal crusade to catch the killer that eluded your father—and save him at the same time. When would be a good time?"

"Leave my dad out of this," I said.

"Are you hiding something, Myron?" she asked.

"What?"

"Do you know more about the killer than you're letting on? There is a theory now that you're involved in the killings. How do you comment—"

Alesha never let Betty get out the rest. With a hand on each of Betty's most prominent features, my former partner gave the reporter a hard shove into the crowd. Betty, her ampleness bouncing the whole way, didn't quite go down, but her stumble did knock the reporters behind her back like bowling pins, clearing a path to the gate. Alesha, Tim, and I hustled up the narrow stone steps before the reporters had a chance to recover.

The two young cops on the porch both looked at me warily, but I ignored them this time, following Alesha and Tim into the house. As we entered, a burly, silver-haired man dressed in a sleeveless white T-shirt and gray sweatpants was coming out, carrying a crying boy on his shoulder. An older woman in an aquamarine bathrobe followed behind him, ushering a glassy-eyed girl in front of her. Both kids were still dressed in pajamas. I held the door open for them, but all of them, adults and kids alike, barely glanced at us. One of the cops preceded them to the gate, helping them through the mob.

We passed a half-dozen cops on our way to the kitchen, turning sideways to avoid one another in the narrow halls. Our feet echoed on the bamboo floors. Pictures of the kids hung on every wall, blue frames to match the powder blue walls, the same color as the outside. We found LuAnn Conrad in her pink silk nightgown in the dining room off the kitchen, staring blankly at her refection in the polished walnut table, a white shawl draped over her shoulders. We also found Branson squatting in front of her, talking to her in a hushed tone.

Nearby, on the stone-tile kitchen floor, I saw a blue tape outline in the shape of a man's body. Three police techs snooped around the area, dusting for fingerprints. Brent Conrad was already gone. A jar of open peanut butter still lay on its side near the tape outline and filled the air with the odor of peanuts. The smell was a bit jarring, bringing back memories of school lunches, cafeterias, and bread so white it was probably more chemical than wheat. No dead-body smell. Peanuts.

Seeing us—seeing *me*—Branson frowned.

"I thought I made myself clear," he said.

"You did," Alesha said.

"And yet here he is."

"Yep."

He glared at her for a few more seconds, then at me, then he shook his head and stood. Looking at him—this compact man in the gray trench coat with the chiseled face and the cut-glass eyes—I tried to imagine him as the Goodbye Killer. The way he stared back, I was pretty sure he was trying to imagine the same thing about me, especially if this was the theory being floated in the press. He spoke to LuAnn in a soft voice that was still clipped and businesslike, as if that was the best he could manage.

"These two in the front us are the detectives assigned to this case, Mrs. Conrad. They will take it from here. Again, I'm sorry for your loss."

She barely blinked. He stepped past us, aiming his index finger at me like a gun.

"Just observe," he said. "Otherwise, I'll throw you in jail for obstructing an investigation."

"I'm just trying to help," I said.

"I mean it, Vale."

"Yes, sir. Understood."

I said this without a hint of sarcasm, but he focused those intense eyes of his on me a while longer. I expected him to offer a critical remark of some sort, but he surprised me by softening his expression. When he spoke again, it was with less intensity—not quite sympathetic or comforting, but at least with no challenge in his tone.

"I'm sorry about Hank," he said. "I saw you filed a missing-person report."

"Yes, sir."

"I'm sure he'll turn up soon."

I didn't answer. For a brief moment, I thought he might actually pat me on the shoulder, but then he turned and left. I considered asking him to assign a few detectives to find Dad, but I doubted that request would have been received well. Alesha and Tim had already pulled up chairs next to LuAnn Conrad, who showed about as much reaction to all of our activity as a portrait. They started in on the questions, but it was standard stuff, the type of questions that in ordinary circumstances might have led somewhere but likely wouldn't yield anything with our particular killer, and getting even a mumbled reply out of her proved challenging.

Why him? Of all the thousands of people living in the Portland area, why Brent Conrad? Why not his neighbor? His racquetball partner? His tax accountant? He was a good man, sure. But Portland was full of good men and good women. Why this one? The inescapable conclusion was that there was no why, at least not why him instead of others. Once the pool had been narrowed, based on the potential virtue of the victims, these were random killings.

The question, then, was how did the Goodbye Killer find them? How did he pick them out of the haystack? If it was true that he was not a ghost or a flesh-and-blood human but something in between, that he, in fact, possessed unique abilities even rarer than my own, then the answer might be that he just *saw* good people the way I saw ghosts. And yet that theory didn't quite jibe with me. Standing there, watching LuAnn Conrad mumble that she didn't remember anyone strange calling or stopping by recently, I asked myself how I would find out about somebody like Brent Conrad or Jasmine Parker—and then I realized the obvious.

"Mrs. Conrad," I said, interrupting them. It may have been my abruptness that jolted her out of her mental daze, because she turned and looked at me.

"Yes?" she said.

Alesha raised her thin eyebrows at me. Tim, as usual, merely looked patiently agreeable, as if life were one continuous game of pinochle.

"Was your husband in the news recently?" I asked.

"In the news?" she replied.

"Yes. The newspaper. Television. Something online."

"No. I mean, not recently."

"How long ago? In what way?"

"Oh … Well, it was so long ago. Years, when Kort was just a baby. That can't—that can't have anything to do with this."

"Tell me about it," I said.

"Well … It's been so long. The *Oregonian* did this feature on Habitat for Humanity when former President Carter was in town. It was mostly about Carter, but there was this sidebar about—about Brent. About all that he'd done. We've … we've still got it framed somewhere. Maybe in the attic. I don't know. It's been—been so long …"

She started to cry. Tim reached out and patted the woman's back. While he comforted her, Alesha stood and took my elbow, guiding us to the corner. Next to us, the morning light shone through a shelf of yellow vases, jars, and cups.

"What are you getting at?" she asked.

"If they're totally random," I said, "that would be one thing, but he only targets Good Samaritans. Jasmine Walker was written up in the college newspaper."

"But many of the past victims were pretty anonymous people. I don't think all of them got in the newspaper. Somebody would have made that connection earlier."

"I know, which is why we really have to dig. He puts potential victims on a list or something. He waits for his moment. "

"That was a long wait."

"Well, something happened to stop him for a while. I don't know what that is yet."

"Fear of getting caught."

"No, something else."

"What, then?"

"I don't know," I said. "But I think finding when each of the past victims got some kind of press might help. A lot of people get in the paper at some point, which is why an article years in the past doesn't seem like a big deal. If we find a person or two that really *didn't* get in the news, even in the smallest way, then maybe we'll find somebody the killer knew personally."

"One of the first few victims, maybe," Alesha said.

"That's what I was thinking," I said.

"It's not much of a theory."

"Got something better?"

"Nope."

"Then we're in trouble," I said, "because we both know you're the smart one."

She flashed one of her dazzling, trademarked Alesha smiles at me. It lasted only a second before she seemed to remember herself, that she was supposed to be unhappy with me—about Jak, about not working the case in the way she would have preferred, something, who knows—but it felt so good to see it that I actually laughed. It wasn't a big one, given the moment, but it was enough that it put a fissure in the barrier between us. I realized how much I depended on her. As complicated as our relationship was, I needed her to keep me grounded. Alesha, with all her talk of new-age astrology; healing crystals; and karma-inducing, positive-energy-creating, toxin-cleansing mental feng shui, was my strongest tether to the world of the living.

"We'll hit the library after we finish here," she said.

"I'll bring my library card."

"Good, because I never got one. I buy all my books on Amazon."

"Expensive."

"But I get free shipping. Plus I can write all over my books. I like to write notes in them."

"Sacrilege," I said.

She returned to LuAnn Conrad. While listening to them, I suddenly caught a whiff of cigarette smoke. Somebody lighting up at a crime scene? Then, getting a stronger take on the odor, the distinctive skunk-like smell, but sweeter, without the nauseous undertones, I realized it wasn't cigarettes but marijuana. Incredulous, I glanced around the room, expecting to see one of the techs inexplicably with a joint in his hand, but everybody was hard at work. I almost commented on it, then realized that there was probably a good reason nobody else detected it. As pungent as it was—the tingle in my nose, the sting in my eyes, even the sagelike taste of it on my tongue, most likely memory echoes from my brief foray into weed as a teenager—I was probably the only living person in the house who experienced these sensations.

I spotted a slight haze in the air down the hall off the living room. With Alesha and Tim still busy with LuAnn, I stepped quietly away from them. None of the techs so much as glanced at me. I followed the smell past framed pictures of the kids at every age, past an open bathroom, past two closed doors to a third one, the last. The smell was strongest here. I used my elbow to press down the lever-style handle—no sense leaving fingerprints anywhere, if it could be avoided—and eased open the door.

The master bedroom. The marijuana odor was definitely stronger. A big four-poster bed with a plush white satin bedspread dominated the room, the sheets rumpled. The bedposts were cherry, stained a deep red, but the dressers, the end tables, a little desk, and a big standing wardrobe closest were antique white, painted in a faux-distressed style. Puffs of smoke emanated from beneath the wardrobe door. I also heard muffled crying. A child, it sounded like.

I eased the bedroom door mostly closed behind me, then, my heart picking up its pace, crept to the wardrobe across a downy gray area rug.

Opening the door and releasing a cloud of brown smoke that made my eyes water, I saw nothing at first but a closet packed with suits, coats, and dresses. Boots and shoes lined the bottom, but then I saw one pair of tennis shoes, small ones, with bare ankles sticking out of them. I pushed back the clothes and there he was, a boy of maybe five or six in cutoff jeans and a black and yellow Batman T-shirt. At least I thought he was five or six until he leaned out to look at me and I saw how bald his head was, how shrunken his eye sockets were, how tight his skin was over the hard angles of his bones. His eyes were cloudy and red, and the tears left tracks on his skin like a knife on sandpaper. He might have been closer to nine or ten.

"Aren't you a little young to be smoking pot?" I asked.

He responded with a twitchy shrug.

"Who are you?"

He sniffled. "Is he—is he gone?"

"Is who gone?"

He leaned out a little farther, glanced about, then retreated into the closet. "The one who took Brent."

I knew who he was now. He was the childhood friend, the one with leukemia. Gavin. I knelt in front of him.

"Do you know who I am?"

He shrugged again.

"I'm not going to hurt you." When he said nothing to this, instead taking another drag from his little marijuana stub, I nodded toward it. "Does it help? Does it make you feel better?"

"It—it makes it hurt not so much."

"That's good."

He held the stub out to me. "Want some?"

It seemed so real, I almost believed I could take it from him. "Thanks, but not my style."

"He's not a ghost," he said quickly. "But he doesn't have a solid body, either. He's something else."

"What?"

Still trembling, the boy shook his head and took another drag, blowing out the smoke from the side of his mouth. It was such an adult gesture that I had a hard time reconciling it with his other behavior, which was more fitting of someone his age.

"What do you think he is, Gavin?" I pressed.

"I saw him," he said. "I saw him—up close. He was hurting Brent. He was hurting him and I yelled at him to stop. He—he turned and looked at me. His face …"

He started crying again. I reached to comfort him, then remembered my limitations. I had to settle for telling him everything would be all right, even though the words themselves probably seemed ridiculous to someone who had suffered so much.

"They're inside of him," he said.

"What?"

"All the people. I heard them. I was so close, I heard them—their voices. They're inside of him and they want to get out."

"You're saying his victims are alive?"

"Not alive. Inside of him. Trapped."

"Trapped," I echoed.

He nodded. I thought about what he was saying, about what it meant, and shuddered at the idea. Everyone in the ghost world had assumed that the Ghost Reaper, as they called him, was killing people twice over: he killed their bodies, *then* he killed them in ghost form, too, somehow obliterating them from existence. That was horrific enough, especially to ghosts who had grown accustomed to eternity as a sort of consolation prize when they found out that there was no heaven. But trapped inside a psychopath—especially one who wasn't a flesh-and-blood human but something different? Something even more terrible? That was more like somebody's twisted vision of hell.

I could accept oblivion. But hell? I had never believed in hell. The idea of suffering on and on without end was truly terrifying. *I'll take you to a better place.* That's what the killer believed he was doing. The better place wasn't oblivion. The better place, at least the way he saw it, was within himself.

Gavin suddenly straightened a bit, his face hopeful. "Maybe," he said, "maybe you can get them out. Do you think you can get them out?"

"I don't know."

"I want to be with Brent. Now he would be able to see me again. We could do things. Have—have fun."

"I can try."

"Please. Please, try. Even if you can't … I don't—I don't want him taking anyone else."

"He didn't take you, though," I said.

"Because I'm sick. He doesn't want sick people. He wants really good ones, like Brent. It's the same reason he didn't take the guy on the street."

This piqued my interest. "What guy on the street?"

Gavin took a long drag from his stub and closed his eyes, blowing the smoke out his nose. "Just some guy. He was standing there on the sidewalk, watching, when the—when he came outside."

"Was it ghost or a flesh-and-blood human?"

"I don't know."

"Did the Ghost Reaper look at him? Or stop next to him?"

Garvin opened his eyes. "Yeah. Yeah, I guess he stopped next to him for just a second and the guy backed up a few steps. That's why I remembered him. I thought maybe he would kill him, too, but he didn't. He just went on past the way he did with me. That's how I know he just wants the good ones. Like Brent."

"Gavin," I said, "I need you to think very hard. Is there *anything* about that man that you can remember?"

"He was all in the shadows."

"Even his shape? Tall or short?"

"Short, I guess. Short for a man."

"Thin or stocky?"

"What's stocky?"

"Sort of like fat."

"Kind of fat, I guess. But not like with a fat tummy. Just sort of bigger."

"His hair? His skin?"

Gavin shook his head. "It was all dark and shadowy. He wasn't in the streetlight. I couldn't see much. I'm sorry. Why, is he important?"

I'd been thinking of Chief Branson. Short and stocky, he could have fit the description. Maybe there wasn't just one serial killer. Maybe there were two, working in concert. Gavin's description of him backing away from the killer as if afraid of him didn't suggest they were working together, but it was impossible to know what Gavin really saw. He was just a child, after all.

"Are you sure there's nothing else about the way he looked that you can remember?" I asked.

Gavin looked like he might tear up again. "I'm sorry," he said.

"It's okay. You helped a lot."

I turned to go, my mind already sifting through what I was going to do next, when Gavin called after me.

"Oh, he wrote something," he said.

"What?"

"The guy on the street, he wrote something down. After the Ghost Reaper passed. Like in a little notebook."

That stopped me cold. Lots of people could have been standing outside the Conrad residence with a little notebook, but I knew of one in particular—and he had every reason to be there, even if he wasn't working with the killer.

Eddie Quincy.

He'd been there in the beginning, working the Ghost Reaper case when it was new, nosing his way into my Mom's life, and here he was again still in the thick of things. I'd dismissed him as an annoying afterthought to the investigation, but now I had to consider the possibility that he was a lot more central. He was *outside* the house. He was outside waiting when the killer left. If he wasn't working with the killer, then he at least knew where the killer was going to strike again before it happened. Otherwise, how could he have gotten there so fast?

"Did I say something wrong?" Gavin asked.

I would have hugged the kid if it had been possible, but I settled for a smile. "No," I said, "you just helped me in a big, big way."

Chapter 13

THE GHOSTS were fleeing Portland.

No other explanation made sense. As I drove across town to my office, the streets teemed with ghosts, dozens on one street, hundreds on the next—colonial soldiers armed with muskets, pioneers in dusty white shirts, men in denim and wool and double-breasted lounge jackets, women in long dresses and short dresses and bright yellow pantsuits. Low-heeled suede shoes and black leather stilettos. Hair decorated with little ribbon bows attached to combs and clips. Hair flowing and loose, carefree to match the bell-bottoms and tie-dye. They walked alone. They walked in pairs. They walked in groups, filling the sidewalks, flowing around the living like water around river rocks. They headed east and west and north and south. I had never seen anything like it.

There were so many ghosts that when I stepped out of the car into the crisp morning air outside my office on Burnside, I caused a bit of a stampede. Two men in bowler hats recognized me and bolted away from my car door, knocking into a woman in a pink pastel dress. She screamed—whether it was because of them or me, I don't know—and then the scream spread like a virus, picked up by women and men. The whole mass of them began to run.

I stood there clinging to the door long enough that eventually Alesha asked me what was wrong.

"Nothing," I said. "Sorry—just thinking."

"You sure you don't want to come to the library with us?" she asked. "It was your idea."

"Maybe later. I told you, I've got to take care of a few pressing things at the office first. Follow-ups on my dad."

Seeing the way she squinted at me, I knew she didn't quite believe me. I didn't blame her. But what could I tell her? I wanted to see if I could track down a long-dead reporter? One who might have some connection to a serial killer who wasn't quite human and who wasn't quite a ghost?

She told me she'd call later. I watched them pull into the street, the car exhaust pluming in the air. Some of the ghosts in the road didn't even bother to get out of the way, and the car passed right through them. When enough of the ghosts had fled, I saw my old pal Elvis, the king of hot dogs, at his yellow cart not far from my office door. Someone had knocked his white chef's cap off, and he was retrieving it from the ground, muttering to himself.

I walked over to him. A man in a business suit stepped out of the laundromat across the street, shirts in plastic draped over his arm. He didn't react when he glanced at me, and I realized there was at least one upside to all this craziness. For the time being, I could tell the living from the dead, because the living didn't fear me.

Not that there were a lot of living people on the street, either. They may not have been fleeing the city, but it was obvious people were mostly staying indoors.

"What's happening?" I asked Elvis.

"You know what's happening, pardner."

"They're that afraid?"

"You got it."

"But you're not?"

"Oh, sure. Have to be not just dead, but dead in the head, not to be a bit scared. I was scared back during the war, even though they just had me flying in to sing a few songs for the guys who really had something to be scared about. But I won't let nobody run me out of town."

"They seem to be more afraid of me than the Ghost Reaper."

"They don't know you. Not like I do. When people get real scared, they start getting scared of everything they don't know and don't understand. How goes the case?"

"I may have a lead. Do you know a reporter named Eddie Quincy?"

"Sorry, pardner. And I know a lot of newsy types. What outfit he work for?"

"Nobody now. He's been dead a while."

"That don't stop most newsy types. You think he's tangled up in this thing, huh?"

"Maybe. But he definitely knows more about the killings than he's letting on."

"Well, you describe him to me and I'll keep my eyes out for him."

I did. When I was finished, Elvis offered me a hot dog, and like usual, I told him I'd take one if it were possible. I retreated to my office, sinking into the chair, and mulled over how I was going to find Eddie Quincy—and even if I did find him, how I could get him to talk to me about what he knew. Except for a few gurgling pipes, the building was mercifully silent. I was so immersed in my thoughts that Patch had to scratch at the window for nearly a minute to get my attention. I let him in and he hopped onto my lap, purring. Patch may not have been an ordinary cat, but his purr had the same therapeutic power.

Outside, the morning traffic picked up its pace, tires thumping through potholes. The brightening sunlight revealed each little divot and scuff mark on my mostly bare white walls. I turned to the computer while Patch perched on my lap, occasionally nuzzling his head against my chin.

Who was Eddie Quincy? I needed to know more about him, and the first place to start was probably with Eddie's own writing.

I'd already read *The Killer Who Wasn't There,* which certainly sensationalized the Goodbye Killer even if it didn't give me much new information, but the one thing I'd skipped in the book had been Eddie's biography at the back. I brought up the e-book and jumped to the bio page. It was only a paragraph, and despite the breathless language, there wasn't a whole lot there I didn't already know. Author of ten books. Worked as an investigative reporter before turning full time to "chronicling the dark psychology of some of the world's most notorious serial killers."

Hoping for better leads, I moved on to the Internet. The first thing I noticed was that there had been a resurgence in both sales and reviews of Quincy's books, starting with *The Killer* but extending to his other titles as well. How convenient. If he wanted to boost his book sales, what better way to do it than to revive interest in the case that had put Quincy on the map? Even if Quincy wasn't the killer himself, or working with him, he certainly was benefiting from the renewed attention. This had occurred to me before, of course, but until Gavin spotted Quincy outside the Conrad residence, I had just thought this was a fortunate coincidence. Now the benefit seemed much more deliberate.

The key question seemed to be: Who was Quincy working with in the world of the living? Find out who that was, and I had a hunch I'd get a lot more answers. A more thorough Internet search quickly brought up Quincy's obituary—not on the *Statesman Journal* website where he'd once worked (everything more than two years old was behind a firewall), but one someone had copied and pasted into a Goodbye Killer forum. Unfortunately, I didn't learn much other than that he'd died of lung cancer twenty-two years ago. There was no mention of surviving relatives. A little more digging led me to some ancestry research someone had posted on a low-tech public website, where I learned that Edward Quincy of Scio, Oregon, was an only child and that his parents, who'd been old when he was born, had preceded him in death by about ten years.

I was lost in thought when Patch meowed loudly and placed his paw on the computer screen. For a hopeful moment, I thought he might have been offering me some kind of deep insight, some cosmic feline connection he had to the truth that eluded us poor humans, but then I realized he was merely following the mouse pointer. Ah, well, even a cat who can see ghosts is just a cat in the end, with cat instincts and cat needs. I swept the pointer left and right, prompting Patch to swipe at the screen a few more times. We were two peas in a pod, Patch and I, both of us straddling two worlds, and yet here we were entertaining ourselves with a mouse pointer. What would we do without each other? If I was gone, who would entertain my furry little friend?

This thought shook something loose in my brain, something Eddie had said when we talked at the bar. He'd said that the money from his books went to a "scholarship for young writers." I didn't think anything of it at the time, but now I wondered. Would someone like Eddie Quincy really donate the money from his books to a bunch of anonymous kids out of the goodness of his heart? People were complicated, so it was possible, but his money was going somewhere—that was for sure. Who would know? Well, the people writing the checks, that was who.

I looked up the publisher on the copyright page of the e-book. It was Night Visions, an imprint of Mandelson & Steeves, one of the huge media conglomerates. They had a New York address. The computer's clock put the time at a hair before 11 in the morning, which would make it almost 2 p.m. back east. Another search on the Internet and I had the name of Myron's editor—Jonathan Delaney—and a customer-service number. I called that number and was soon transferred to the editorial department. A young woman who sounded about fourteen years old answered. I asked to speak with Mr. Delaney.

I heard a plastic crinkle in the background, like a bag of chips. Sure enough, when she spoke again, it was with a bit of a crunchy mumble. "Oh, I'm sorry," she said, "he's at a conference until Monday. Would you like me to direct you to his voice mail?"

"I'm afraid it's a bit urgent," I said. "Perhaps you can be of some help."

"I'll do my best, sir. What do you need?"

For a few seconds, I debated which approach to take. Often the truth—or something close to the truth—really was best, but with my name all over the national news, I sensed she might shut down quickly if she found out who I was.

"Well, it's a bit of a sensitive matter, Miss—can I ask your name?"

She hesitated. "Alice Sampson."

"Yes, Alice. I'm William Katzberg with the IRS Fraud Division. I'm going to breach a bit of protocol here, Alice. I shouldn't be telling you this at all, but I'm afraid we're investigating Mr. Delaney—him and one of his clients."

"Oh no."

"I'm fairly certain it's an error. I'm trying to get to the bottom of it, but my boss wants to hand it over to the attorney general's office for prosecution."

"Prosecution!"

"That's why I need some information quickly, Alice. One of Delaney's authors has been deceased quite some time, and we need to know exactly who is receiving the royalty checks. I have some information I've gotten from tax returns, but it's incomplete. I think it's an error on the IRS side, but my boss insists it's fraud." I lowered my voice to a conspiratorial whisper. "Personally, I think he's just trying to cover his ass, because if he has to admit that his department screwed up, well, there goes his promotion. You get my drift, Alice?"

"Yes."

"I probably shouldn't be telling you this, but I really don't like the guy. So what I want to do is insert that royalty information and make it look like it was there all along. But if I don't do it right now, it won't happen. Can you help me? We can get your boss out of this scrape and stick it to my boss at the same time. I can also tell you, Alice, that I have ways of communicating to Mr. Delaney just how helpful you were with this."

I could hear the gears turning in her head. The implication, of course, was not only that Mr. Delaney could be told how helpful she *was*, but he could also be told how helpful she *wasn't*.

"Who's the author?" she asked finally.

"His name is Eddie Quincy."

"Oh, him."

"Yes, I bet his books have been selling better because of that awful stuff in Portland. That's part of why Quincy's tax returns were flagged, which led us back to Mandelson & Steeves—and Delaney."

When Alice spoke again, she had lowered her own voice to a whisper, with a bit of a cloak-and-dagger tone. "Well … Let me see. I think I can get that for you, sir. Can you hold for a moment?"

"Um … Yes, but just for a minute. I'm actually supposed to meet my boss in about half an hour."

"Oh no."

"That's why I said it's urgent."

"I see. I'll—I'll be right back."

There was a click and then I was listening to classical music. A few minutes passed, long enough that I worried she might have talked to someone else in the office and the game was up.

"Mr. Katzberg?" She sounded out of breath.

"Call me Will, Alice. What did you find?"

"Well, the royalties are paid to a trust set up in Quincy's name. It's called the Northwest Young Writers Advancement Fund."

I wanted to laugh and cry at the same time. So Eddie wasn't lying.

"Sir?" Alice said.

"Still here," I said. "Does it say who's handling the trust?"

"Um … yes, sir. It's a firm out of Portland. Akelton & Moore. Um, it does say here that it's supposed to be anonymous, so I guess the recipients aren't supposed to know the money came from Quincy's books. You're not—you're not going to tell anyone this, are you? Except for putting it in the, um, paperwork."

The name seemed familiar, and I didn't think it was just because I'd heard of them. They were not only one of the biggest CPA firms in the country, but they were local, too, started by a couple of college friends who graduated from Oregon State University nearly fifty years back. No, the name jogged my memory in a more recent way. Why? Maybe it was just because I'd seen their name on a T-shirt or a banner, as they were involved in lots of local charities. That distinctive A&M logo of theirs, with the *A* and the *M* partially overlapping, was hard to miss ...

A&M.

It came to me then, in a flash. I knew exactly where I'd heard A&M mentioned recently—and I also knew it couldn't be a coincidence. The elation of discovery, that rare feeling that every detective gets to experience now and then when a missing piece falls into place, only lasted a fleeting second. Replacing it, with all the pleasantness of something rotten sliding into my stomach, was a mix of rage and disappointment and embarrassment.

It was impossible to feel good when the missing piece led you directly to the woman who had somehow captured your heart.

Chapter 14

I DECIDED TO WAIT until I calmed down to call Jak, then changed my mind and called her immediately. It wasn't a good move. The quaver in my voice prompted her to ask what was wrong. I snapped at her that there was nothing wrong—I just wanted to meet her. How about now? After a bit of hesitation, she said she could be at my place in half an hour. I asked if we could meet at her place instead. After an even longer hesitation, she said her place was a total disaster—her housekeeper was out sick this week—so she'd prefer to hold off on my seeing it until she got things in order.

I told her fine, half an hour at my place, but then I called Alesha and asked her to give me the address for one Jacqueline Worthe from her DMV record. Alesha sounded downright gleeful at my request, prodding me about what was going on, and I snapped at her, too, telling her I just needed this favor for now.

Ten minutes later, I stood in front of apartment 201B of a shabby eight-plex in northeast Portland. The exterior was not only an ugly color of green, but it was different shades of green, a spectrum between lime and algae as if someone had done touch-ups with whatever green paint was cheapest. Live oaks and Douglas firs cast the whole place in deep shadow. Her place was up a set of wooden stairs that creaked and wobbled under my feet.

An old man dressed in overalls and a grease-stained white T-shirt sat hunched on a milk crate outside the other door at the top of the stairs, 201A. He held a long pipe and squinted at me suspiciously under his drooping eyebrows. Smoke that smelled of tobacco and oranges curled around his face. I nodded toward Jak's door.

"She in?" I asked.

The pipe dropped from the old man's mouth, bounced against the wooden slats, and fell to the cracked concrete below. He gaped at me.

"Ah," I said, "not a member of the living, huh?"

"You—you—you—" he stuttered.

"Tell me something," I said. "You seen another ghost coming to her place? A short balding guy who goes by the name Eddie Quincy? He might be—"

I didn't get to finish because the old man bounded off the milk crate and into the other apartment, straight through the door. I'd tried to keep my voice down, but it still must have carried through the thin walls, because Jak's door opened and there she was, dressed in a black turtleneck and designer jeans, her blond hair swept back into a tight ponytail. As I'd expected—and really, hoped—she looked shocked to see me. More than shocked. Ashamed, maybe. And a bit betrayed.

"Surprise," I said.

Her eyes flared. I thought maybe she was going to slam the door, but then she bowed her head and gestured for me to enter.

Her apartment wasn't a disaster, but it wasn't the kind of place that a housekeeper visited either. A pine futon covered with a Native American blanket. White IKEA bookshelves, sagging under the weight of all her books. A green Formica kitchen table with metal legs, a laptop open and running on top of it, with spiral notebooks and lots of loose paper scattered around. Posters from famous pulp movies. The whole thing, even with the bedroom I could see off the kitchen, was hardly bigger than my living room—and my living room was on the small side.

"Well," she said.

"Nice place," I said.

"Don't do that."

"What? It's a nice place. I'm just being honest."

"Myron—"

"We should always be honest, right Jak? That's what they say. Honesty is the best policy."

She rubbed her forehead. In the silence, I heard the dripping of her kitchen faucet and the hum of her refrigerator. Next door, I heard someone talking in a low, agitated voice, and I wondered if it was the old man. I wondered if the person he was talking to could hear him.

"I'm sorry," she said.

"Ah, straight to the apology," I said. "Points for that. So how much of it was an act, then? Did you feel anything for me at all?"

"What? Of course I do!" Her eyes misted up.

"You're certainly a good actress, that's for sure," I said. "I think you missed your calling. What I want to know is how much of this was Eddie's idea."

"Eddie? What are you talking about?"

"Come on! You know exactly what I'm talking about. I'm talking about your father here, kiddo. Don't play dumb. I followed the money."

She shook her head. "My father? Myron, I really have no idea what you're talking about. I've never met my father. I *told* you that."

Even though I shouldn't have, I believed her. Even though she'd lied to me once and had every reason to lie to me again, there was something about her tone that sounded authentic. Maybe she was just acting again—the femme fatale from some of those pulp movies on her walls conniving her way to some new purpose—and maybe I just *wanted* to believe her, but I decided that coming at her with a lot of rage wouldn't get us anywhere. It wouldn't hurt me to at least pretend she was telling the truth. She couldn't fool me a second time.

I gestured to the futon. "Maybe we should sit down."

"But what about my father?"

"Let's sit down and talk about it," I said. "We'll figure it out together."

"Myron—"

"Sit. Come on."

She turned to the futon, hunched and small, arms tucked around her waist. We sat next to each other, a few inches more distance between us than would have been there yesterday, the thin mattress sagging to the wooden slats beneath it. I detected a faint whiff of something sweetly alcoholic coming from the blanket, a bit of spilled wine perhaps. Jak, all of her bravado gone, stared at me with the wide-eyed fear of someone awaiting a cancer diagnosis.

"Is there anyone else in here?" she asked.

"What?"

"You know, ghosts."

"Oh. No, just us."

"Okay."

"You told me that you earned most of your money from PayPal donations," I said. "That's not true, is it?"

"Well …"

"Jak, come on. You get regular payments from something called the Northwest Young Writers Advancement Fund, right?"

"It was a contest," Jak said. "I won it about—about eight years ago. Why? What's that have to do with my father?"

"How did you find out about it?"

"There was a letter that came in the mail. A brochure thing. It said I could win twenty years of payments of $2,000 a month. I just needed to email a sample of my writing."

"Did you ever meet anyone involved?"

"No, they just sent a congratulations letter. They told me they set up the fund with a broker at A&M, and all I had to do was go in and work with him to make sure I got my payments. I kept thinking it might be some kind of scam, but it wasn't."

"And you never thought to investigate this program? Someone like you, who writes all kinds of investigative pieces?"

"No. I thought about it. But Myron, it seemed too good to be true. I didn't want the bubble to burst. It started when I was just barely eighteen, just out of foster care, just finding my way. I got a job as a waitress at one of those Hooters-like places. It was kind of demeaning, getting hired mostly because of my boobs, but at least I wasn't stripping. I thought about that, you know. Stripping. It seemed like an easy way to make some money, maybe sock some away so I could do something with my life, go to college, something. After six months of serving beer and letting guys *accidentally* cop a feel so I could get a good tip, I was really thinking about the stripping thing. There was this guy who came in that said he'd give me a shot if I wanted to come into his strip club some Friday night. I was in a really dark place. Then one night, after a lot of drinking, I picked up the phone to call the guy—then decided to swallow a whole bunch of pills instead."

"Jak," I said.

"It wasn't the first time, actually. I even swallowed them this time around, but then I made myself throw up in the toilet. That's also when I started blogging—and I blogged about all this stuff. I was brutally honest. People really liked it. That's how the Young Writers people said they found out about me—through my blog. They asked me to submit."

"I see," I said.

"And Myron, I wanted to tell you. Remember when we were lying in bed right before your—your mom showed up? I was going to tell you then. It's just … the PayPal stuff doesn't do as well as it used to. And the money from the program, they miss months now and then."

"What?"

"They finally wrote me a letter this month saying that there should be a check coming within a few months that would make up for the missed ones, but yeah, it had gotten to the point in the last year where they had missed about every other month."

"You told me you moved all over the place. Was that true?"

"Yes! Myron, I—I only lied because I was ashamed of how much things had fallen. After the recession, the donations started to dry up. A lot of bloggers saw the same thing. And then with the contest money getting erratic, I actually had to apply for food stamps. Food stamps! Me! It was horrible. I really was doing as well as I said a couple years ago."

"How long have you lived in Portland?"

"Maybe six months."

"Why did you move here?"

"Oh, lots of reasons. I'd sometimes have discussions with people in my comments section. People kept saying I should give Portland a chance because it would probably fit my personality. I mean, I *was* from Oregon originally. At least that's what my mom said, before she moved us down to Los Angeles. Myron, *please* tell me what this has to do with my father."

"Where in Oregon?"

"Huh?"

"Where were you born?"

"My birth certificate says it was Salem. I had to get a copy when I wanted to get a job. No father listed. Myron—"

"Salem. These discussions with people on your blog. The people who said you should move to Portland. Do you know who they are?"

"Nah. I mean, some of them may use their real names, but they're probably just handles. And even if I could track that stuff, I didn't."

"So it could be the same person?"

"Huh?"

"The same person," I said. "It could be the same person writing under different names."

"Well, I guess. I think I would have noticed if I had a heavy concentration of the same IP addresses, but people could be logging in from different locations or devices. But why would somebody do that?"

We had reached the point where I needed to tell her about Eddie Quincy. I still couldn't conclusively prove that he was her father, but there were just too many coincidences. It explained the weird way he had looked at her back at the Mistwood: that hadn't been lust, just surprise at seeing his daughter. Jak was born in Salem. Eddie worked for the newspaper in Salem. The money was coming from A&M. The money was starting to dry up, probably because of low sales, and yet she got a letter right when his sales would have taken off because of the renewed interest in the Goodbye Killer case. Eddie had told Mom that he had somebody who could write the next book for him. Who better than Jak?

"You hate me," Jak said suddenly, filling the silence.

"I don't hate you," I said.

"I wouldn't blame you for hating me."

"I don't hate you, Jak. Seriously. I'm not happy you didn't tell me about your real living situation, but I get it now. And the last week—" I shook my head. "It was very fast, okay? And when my father went missing … I'm sorry if I pushed you away. Hey? Hey, what's wrong? It's okay."

She'd started crying, big gulping tears. I'd always felt helpless when a woman cried, as if I were watching a mugging in progress on a closed-circuit television and there was nothing I could do to stop it. Like an idiot, I watched for a long time before taking her hand. Her skin felt both sweaty and cold.

"Sorry," she said.

"Don't worry about it. You can cry in front of me."

She finally brought the crying to a sniffling stop, grabbing a handful of tissues from a box on the coffee table and dabbing at her face. "I don't like crying. I try not to do it. I want you to see me as strong."

"You can be strong and cry. I'd cry more if I could. It's good for you. Cathartic."

"When's the last time you cried?"

"I don't remember. I tried to cry when Billie left. Wanted to. But it's like something's missing, like … I don't know, like I'm sitting in a car but I don't have the key."

She nodded and put her other hand on top of mine. We sat like that, looking into each other's eyes, and I watched the strength flow back into her. Spine straightening. Shoulders squaring. Head slightly cocked to the side, the confidence returning to her eyes. It might have been an act, but then, that was how it was for all of us a good percentage of the time. We were all acting, trying to fool everyone into a willing suspension of disbelief that it was all real, as they say in the theater. It was just a question of how much we could also fool ourselves at the same time.

"All right," she said. "Hit me with it. What does all this have to do with my father? Don't tell me you think he's the Goodbye Killer."

"Maybe," I said.

"Really?"

"Or maybe not. Maybe he's not even your father. Jak, remember when you told me that you sometimes felt like you could sense your father around? What did you mean by that? Do you mean you hear him speaking to you?"

"No," Jak said, "not speaking. More just a—a presence, I guess. Like he's sometimes watching me. Not in a creepy way. More like a father looking down at a baby in a crib. I know that sounds silly. Myron, you've got to tell me what you know right now. This is driving me nuts."

She was right. I'd withheld the information long enough, so I told her everything. I told her about Eddie Quincy, the onetime newspaperman from Salem, Oregon, who became the true-crime writer of *The Killer Who Wasn't There*. I told her that there was a very good chance that the Northwest Young Writers Advancement Fund was just a cover so he could funnel his royalty money to her via A&M without her knowing where it was coming from, something he must have set up with his publisher when he was dying of cancer. I told her about what Mom had said about Eddie having a connection with a living person who could write another book about the Goodbye Killer. I told her about how Gavin had seen him outside the Conrad residence. I told her he might have been working with the killer.

It was a lot to take in at once, like a boxer in the ring absorbing a flurry of body blows. She handled it like a champ, steely-eyed, her posture and demeanor already far removed from the fragile creature she was just moments ago. When I was done talking, she got up and went to her laptop, pecking away at the keyboard. She read for while, typed a bit more, read again.

"Not exactly a Brad Pitt in the looks department, is he?" she said.

"Not exactly, no."

"But I do see some resemblance. I mostly look like my mom, though. Thank God. I wonder what she saw in him."

"We still don't know for sure it's him," I said.

"Oh, it's him. Everything fits. Everything you said makes sense—and there was other stuff, too, things my Mom said. When I was little, before she really went down the toilet with drugs, I remember—I have this memory. It's fuzzy, but I remember showing her a little comic-book thing I'd made of pictures and whatever words I knew how to write. I told her I liked making books, and she said she wasn't surprised. She didn't say why—she would never talk about my father, no matter how much I asked her—but that comment always stuck with me. Funny. I've even read his book already. Thought he was a good writer. Not as good as me, of course, but not bad."

Her smug grin was a welcome sight. I knew she wanted me to smile in return. I knew she wanted a lot more than that. It was all in the lingering stare, the tilt of the hips. If anything, the attraction between us was even stronger than before, electrified by all the recent tension.

That was my body talking, but this time it was critical that I didn't give in to it. I had to do what was right for both of us. I'd entered her apartment already knowing what needed to be done. A little lust didn't change anything.

"Look," I said, "we need to talk."

Chapter 15

IT WASN'T EASY leaving Jak that night. Alone, I tussled with the sheets for a couple of hours before finally giving up and settling in front of the television with one of the Coors I'd picked up on the way home. I actually didn't like Coors, being something of a beer snob who preferred Oregon microbrews, and only drank the stuff when I was feeling guilty. My theory was that downing a beer I didn't like made it much easier to stop at one. Sometimes the theory even proved to be true.

Outside, silence pervaded my Sellwood neighborhood—or at least for what passed for silence in a Portland suburb. An old truck wheezed past. Some people laughed on a patio a few houses over. A couple of cats hissed and screeched nearby, twenty seconds of grating noise, but then that was gone, too. I ran through the lineup of late-night hosts, didn't find any of them funny, and ended up on one of the shopping channels debating whether I needed a new automated potato peeler. I couldn't remember if I'd used the one I'd bought after Billie left—probably from the same channel, late at night, drinking bad beer and feeling guilty.

I didn't see many ghosts on television, which was the reason I watched a fair amount now when I'd hardly watched it before I woke up with a bullet lodged in my brain. Something about the presence of the cameras tended to scare them off, which meant watching television was one of the few ways I got a glimpse into a world that was once my own, a much simpler, less crowded one. It may not have been all that accurate a glimpse, distorted and warped as television was, but it was still comforting in a way. Yes, the television seemed to remind me, that other world still exists. Yes, you might even get back to it someday.

I was contemplating giving in to the temptation of a second Coors when I heard the rush of footsteps behind me along with fast, raspy breathing. I jumped out of the rocker I'd scooted in front of the television and spun to face my intruder.

It was Eddie Quincy.

"Myron!" he gasped.

That was all he could manage before he doubled over, trying to regain his breath. His scattered strands of hair stuck to his sweaty scalp. His skin, normally an odd orange color, was now an odd orange color mixed with blotchy pink spots. His shirttails stuck out of the back of his plaid jacket and his tan chinos were wrinkled and askew. I wondered briefly why he was having trouble breathing when he didn't need any breath, then I pushed the thought from my mind. Those types of questions only led to more questions, none of which I could ever explain, except that ghosts did many things because they believed they needed to do those things.

"What is it?" I asked. "What's going on?"

"Myron—" he tried again.

"I need to talk to you," I said. "I need to know exactly how you're involved with the Ghost Reaper. Are you the Ghost Reaper? Tell me right now."

"No!"

"Then how are you involved?"

"Myron! No time. It's—it's about Jak. Jak Worthe." He finally got some amount of control over his breathing, straightening a bit and staring at me with his beady eyes. "She's in trouble! You need to go there now."

"What?"

"She's got your gun!"

"What?"

He nodded. "You must have left it there tonight. Or she took it out of your coat. Myron. Myron, she wrote a suicide note and posted it on her blog. Said the guy she's in love with rejected her, so she doesn't—doesn't want to go on. Myron—"

I hustled to the closet and found the holster hanging inside my leather jacket, but no Glock. "This is nuts! She wouldn't do that."

"She will! She will!" he cried. "She's tried to kill herself before. You have to stop her! I tried. I yelled and yelled, but she can't hear me."

I grabbed my phone and called her. It went to voice mail. I tried again: same result.

"Oh no," he moaned. "You've got to go over there!"

I jumped to the computer and brought up her website, scanning the latest entry. Sure enough, there was a long diatribe about how life wasn't worth living once you've lost the man you love, especially when you've known so much emptiness.

"Myron, we don't have—" Eddie began.

"You're right," I said, "let's go."

Shoes, jacket, keys—in thirty seconds, I blew out of the house and jumped in the Prius, buzzing through the dark streets with Eddie fidgeting in the passenger seat. A strong wind rippled the flyers stapled to the telephone poles on Burnside. The city really was strangely empty, not a ghost in sight. I pushed the car as fast as it would go, hoping no cop who needed to make his ticket quota would spot me. The empty streets whipped past. We hit one red stoplight, but no one was there, so I zoomed through it.

I glanced at Eddie. The green glow of the dashboard gave his face a sickly pallor. Or maybe, based on how pinched his lips were, he really was going to be sick.

"Why do you care so much about her?" I asked.

He didn't answer.

"Why were you even watching her?" I pressed. "You always creep around the apartments of cute girls?"

"No!"

"Then why were you over there?"

"I just was, okay?"

"I saw the way you looked at her at the Mistwood," I said. "I thought it was your ordinary dirty-old-man lust, but it wasn't, was it?"

"I just want to help her."

"It's more than that."

"No, no, I just—"

"It's more than that, and you know it. Tell me."

Eddie chewed on his lower lip, the streetlamps overhead streaking shadows across his face. He scratched at his wrinkled chinos, clenching and unclenching his fingers. We made a few more turns and there we were, screeching to a stop in front of Jak's eight-plex. All the lights were dark except one—top left, Jak's place. Eddie started getting out of the Prius, floating through the door, and stopped when he saw that I hadn't taken my hands off the steering wheel.

"What are you *doing?*" he said.

"I need answers," I said.

He settled back into the seat, leaning toward me. "But we're here! She's—she's up there right now—"

"I know what she's doing," I said calmly. "And I'm not getting out of this car until I get some answers, Eddie. How do you know Jak Worthe?"

He leaned closer still, as if to grab me by the scruff of my jacket, before he realized it was impossible—which only turned his face more desperate. "We don't have time! Don't you care about her? You may—may have left her, but she doesn't deserve to die!"

"This isn't about what I feel," I said. "How do you know her?"

"How can you be so heartless!" he shouted.

"I'm doing what has to be done."

"If she dies, it's—it's on you!"

"No, Eddie, it's on you. Tell me what you're hiding from me, and

I'll go upstairs."

He panted and gasped a bit, scrambling around in his seat, glancing at Jak's window and back at me, a lot of frantic movement all packed into a tiny space. His face was so sweaty and red, it looked like he'd just jumped out of a hot tub. There was nothing Eddie could do to save her on his own. I knew this, he knew this, and it gave me a lot of leverage. I was willing to use that leverage, as cold as it might have seemed to him.

"You bastard!" he screamed at me.

"Tell me what you know."

"She's going to die!"

"Tell me."

There was one last hysterical frenzy, a physical spasm that would have gotten me to laugh if the stakes weren't so high, and then he spat out a single word as if he'd been choking on it: *"Daughter!"*

"What?"

"She's my daughter, all right? My daughter!"

"How?"

"We don't have time!"

"Eddie—"

"I—I was young. Working in Salem. Harriet was a temp doing some filing in the office. It was a one-night stand. She wanted the baby. I said to hell with her, but she had it anyway. She moved away! She moved away and I never got to be part of Jacqueline's life. And then—then I got sick, and I thought about her, how I wasn't there for her … Myron, come on! She might pull the trigger at any moment!"

"And all the money from your books went to her?"

"Yes, yes!"

"And you were going to help her write the next book, weren't you?"

"Yes! Now, let's go!"

He turned once again to the door, but I wasn't moving. "And you're not the Ghost Reaper?"

"No!"

"But you know him, don't you? You were outside the Conrad house Friday night. Someone saw you. How do you know him?"

Eddie bit down on his clenched fist. "I don't! I swear I don't!"

"Then why were you outside the house?"

"Myron!"

"Eddie, tell me the truth!"

He blinked his watery eyes at me and spun toward the door and back to me again, his lips moving soundlessly, his whole body a tremulous mass of barely contained energy. A stream of saliva hung from the corner of his mouth. Eddie's seizure-like movements reminded me of the few people I'd had to zap with a Taser back in my uniform days, a ugly sight to behold that always left me feeling ashamed that I'd had to resort to such a barbaric device.

"I'll—I'll tell you!" he wailed finally. "I'll tell you everything! But it's—it's complicated! I'll tell you as soon as we save her. *Please!*"

Before I could reply, he dived through the car door and took two stumbling steps toward the apartment building, only then glancing back at me—a shuddering dark shape in front of overgrown laurel bushes. I glanced at Jak's lit apartment. How much more could I really push Eddie right now? He bolted toward the apartment building, a stumbling, swinging sprint that was half run and half swim.

I followed, scrambling through the tall grass to the stairway. The wind rattled the oak leaves and rippled through my hair, ice cold on my warm face. The moon, finally piercing clouds that covered the sky like coiled rags, laced Eddie's jacket with pallid light. I caught up to him just as he plunged through Jak's front door, and I jerked it open and followed him inside.

She was there at her little kitchen table, the Glock pointed under her chin. The light from the bedroom behind her cast her face in shadow, her sleeveless black T-shirt making her gun arm appear as if it were floating, disembodied. The wind, blowing at my back through the open front door, scattered loose papers on her table and sent them flying.

"Stop! " Eddie cried, waving at her frantically. He tripped over his own feet and went down, landing with a thud before bouncing back into a ragged crawl. "Please don't! Please don't do it!"

But of course Jak couldn't see or hear him. She did, however, take full notice of me, pressing the nozzle of the gun even tighter against her chin.

"Stay back," she warned me. "You can't stop me. I don't want to live if I can't have you."

"Jak, let's talk about this."

"We already did talk about this. You said we were through."

Eddie, bawling like a baby, had crawled all the way to the table. He babbled at her to stop, that it wasn't worth it, that he loved her, and he went on babbling as he staggered to his feet. He groped for her gun hand, his fingers passing through with each futile attempt. He said I wasn't worth it. He said no man was worth it. He said there was so much he wanted to tell her, if only she waited, if only she gave him a chance. During this desperate display, I couldn't help but stare at him—and Jak *saw* me staring.

"What?" she said. "What are you looking at? Is there ... is there someone else *here*?"

"Yes!" Eddie said. "Yes, there is! You know about what Myron can do. I'm here, sweetheart! I'm right next to you!"

"Yes," I said to Jak.

"Who is it?"

"I think you know who it is," I said.

This got her to lower her gun, but only a little. Eddie, encouraged, smiled at her through his tears.

"Yes!" he said. "Yes, put the gun down, Jackie! Put it down."

"My father," she said.

"That's right."

"Yes, yes, it's *me*!" Eddie cried triumphantly.

"Why?" Jak said.

"He wanted to stop you," I said. "He read your blog, and he came to get me. Please, Jak. Put the gun down. I'll—I'll translate for him. I'll tell you what he says."

She didn't move, the Glock still poised an inch or two below her chin. With the shadows, I could barely see her face. In the tense seconds that ticked past, the night yawned through the open door, cold wind racing through the little apartment. Suddenly, Jak shoved the Glock against her chin.

"You're lying," she said. "You're a bastard and you're lying!"

"No!" Eddie protested.

"You're just making him up," Jak said. "You're making him up because you know it's the only way I'll stop. He's not here at all. There's no one here but us!" She closed her eyes. Her finger tightened on the trigger.

"Wait!" Eddie said. "Wait, I can prove it! I can prove I'm here! Myron, Myron—please, tell her. I can prove it!"

"He can prove it," I said.

Her eyes flew wide. "What?"

"He said he can prove he's here."

"Tell her—tell her I know about the first time she almost did it," Eddie said. "When she was … it was back at that horrible foster family. The one with the man who … Tell her I watched her dump all the pills on her bed. She poured a glass of water in a Betty Boop cup. No one else would know about the cup, because she—she cleaned it and put it away. Tell her about Betty Boop, Myron! Tell her!"

I told her. Emotions rippled across her face like an accelerated movie reel—shock, relief, anger, it was all there. Staring to her left, where Eddie stood crouched, she lowered the gun as if hardly aware of its presence. The Glock didn't quite make it to the table, hovering inches over it, but it no longer pointed anywhere in her direction. Eddie expelled a ragged sigh.

"Thank God," he said.

"My father," Jak said, a shiny film over her eyes. "Dad. Can you hear me?"

"Yes," Eddie said.

She looked at me. I nodded.

"Why—why did you leave?" she asked, a hitch in her voice.

"I didn't leave," Eddie said. "Your mother, she left. I wanted—I mean, I know I made mistakes. But if she had been—"

"I was all alone," Jak said, talking over him. "Mom was messed up. I could have … You could have helped me. You could have helped me when you were still alive."

Eddie looked at me with desperation. "Please, tell her! Tell her Harriet was the one who left."

I crossed my arms, frowning at him. Now Jak was looking at me, too, waiting for my translation.

"I don't work for free," I said.

"What?" Eddie said.

"You tell me what you're hiding about the Ghost Reaper, then I'll translate."

"Myron—"

"Tell me what you know, or I walk out the door forever. This is it, Eddie. You'll never get another chance to make things right with her. Jak already knows I want nothing to do with her. She's a basket case and I'm done. You want your moment in the confessional with her? Tell me about the Ghost Reaper."

Jak started to cry, the way a toddler might cry, openly and nakedly. Eddie looked on helplessly, reaching for her a little before retracting his hand, then blinked and sputtered before finally managing to get out a response: "How—how could you be so *heartless?*"

"Me? Heartless? You're the one that just said you thought she was an ugly baby, which was why you didn't stay."

"What? I didn't say that!"

"What's that, you say? You want me to tell Jak that you're not surprised that her mother ended up in jail? Because she was a useless whore?"

He blinked rapidly, and I saw something on his face, something I didn't like. The gears in his head were turning, but not in the way I'd hoped. He didn't look angry; he looked suspicious. I shrugged and started to turn toward the door. The mother comment was probably going too far, but I was out of cards, and it was my last desperate play.

Jak, glaring at me in defiance, again took the gun and shoved it under her chin.

"I'm gonna do it," she said.

"You gotta do what you gotta do," I said.

I took another few steps toward the door. No looking back. I wouldn't let myself look back. My hand was on the door handle. My hand—despite my best intentions, visibly trembling—was opening the door.

"You're lying," Eddie said, suddenly calm.

"What?" I said.

"This—this is some kind of setup," he said. "You're trying to trick me. You're trying to trick me into telling you things."

"What's happening?" Jak said. "I swear, I'm going to pull the trigger!"

"She almost had me," Eddie said. "It was a good trap—the suicide note, the gun. You did this to get me to tell you about the Ghost Reaper. You want to know who he is. You think I know. But what if I don't know? What if I don't have the faintest clue?"

"We both know that's not true," I said.

"Yeah, well, even if I did, why would I tell you? It's not time yet. It will be time soon. It will all come out—and this one here, my little girl, she's going to write about it. It'll make us famous. It'll make us both famous."

His panic abated, he gazed at Jak with such adoration—the way only a proud father can look at his daughter—that I momentarily forgot that this man was probably responsible for the deaths of countless innocent people. I looked at her, too, and she looked back, eyebrows arching ever so slightly, her thespian mask briefly falling away. She wanted to know what was going on. The game was up: that was what was going on.

"He knows," I said to Jak.

The gun dropped just a little. "What?" she said.

"He knows you're faking. It's all right." I took a few steps toward him. "Eddie, it doesn't matter. You can still do what's right. You can tell me who the Goodbye Killer is, and maybe we can stop him from killing other people."

"I haven't done anything! I'm a writer. I just write about it, that's all."

"At the very least, you're allowing him to kill people. And maybe you're even telling him who to target."

"No!"

Jak set the Glock on the table, the clunk on the wood sharp and loud. Behind us, the wind still moaned and whistled through the open front door. Following my gaze, she turned and faced Eddie, all that rage and despair gone as if she'd flipped a switch. There was something disturbing about how easily she could do that. She had a future on Broadway if she wanted one. Or in politics.

"Dad," she said. "Dad, please tell us who he is. I can still write about it. But it's got to be the truth. All of it."

Eddie swallowed hard. "Jackie, you don't—"

"It's the only way," she said, talking right on top of him.

"It—It has to build up," he insisted. "The hype has to build. It has to be big—"

"You want to help me, this is it. Tell Myron the truth. Tell *me* the truth. Then maybe—" Her voice choked off the words, and she had to shake her head and try again. "Then maybe you and me, we can pick up the pieces a little. Maybe we can have something. But you don't tell me the truth right now, we have nothing. And I'm not going to write about any of this. I promise you, *none* of it. Yeah, maybe I won't kill myself, but I'll throw my computer into the Columbia River before I let another innocent person die. Not if you can stop it. And I know you can, Dad. Do this. Do what's right."

He began to cry. His face, that rumpled, pasty white face of his, crumpled like newspaper in the rain. He reached for her, but of course she couldn't see this, so he turned to me.

"Myron," he implored, "Myron, tell her that I love her. I want her to know that. I know I wasn't—I wasn't there for her, but I love her. Tell her."

"The truth, Eddie," I said.

"Okay, okay, just tell her first. I *promise*, I'll tell you everything. You won't like it, you probably won't even believe it, but I'll tell you. The killer is someone you know. But Jackie is going to hate me afterward, so I want her to know I love her first. Can you do that, Myron? Please tell her. You love her, too. I know you do. Just tell her. It's all I want. Tell her."

Jak looked at me, waiting. Even with her face streaked from tears—fake or real, it was hard to say—even as haggard as she appeared in that sleeveless black T-shirt, her hair loose and disheveled, even then, she was beautiful. And I did love her. I still didn't know exactly what kind of love it was, but I knew it was more than lust. Maybe I was a fool for giving Eddie anything, but I had always been a sucker for sentiment—and I knew, looking at Jak's lovely face, that I wasn't doing it for him.

"Your father wants you to know he loves you," I said to her. "He's sorry for not being there for you, and he loves you."

Jak closed her eyes and swallowed. If this was all an act, then she was doing an Oscar-worthy job of it.

"Thank you," she said.

"The truth," I said to Eddie. "What did you mean, the Ghost Reaper is someone I know?"

"Right, right. Of course. You're not going to like it."

"Eddie, *now*."

"I just want you to know that I didn't make him this way. The Ghost Reaper—it's something else inside him. Some kind of ... creature, or other person. There is nothing like him. He just kept it trapped inside himself for many years. Look, when I tell you everything, you're both going to think—well, you'll think I brought out his monster. But I didn't. Not really. It was always there. It was just a matter of time. So you can't blame me. I never killed anyone."

"Eddie!"

"Yes?"

"Who is it?"

He tipped his head, resigned, and the answer was right there. A light would shine through his fog of words. It may have been because of this, my heightened sense of anticipation of what he was going to say next, that I didn't notice the strange, queasy feeling taking root inside me until it was so powerful, it raised the hairs on the back of my neck.

The dread.

The impending awfulness.

The curtain of darkness sweeping over my thoughts.

I recognized it for what it was only a split second before the front door, already partially open, slammed against the wall.

A frigid wind blasted me in the back hard enough that I stumbled to my knees. The temperature dropped all at once, like cold hands pressing in from all sides. The air smelled of dank earth and rotting flesh. I was facing Jak, not the door, when it happened, so the first thing I saw was her face, her hair blown straight back. She'd run the gamut of facial expressions in the past few minutes, but this time I had no doubt that the emotion in those widening eyes was genuine. True fear. In my line of work, I'd had more than a few chances to witness true fear on someone's face, and this was it. True fear left a mark on my mind, a mental scar that never faded, that always resurfaced to haunt both my dreams and my waking thoughts. This is what I saw on Jak's face.

She saw it. It wasn't invisible to her. *She saw it.*

The light in the room, though it did not go out, changed. With the air swirling, rattling cabinet doors and posters on the walls, the light dimmed gray and lifeless. Someone screamed. I think it was Eddie, but I was still on my hands looking up at Jak.

I watched her pick up the Glock. I watched her pick it up, aim at whatever was coming through the door, and fire.

Click. Click. Click.

Empty. Of course it was empty. I had insisted that the cartridge be empty, because there was no way I was allowing her to point a loaded weapon at her temple just for some ruse. And what did it matter? Would physical bullets really have stopped whatever was coming through the door? Jak firing at it, though, did accomplish something else.

The Ghost Reaper was furious.

How else to explain the anguished cry from behind me, piercing through the roar of the wind? The rustle of ripped fabric? The sense of heaviness as the creature bore down? It was only then, rising to my feet, that I finally turned in the maelstrom and saw the thing with my own eyes. A week earlier, I had caught one fleeting glimpse of him on top of the building across from Jasmine Walker's dormitory, so I was already steeling myself for whatever terrible thing I was about to behold, but it still didn't prepare me.

It may have had a vaguely human shape, this towering, black figure, with something that resembled a head under its billowing hood, something like fingers groping out of its dark sleeves, and something like a body inside the tattered layers of its cloak, but that was as far as the comparison could go. The fingers were like twigs coated with coal, dusty and black. He—if it could be called a he—was so tall that even bending low, the fraying tip of his hood brushed against the ceiling. The wind whipped the cloak back and forth against the skeletal body underneath, grotesquely thin and bent at odd angles; nothing living could have a shape like that. The fraying ends of the cloak groped like the tentacles of an octopus. The way the air turned darker around its body, thick with soot or ash, camouflaged it in perpetual shadow. It was like trying to look at the thing through smoked glass. The swirl of air changed what I saw by the second, bending the shadows, twisting and melting the thing before forming it once again. It was never stable. It never looked the same for more than a second.

Then it lifted its head—and I saw dozens of faces staring back at me, all of them screaming.

It was both this, a tapestry of terrified souls, *and* a face of its own, as if all the contorted and anguished expressions of other people were projected like a film onto a projector screen. I could only bear to look at it directly for a second, but I saw a skull-like face, silvery white, long and thin like a blade, with only darkness where the mouth, nose, and eyes should have been. The other faces flowed in and out of those dark sockets—a river of pain and agony, a rippling skin of terror. And then, as the Ghost Reaper neared, sweeping in like the sudden onset of night, I saw all those faces merge and coalesce. I saw them form one face. I saw them form themselves into *my* face.

My face was screaming.

Daggers in the eyes. That's how it felt, staring at the Ghost Reaper, the fear transformed into an agony burrowing into my brain. I looked away. I had to look away or be consumed. I felt a real scream rising up in my throat, but I clamped it down. I heard a voice, and it was my own voice, comforting and clear inside my brain: *Come with me, Myron. Come with me and I will take you to a better place.* The Ghost Reaper moved closer, and I thought it was going to take me, but then that great mass of rippling rags hesitated, slowed, stopped, then even more suddenly launched itself at Eddie.

Shouting and blubbering this whole time, Eddie had backed himself against the far wall, his pad and pen clutched in front of him as if they were some kind of talisman that could ward off evil. In the tornado of darkness and fog that swirled around him, his few strands of hair stood on end, vibrating like reeds in a storm. The Ghost Reaper rose over him.

"We—we had a deal!" he cried. "We—"

And that was it for poor Eddie Quincy, the intrepid muckraker with the long-lost daughter. One moment he was there, cowering and whimpering, and the next he was not Eddie but a thousand fragmented pieces of Eddie breaking apart like a puzzle, glowing a phosphorescent blue and disintegrating before our eyes. Those pieces circled in the air, spinning around in the tornado, breaking apart into even smaller pieces, crumbling particles of his former self, then only dust—a pulsating blue dust flowing into the Ghost Reaper's hood. There was a sound like a huge intake of breath, a rush of air, a rattle of a throat. Eddie's face was the last to go, holding its form until the final second, all that terror still visible, until it, too, burst and broke apart. The last of him, in a flickering blue mist, vanished into the hood.

The Ghost Reaper turned to Jak.

She still sat in terror, pointing the Glock in its direction. Did she see it fully? Did she see what I saw? If not, she certainly saw something equally horrifying. Her own face was so gripped with fear, the eyes recessed, the skin pulled taught across the bones, that she hardly looked like the same person. The great undulating cloud of rags and shadows that was the Ghost Reaper moved suddenly toward her.

I had to act.

It was a race, the two of us trying to get to Jak first. Fear put glue in my bones, turned my feet to cement blocks. I pushed through it. Someone was screaming. Was it Jak or the Ghost Reaper?

With an anguished cry of my own, I launched myself toward her, sliding my body between her and the Ghost Reaper at the last moment. She was in the chair, and I was still partly on my knees, the Ghost Reaper bearing down on us.

My own voice rattled again in my mind, clear even as the wind roared in my ears: *Myron, give her to me. I will take her to a better place. Give her to me now.*

There is fear. There is terror. There is horror. I had seen plenty of evil, both before and after I walked with the dead, and I had experienced what I thought was the full spectrum of fear. But now I saw there was more. There is something beyond those feelings, some indescribable emotion that springs from the primal part of our brains. This thing—this feeling—when it takes hold, it takes hold of *all* of you. It has control of your body and your thoughts. You are no longer you. You are something else, not quite a person and not quite real, something that can only dangle like prey before a spider. It is nature's way of saying the game is finally up. It is nature's way of sparing the real you from a horror too consuming to comprehend.

And yet the game wasn't quite up. The Ghost Reaper, looming before me—close enough that I felt the cold emanating from it in waves—hesitated. Why didn't it take us? Behind me, Jak let out a gurgled cry, but she was still there. The face, those many anguished faces, peered down at me. Inched closer. I would not close my eyes. I refused to close my eyes. If this was the end, then I would meet it with my eyes open—and I saw, inside the Ghost Reaper's gaping eye sockets, inside the dark, empty holes where the nose and mouth should be, a profound and ancient emptiness. It was like staring into a deep abyss and knowing that if you jumped, you would just go on falling forever.

The three of us crouched in the center of a swirling black cyclone. Blue particles appeared in the air, glowing and flickering, the black turning bluer by the second. Jak's sobs fell silent. Then I knew. The ghost inside her was breaking apart, just as I had seen Eddie break apart. Even as I tried to protect her, the Ghost Reaper was taking her. I was slowing him down, but he was still taking her. I had to act now or she would be lost forever. But how?

I remembered what the priest had told me.

The Department, he'd said, *wanted* the Ghost Reaper to take me. They thought that if it consumed me, my strange ability to straddle two worlds might infect it like some kind of virus. There was a reason the Ghost Reaper did not take me. It must have been afraid of exactly this possibility.

If I sacrificed myself, she might be saved.

If I sacrificed myself, I might destroy him.

Winston Hopner had moved me into this position, knowing full well that I would be forced to make this choice. I was a pawn in his game, a game that would allow him to eliminate both the Ghost Reaper and me at the same time, but it did not change what I needed to do. There was no time to feel bitter. Either I sacrificed myself or Jak died. Those eye sockets gaped large and black before me. The mouth, that infinitely black mouth, inhaled a steady stream of blue dust—Jak's essence, taken bit by bit.

I shoved my hand directly into the Ghost Reaper's mouth.

No half-measures. In the roaring wind, I plunged my arm deep into that void, to the wrist, to the forearm, to the elbow. Cold. So very cold. I leaned forward, pushing in deeper, to the shoulder, to the edge of my neck.

I felt something warm and feathery brush against my fingertips, and suddenly I was no longer me. I was someone else and I felt a sinister need take hold of me, a desire to take, to consume. I needed joy. I needed it so very badly, even if it meant taking it from others. This feathery feeling, this was some buried joy within the Ghost Reaper. This is where he kept what he had stolen. I would take it from him.

I would take it and it would be mine.

A tortured cry filled the room, coming from all sides, swirling around us with the wind. The Ghost Reaper's face jerked back, away from me, spitting out my arm in a cloud of blue dust—smelling sweetly rotten, like spoiled fruit. Like a massive moth fluttering in retreat, the Ghost Reaper surged backward toward the door, all the fraying, ragged threads of its cloak snapping and whipping at the air like vipers. Still gripped by a desire to *take, take, take,* I jumped to my feet and roared at my assailant.

All that violent energy, that rippling, undulating mass of moaning wind and crackling fabric—it slipped through the door and expelled itself into the night. I pursued a few steps, but already the dark hunger was fading. Reaching the door, I remembered why I had been willing to sacrifice myself—the young woman behind me.

I glanced over my shoulder and saw her, slumped backward over her chair, staring at the ceiling.

Thinking she was dead, that my effort had all been in vain, I hurried to her side. Already the frenzied wind had died to a mere whisper, a cold breeze on my warm face. I scooped her up in my arms. Her pretty little face stared impassive, eyes wide and unblinking. Not at the ceiling. Not at anything. Her body felt cold and heavy. Even her hair, falling loose over my hands, felt as if it had been coated in ice.

Then she took a breath. It was not a big, gaping breath but a tiny one, a hiss of air over her lips. She blinked. One time, she blinked, continuing to stare beyond me. Breathing. Blinking. Signs of life.

"Jak?" I said.

No answer. She blinked again, but it was automatic, like breathing. Her body held on but she was somewhere else, deep inside. From the corner of my eye, I glimpsed the shape of a person in the doorway, dressed in black. I looked, expecting a return of the Ghost Reaper, and there was my father.

He wore an old wool trench coat that looked as if it had been pulled from a dumpster—and probably was, stained and scuffed, the elbows worn through, the color uneven, more gray in some spots than black. Bits of leaves and twigs stuck to the coarse wool. The thick material gave him the appearance of more bulk than he actually had, almost as bulky as he was before the disease took hold—a big, powerful man who filled the doorway. I spotted a bit of the powder blue collar of his sweater underneath, the same sweater he'd been wearing when he disappeared. His fringe of silver hair stuck out at odd angles. His skin tone had darkened in the past week, and I thought it might have been from the sun until I realized it was just a layer of grime. The grease stain on his neck resembled a deep gash from a knife.

The killer is someone you know.

Eddie's words jumped into my mind. The terrible possibility that the killer was right here, that he had been right here all along, came down on me with the precision of an executioner's ax. My father? The Ghost Reaper? I told myself the Department would have known … and yet maybe they did. Maybe this is what they wanted, for me to confront him, to have to be the one to stop him.

A sudden wind fluttered the bottom of Dad's trench coat. He stared at me with the same uncomprehending eyes that I had gotten used to in the past few years, but there was also a flicker of recognition. He knew me, or at least some part of him did.

"I … I have to stop him," he said, his voice rough and halting. "It's my … my fault. It's locked up inside me, and I can use it. I don't—I don't want you to get hurt."

I tried to speak, just to call to him, but my own throat was clenched tight. I took a step toward him. The recognition in his eyes, the part of him that knew me, vanished, leaving the cold emptiness I had come to know so well.

He sprang from the room, thumping down the stairs outside.

I ran to the doorway and saw him stumble down the last few steps and scramble toward the street, but then I stopped. Jak needed my help. Hospital, doctors, something.

Filled with both sadness and dread, I watched my father slip into the shadows of the oaks across the street and disappear.

Chapter 16

WHEN IT CAME DOWN TO IT, the problem wasn't physical, at least that the doctor could tell. Jak was in shock. He may have used other words as well, something more clinical, something about acute psychological trauma, but *shock* was the word that permeated my mental fog.

"We can keep her here another day," he said, his voice distant and languid, "but we need to talk soon about getting her into a facility more appropriate for her condition. She drinks and eats when someone feeds her, but that's about it. She needs people trained to help coax her out of this mental state. It may take some time."

Jak lay still in the hospital bed before me, staring blankly at the ceiling, her blond hair fanned out on the white pillow. She blinked, she breathed, but otherwise she could have been dead. Except for the muffled voices of the nurses at the station outside, the room was quiet—no heart monitor, no IV bag, just this pretty blonde lying silently in the bed. The dozen red roses next to the bed, the ones I'd brought in two days earlier, had already started to wilt.

It was Monday morning, early. How early I couldn't say, since I hadn't spent much time looking at the clock, but the light shining around the crack in the curtains had the slanted quality of dawn. Mercifully, Alesha, when I'd called her, had agreed with my suggestion not to report this one to the police, which kept the press from knowing and afforded Jak the quiet she needed to recover.

I looked at the doctor, finally seeing the young man who'd been speaking to me, a kid in a white coat who couldn't have been more than thirty and looked more like fifteen. With his perfectly parted hair, scholarly wire-framed glasses, and stethoscope draped around his neck, he looked like how a high school drama student thought a doctor would dress.

"How much time?" I said.

"There's no saying," the doctor replied. "It could happen at any moment. It could take years."

Years. I thought about my own stint in a coma, a real coma, years ago. I thought about the time after that, as I tried to adjust to the new world I found myself in, when I had to be put into a facility with padded walls. I thought about all of this and felt the guilt growing inside me, spreading like a virus. This wouldn't have happened if I hadn't asked her to go along with the idea of tricking Eddie. I reached down and took her hand. It felt small and limp, but warm. There was hope yet.

"I'm sorry," I whispered.

The doctor, proving he was wise beyond his years, said nothing.

EMERGING ONTO THE SIDEWALK outside Providence Portland Medical Center, I ran into Alesha and Tim approaching the brick building.

"The kid going to be okay?" she asked.

To Alesha's credit, there was no a hint of jealousy in her voice this time, just genuine concern. A bank of storm clouds gathered on the western horizon. In the flat light, Alesha's skin looked darker than usual, and her monochromatic outfit only seemed to accentuate it— black leather jacket, gray V-neck shirt, and gray cotton pants. Tim, his red hair sculpted like glazed clay, looked, as always, as if he'd just been bought at the store and taken out of the packaging.

Across the parking lot, two men in white togas hurried barefoot along the sidewalk. Although I couldn't say for certain that they were ghosts, odds were high that they were, and seeing them made me realize just how few ghosts I'd seen lately. A hospital would usually be teeming with them, but I couldn't remember seeing one.

"I don't know," I said.

"Give her time," Tim said. "She'll come around."

"You sure you don't want to report this?" Alesha asked.

"I'm not sure of anything right now," I said. "But if I can keep the press away from Jak's bedside for as long as possible, that can only help her. And what are we going to report?"

"And you never got a good look at his face?"

"I *told* you. He was wearing a cloak. The hood hid his face."

"But why come after her?"

"To get to me, I guess. To punish me. My name's all over the news. I'm the son of the man who pursued him before. He must be getting scared."

Alesha frowned. I'd seen that expression on her face before, when she was questioning a witness and didn't believe what she was hearing. The story I'd told her—that I'd gone to Jak's place when I read the suicide note on her blog and found the Goodbye Killer in his black cloak leaning over her when I got there—was flimsy, no doubt about it, but what else could I tell her? The truth? Not now.

"But Jak saw him?" she asked.

"Yes."

"So she could ID him?"

"Maybe."

"What do you mean, maybe? Didn't she look him right in the face?"

The image of that tapestry of screaming faces leapt into my mind and I forced it away. "I don't know what she saw, okay, Alesha? She saw something terrible, that's all I know, something that made her mind shut down. I'm sure when she wakes up, she'll be able to help us. But there's no point in interrogating someone who's basically in a coma."

"I *wasn't* going to interrogate her," Alesha fired back.

"I just want to focus on catching this guy," I said.

"We all want that," Tim said.

"Shut up, Tim," Alesha said.

"Right, sorry," Tim said.

"Don't apologize either. Jesus. It's like I picked you up from Sunday school or something. You can at least pretend to be a real cop."

"Alesha," I said, "come on. Tim is just trying to help."

"No, it's okay," Tim said. "It's a stressful situation. I understand."

Alesha groaned. "There he goes again. Man, doesn't anything get to you? Just once, I'd like to see you lose it a little. Throw a few random curse words around. Or flip someone the bird. I have some books that will help you develop your chi, but you can get started in a more simple way. There, see that old lady with the walker coming out of the hospital? Give her the finger."

Tim chuckled. "I'm not sure what that would—"

"Come on, do it. It'll feel good."

"All right, knock it off," I said. "Tim's right. We all want the same thing here. Did you guys find out anything about the victims, anything that could help us? Alesha?"

Alesha wrested her attention away from Tim reluctantly. "No, and we've been over it and over it, Myron. Just random people—good people, too good, really. A few got in the paper for one thing or another, but some didn't. We focused on those and the first few victims, like we talked about. The only connection we found was that the first two victims were within a quarter-mile of each other."

"I remember," I said. "That's why my dad and Sal focused on the Hillsdale area, even after the other murders. But nothing ever came of it."

"Nope," Alesha said.

She was still studying me as if I was holding something back. I was holding *a lot* back, including that I was fairly certain that the Goodbye Killer was my father. *It's locked up inside me, and I can use it.* Did that mean he was going to use the monster somehow against himself? Maybe the Department, by allowing him to start seeing through the fog of Alzheimer's, was inadvertently giving him a way to conquer his inner demon.

Or was it the opposite? The Goodbye Killer had been around before Dad's mental illness really took hold, after all. In fact, the reason the inner monster went dormant may be *because* of the Alzheimer's.

But what about Jasmine Walker? Her death had been before the Director agreed to my request to do something about Dad's mental illness in return for my help. I was missing a piece of information, a critical piece, but I didn't know what it was.

"Those first two victims," I said, "did they have *anything* else in common? They were both women in their thirties, right?"

"Right," Alesha said. "The only thing was that they both had children who went to the same school. According to the case file, though, your dad and Sal followed up on that and nothing came of it. The kids were in different grades and didn't know each other. One was a boy, seven, the other a girl, eleven. The parents had never met. Even with the later murders, they went back to that a couple times, thinking there had to be something about the school, but there was nothing— and no kind of link like that later."

Then it came to me, that conversation all those years ago that Sal and Dad had while I hid under the desk. Dad had something about the children of some of those first few victims, how he couldn't let them down. *He'd said that one of them had said he wanted to grow up to be a police officer.* The comment had stuck with me because I already knew I wanted to be a police officer as well, so I felt a kinship with this child. It hadn't seemed significant at that time, but now I wondered: Why did this boy tell my dad he wanted to be a police officer? If his mother had just been killed, would he really say something like that? He would have been in shock. No, it was much more likely that Dad had met this boy before the murder.

"What is it?" Alesha asked.

"Hmm?"

"You got that look on your face. Like you just thought of something."

I considered whether to bring her in on my thoughts. Once I implicated Dad in any way, the wheels of justice would start to turn in his direction. "No, just racking my brain."

"Myron," she said, "if we don't work together on this—"

"It's nothing, really. I've just had this nutty idea that Clive Branson was behind this somehow."

"The chief?" Tim said. "Really?"

"I told you it was crazy. Just had this gut feeling, which is why I haven't brought it up with you before now. Look, guys, I'm totally exhausted. Can we pick this up later? I want to go home and get some rest."

"We could do some checking on his whereabouts at the time of the murders," Tim said. "It would at least be a place to start."

"Yeah, you guys should do that. Let's check in tomorrow. I need a day off from this madness."

Alesha continued to give me a skeptical eye, but eventually she gave me a perfunctory nod.

"Get some sleep," she said.

WITH ALESHA AND TIM driving behind me for a few blocks, I made sure to head for Sellwood until they turned toward the police station. Then, a few blocks later, I did a U-turn and made my way across the Morrison Street Bridge, heading east on US-26 toward Forest Grove, the morning sun so bright in my rearview mirror that I had to adjust it to keep from getting blinded. It was true that I was exhausted, but I had no intention of getting any sleep. With Jak at least stabilized, I needed to talk to the two people who knew Dad best.

Just before the Forest Grove exit, I saw the black limousine in my rearview mirror. I pulled off into a Rite Aid parking lot. When the limo parked next to me on the right, I got out of my car and headed to the other side just as the limo's driver's-side door opened and Fist leaned his big white head out, mirrored sunglasses gleaming in the sun.

I opened my leather jacket and put my hand on the Glock. He saw me and placed one leather boot on the black asphalt anyway.

"I wouldn't," I said.

He froze like that, one foot in the limo, one foot out, his face about as expressive as the light pole next to us. His eyes were hidden from me, but I imagined they were filled with terror at my bold move. The tinted rear window whirred down, and I saw the top of a white bowler hat. Hopner started speaking before his hawkish face came into view.

"Mr. Vale," he said.

"What do you want?" I said.

With the window rolled completely down, he leaned out a bit, his chiseled cheekbones and neatly trimmed beard so real, so vivid, that it was hard to believe that he was a ghost. "Are you really going to shoot my assistant right here in broad daylight? I'm afraid that would not be helpful to your investigation, facing a murder charge. Remember, unlike me, Fist is still very much among the world of the living."

"As long as he remains in the limo," I said, "he'll stay that way."

"How generous of you. You seem quite confident of yourself, Mr. Vale—Myron, rather. Perhaps you are forgetting who you are dealing with here?"

"I'm dealing with somebody who has set me up to take a fall," I said.

"Pishposh," Hopner said. "Whatever gave you that idea? I have only come for an update. You have been very bad about answering your emails lately."

"You know who the Reaper is," I said. "You've always known."

"Don't be ridiculous."

"You wanted him to kill me. Maybe you wanted us to kill each other."

Fist, growing impatient, started to lean out of the limo. I answered this by starting to pull the Glock out of its holster.

Winston sighed. "Fist, get back in the limo and shut the door. Making a scene in a drugstore parking lot will not help any of us."

With a grunt, Fist put his leg back in the limo and shut the door. The grunt was the first sound I'd heard him make. Progress. He wanted to open up to me, I could feel it. Soon I'd have him reciting Shakespeare's soliloquies until his voice grew hoarse.

"Who is the Goodbye Killer?" I asked Hopner.

"I have no idea."

"You're lying."

"Oh, that is such an unpleasant word. I'd suggest you not throw it around so casually."

"Is it my father?"

"What? The man who could barely tie his shoes a week ago? Come now, Myron. I'm disappointed. I thought you would have made more progress by now. How many more victims have to die? How many more of my people have to flee the city? We have a name for what Portland's becoming. You've heard of the term *ghost town*? Well, for us, this is becoming a *ghostless* town, which is far more disturbing."

"I'm kind of liking it," I said.

"You won't when you see what Portland becomes. There is a certain balance that ghosts bring to a city, a certain energy. Without that balance … well, let's just say that disturbing things can happen. People are affected in strange ways. If you think the Ghost Reaper is bad, that would just be the beginning. It's happened before. Germany in the early 1930s, for example. Rome at the end. It's not something you should wish for, trust me."

"Who is the Goodbye Killer?"

"I told you, I don't know."

"Of course not," I said. "You're only the *Assistant* Director."

He tried to hide the flash of anger that passed over his face, but I still caught it. "It's true that the Director has powers of insight that I do not have, but even he does not know all. There really is no vast conspiracy. There is only a terrible killer on the loose, one who is quickly creating a situation in Portland that is setting the stage for something much more awful. You think you know our world, Myron? You don't know it at all. You need to solve this case. Everything is at stake—the very foundations of the world itself."

"No pressure, huh?"

"If we could have done it ourselves, we would have done so by now."

"If you *could* have done it," I said. "Interesting way of putting that. You need someone to sacrifice themselves to take him down, somebody not like everybody else. Somebody like me."

Hopner regarded me coolly. Next to the window, I saw my reflection in the shiny black paint, my unshaven face and the bags under my eyes. The limo's idling engine produced a low, steady hum, the exhaust pipe puffing out clouds of white smoke that curled over the trunk and dissipated into the crisp morning air. The people in their cars, oblivious to the crisis unfolding in their city, cruised past us.

"Solve the case," he said sternly. "We're running out of time."

"What about my friend Jak? Can you help her? Can the—the Director do something for her, the way he did something for my father?"

"It's not the same," Hopner replied. "The Worthe girl, she saw something that makes her want to hide from the world. Only time will tell if she's ready to face it again."

"But—"

"All you can do, Myron, is give her a world she wants to live in again. To do that, you need to stop the Ghost Reaper. You may not think highly of me, or the Department, but that doesn't matter. There is no one like you, and you have a job to do that no one else can."

Before waiting for me to reply, he rolled up his window. I stood in the parking lot and watched them go, pretending that my tough-guy act had scared them away.

Chapter 17

I FOUND MOM in Dad's room at the Mistwood, awaiting his return. She sat hunched on Dad's neatly made bed, the way it had been left the day of his disappearance, her hands folded in her lap, her skin even whiter than usual—no makeup, eyes puffy and red. She wore a blue silk shawl draped over a gray wool sweater patterned with white roses. Both the shawl and sweater were much too large for her spindly frame.

When I stepped through the door, she looked up from her place on the bed, hopeful, but the hope quickly drained away when saw that it was me. Alone.

"Myron," she said.

Her voice sounded so anguished that I couldn't even take pleasure in her calling me by my first name. I closed the door behind me and sat next to her on the bed, the mattress sagging under my weight when it hadn't under hers.

"No sign of him?" I asked her.

"No." She sighed. "It's so empty around this place now. So many residents, leaving."

"You mean the ghosts?"

241

"I don't think we need to label them. They're just people, after all."

"Well …"

"Isn't that what that Martin Luther King tried to tell people? Not to judge people by—by their appearance."

"Does he still preach that?"

She gave me a queer look. "What an odd thing to say. You know as well as I that someone shot that poor man. He's not around to do any preaching."

I didn't know what to say to that. She went back to staring at her hands. It was sometimes hard to know whether she was fully aware of what she was—meaning she was just messing with me—or whether she truly was as confused about the state of her existence as she seemed. If reality itself confounded her, how was I going to break it to her that her husband may be a serial killer? *Not* breaking it to her was no longer an option.

"I need your help," I said.

"Oh?"

"But there's something I need to tell you first, and you're not going to like it. It's about Dad."

She turned to me then, this sad, frail woman, and I saw that I had her full attention. There was no way to soften the blow, not really, so I just laid it out as quickly and clearly as I could. I told her what happened at Jak's apartment. I told her why I thought it might be Dad. I told her that if we were going to stop him, and soon, I needed her help thinking of a way to draw him out. Nobody knew him better than she did.

"Impossible," she said, when I was finished.

"Mom—"

"No, no, it can't be. Not your father." She straightened, eyes narrowing, all that sagging defeatism replaced with brusque defiance. "How could you even think that? You know that's not the kind of man he is."

"I don't want to believe it," I said, "and I don't know it for sure. But those kids of the first few victims, they went to the same school. Do you have any idea how he might have known them?"

"It's nonsense! He—he couldn't have done it! I know that one of those poor people, this lady, she died when we were vacationing in California. Disneyland. We took you for your birthday. Do you remember? I remember because this lady, she was the second one and Hank got the call from Sal while we were down there. He took it so hard. That's when he knew it was a—a—what do you call it?"

"A serial killer," I said.

"Right. Right, a serial killer. That's when he knew. I remember it because things were starting to get better for us. Then this woman died and … and it was so much worse than before. He pulled away. He started drinking a lot. He was always out, either with Sal or on his own. And me …" She shook her head.

"You and Sal?" I said.

She nodded.

"Was Maria sick then?"

"No! I couldn't have done that to her. They were separated at the time. And Hank and I … Well, I didn't know if we would last. Oh Myron! Maybe your father doesn't want to be with me anymore, but a killer? No. He would have had to be in two places at the same time."

"Maybe he was," I said.

When she gave a queer look, I explained how the Goodbye Killer, or Ghost Reaper, was most likely not just one person, but some kind of manifestation of that person, like a split personality. Her defiance turned to befuddlement. I felt bad heaping all of this on her when she already had a hard enough time keeping it all together. But what else could I do? I couldn't let any more innocent people die.

"Nonsense," she said. "It sounds like … like some crazy ramblings of a drunkard. Have you been drinking, Myron? I don't understand where this is all coming from. Why are you telling me all of this? Are you just doing this to hurt me? I know you hate me. I've always known it. But this—"

"I don't hate you," I said.

"—this—this is just so *hurtful*. Your father is *not* a killer."

"Maybe so," I said. "But the best way to prove him innocent is to find him, and that's something we want anyway. The question I asked you, about the children of the first two victims. Think hard. One of them told Dad he wanted to be a cop when he grew up. That's not something a kid would say after his mother was just murdered. When would that have happened?"

"I don't know," she said.

"Think!"

"Don't yell! Please!"

I saw the fissures forming, like fine cracks in an expensive vase. Her eyes welled up with tears and her bottom lip trembled. I needed her to keep it together a bit longer, because a plan was starting to form in my mind, a plan to flush Dad out into the open, and Mom was going to play an integral part in it.

"It's all right," I said, trying to sound as soothing as possible but mostly failing. "You don't remember. It's okay, really. Again, maybe it's nothing. But there's someone else who might remember—and we're going to go see him together."

Chapter 18

A HALF-HOUR LATER, I parked the Prius in front of Sal's sandwich shop. The *Open* sign was not yet illuminated, but I saw him pulling a tray of hoagie rolls out of the oven. A drizzle had just started to speckle the front windshield, the promise of rain in all those gray clouds finally realized. The digital clock on the dashboard read 9:33 a.m., but the light was so flat that it felt like either dawn or dusk. A lone homeless person pushed a squeaky shopping cart on the far end, his gray sweatshirt hood dotted with raindrops. Mom, sitting in the passenger seat, heaved out a great sigh.

"Why am I here again?" she asked.

"You might have ideas," I said. "If it's true about Dad—"

"It's not," she insisted.

"—then we're going to need to come up with a plan to draw him out," I continued. "You two know him best. I need you to brainstorm and come up with something."

"But Sal won't see me," Mom said. "He won't even know I'm there."

"I realize that, but you can still contribute to the conversation. I'll hear it."

She didn't reply, or even nod, but she also didn't protest. I got out of the car, and she followed. I stepped up to the glass door and lifted my hand to knock but watched Sal for a moment instead. He

245

didn't see me; he was so focused on his work, his eyes bright, his thinning hair wet and slicked straight back as if he'd just gotten out of the shower. When I'd seen him in his apartment before, he'd seemed lost, withdrawn into himself, but he had much more energy while working. For the first time, I understood why he'd opened the sandwich shop when he left the force. It may have seemed like trivial work, but the repetition of trivial work could provide its own refuge from dark thoughts.

I tried the door and found it locked. At the rattling, though, he looked up and saw me.

"Myron," he said, opening the door. His voice had a cheerful, vibrant fullness, not at all like the sullen person I'd seen last time. "I figured you'd be out looking for Hank."

That wonderful aroma of recently baked bread wafted into the open air—one of the most welcoming smells known to man, if I was to be the judge. Someone should really bottle that smell and sell it.

"We need to talk," I said. It came out a little harsher than I'd intended. "It's about Dad. I need to ask you some questions."

"Okay. But can it wait until a little later? I'm kind of busy getting ready to—"

"I know about you and Mom," I said.

A flurry of emotions swept over his face—disbelief, embarrassment, and maybe even a little anger, too. I watched his eyes harden as they focused on my own. "Let's go upstairs," he said.

He let me inside, Mom slipping in just before he closed the door. He tossed his apron on the counter, then led us up the rickety stairs. I glanced at Mom and saw that her eyes were big and round, a rabbit trapped in a snare. The last time I'd ascended these stairs, I'd felt the presence of the Ghost Reaper, a feeling that had been confirmed when we'd gone inside, but I felt nothing now.

I expected to find the same grimy apartment and was surprised that it had undergone a bit of a makeover since my last visit. The dishes in the sink were gone, the metal basin scrubbed shiny, the counters clean, the floor swept. The carpet was still threadbare, but it had been vacuumed to an inch of its life, and the futon was covered in a bright green afghan rather than a black sheet. Even the smell of cigarettes was gone, replaced by some kind of pine air freshener. No one would want to feature it in *Better Homes & Gardens,* but at least there was a whiff of hope about the place now.

"Oh, it looks better," Mom said.

I glanced at her, and she must have realized that she'd just confirmed she'd been there before, because she swallowed hard.

"I just came to check on him a couple of times," she said.

"What's this about, Myron?" Sal asked, oblivious to her comments.

"It's about finding Dad," I said, "but I want to start with your affair with Mom first. I'm sorry to be blunt about this, but there's no point in beating around the bush."

"Well," Mom began huffily, "I wouldn't exactly call it—"

"Oh," Sal said. No denials, no protesting that he was misunderstood, just a slight perfunctory nod. "Okay. Yeah, it's true. It lasted about a year."

"I think it was more like a few months," Mom interjected.

"Maybe a year and a half," Sal added.

"He's exaggerating!" Mom said.

It took a fair amount of willpower to keep myself from shushing her. "How did it start?" I asked.

"I don't know, really," he said. "Neither of our marriages were going well. We just started talking, opening up about our problems. One thing led to another. Myron, I'm sorry I didn't tell you before now. Your mom and I agreed to never talk about it."

"Well, that part is true at least," Mom said.

"Did Dad know?"

"Heavens no," Mom said.

"I don't think so," Sal said. "If he did, I'm pretty sure I would have taken it on the chin pretty hard. How did you find out, anyway?"

It wasn't a question I'd been prepared to answer, since I couldn't very well tell him I'd heard it from Mom herself. "I found a note Mom wrote, something I think she was going to give to you. It made it pretty obvious."

"Oh," he said.

"That's a lie," Mom said.

"Stop," I said.

"Huh?" Sal said.

I hadn't realized I'd spoken the word out loud until Sal reacted. "Stop," I repeated. "She said in the letter that the two of you needed to stop, but she obviously didn't send the letter, so I guess she had mixed feelings about it."

"Well, *really*," Mom said.

"She was just confused, like me, Myron," Sal said.

"How dare you!" Mom said.

"We both were still very much in love with our spouses," Sal said. "I want you to know that. Maria and I … well, the hunt for the Goodbye Killer had really taken its toll. I'd kind of pushed Maria away. She even went to live with her mother for a while. Hank was out drinking so much that he was pretty much out of Eleanor's life, too. Then I finally started taking my pills—Eleanor helped me with that—and things got better. Your dad, he got sober, went to some meetings, turned his life around. Maria came back."

"And it was over, just like that?" I asked.

"I did care about her, but I don't think it was ever really about us. She's quite a woman, Myron. I was in a dark place and she helped bring me out of it. I hope I helped her, too. I certainly did everything I could to make sure Hank didn't go too far over the brink. Maybe it was just my guilty conscience, but I don't think so. I loved them both. I would have done anything for them."

Mom had no answer to this, but I saw that her eyes had taken on a misty sheen. I decided it was time to level with Sal.

"About why I'm here," I said. "This is going to sound pretty crazy. I don't know how else to say it other than to just say it … I think Dad might be the Goodbye Killer."

Sal's blinking was so slow and mechanical, I half expected to hear gears whirring behind his eyes. Mom let slip a little whimper.

"I know, crazy," I said. "And I'm the last person who would want to think this, but there are some things that—"

"That's impossible," Sal said.

"It may seem—"

"No, it's *impossible*. I was with your dad when we actually *saw* the Goodbye Killer. There's no way he could be in two places at the—"

"And what did you see?" I asked.

"What?"

"I heard you, when I was just a kid. I was hiding under Dad's desk when you two talked about what you saw. You said it wasn't human."

"Oh," Sal said, waving at the air dismissively, "that was just the pressure getting to us. It makes you imagine things."

"But what if it was true? What if it's something else, something like a … spirit residing in someone? Maybe it's like being, I don't know, possessed. Maybe Dad doesn't even really know it's there. I know, I know, this is crazy, but … I saw it, too, Sal. I saw what you guys saw. I know it takes a big leap, but take that leap for a second. What does your gut tell you?"

I saw the disbelief in his eyes, but there was something else, a kind of recognition of some unpleasant fact that he hadn't wanted to face.

"No," he said.

"I don't want to believe it, either."

"It's just the stress getting to you, Myron. With your dad missing—"

"It's not the stress."

"—you're just grasping, your mind exhausted. I understand. What you need is sleep."

"It's *not* the stress," I insisted. "A child of one of the victims told Dad he wanted to be a police officer when he grew up. When did he tell him that?"

"What?"

"That's not something a kid would say right after his mother was murdered. And the kids of two different victims went to the same school."

"Oh, that," Sal said. "We did some school visits back then. You know, talk to kids about what it's like being a detective. That's probably where your dad met them. Just a coincidence."

"Or it's where Dad decided on his next victims," I said.

"No! It's not your father. It can't be. Hank Vale is a good man. There is no way he would—"

"I need your help catching him."

"—would ever do something like that. Never!"

"He doesn't know what he is!"

Sal slapped me. I'd been leaning in close, my voice rising to match his, and the blow caught me off guard—an open-palmed strike to the right cheek that made my eyes water. By the time I'd recovered enough to realize what had happened, Sal was jabbing his finger in my face.

"Watch your mouth!" he bellowed. "That's your father you're talking about! He would—he would never hurt innocent people! Never! You hear me? I don't care what that, that *thing* is—it's *not* Hank Vale. Get this through your head! The Ghost Reaper is *not* your father! You may have stopped believing in him, but I haven't. I will never—never stop believing in him. He's a better man than me. Than you! Than both of us put together! You hear me? *You hear me?*"

Mom, sobbing openly, turned to the refrigerator. I rubbed my cheek, trying to keep my adrenaline in check. His outburst came out in one big blizzard of words, so it took a few seconds before I realized the little nugget of information buried inside of it.

He'd called it the Ghost Reaper. Not the Goodbye Killer.

The Ghost Reaper.

I did everything I could to keep my surprise from showing. He was still glaring, still pointing, breathing hard enough through his nose that I could hear it even over mom's siren-like wails. If he realized he'd made a slip, he certainly didn't show it. Was Sal the Ghost Reaper? I raced through the possibilities, trying to think if there was any other reason he would know it was called the Ghost Reaper among the non-living. Did he see ghosts? He didn't appear to see Mom. Maybe, if he *was* the killer, he really wasn't aware of what was inside him.

"What?" he snapped. "What is it?"

"Huh?"

"You want to say something. I can see it."

"No. No, I … I think you're right, Sal. I'm sorry. I don't know what came over me. Maybe it's the stress after all."

His face softened a little, though when he spoke, his voice still carried a hard edge to it. "You need to get some help, Myron. Trust me on this one. Get some help before you let wild theories ruin your life."

It came to me then. The truth had been right there in front of me all along. Eddie Quincy had said that the Ghost Reaper just needed a little nudge. I thought of something that could cause that nudge, and the proof of it was probably in the apartment.

"You're probably right," I said. "I'll get some help. I just—man, I'm not feeling well. I'm feeling a little sick."

"You want a glass of water?" Sal asked.

"No, no, I'm just … Can I use your bathroom for a second?"

"Sure, sure, go."

Feigning a bit of wobbliness, I staggered to his bathroom. As I'd hoped, my mother's concern for her son's welfare broke through her spell of despair enough that she watched me go. I made a motion with my eyes for her to follow, and, somewhat reluctantly, she did. When we'd both entered the little room, I closed the door, catching a brief glimpse of Sal gazing at me from the kitchen.

"What is it?" Mom asked. "This is strange, the two of us being in the bathroom like this."

I turned to the pill bottles lining the green tile around the sink. The doxazosin, the one for prostate issues, was empty. The Lexapro, the antidepressants, appeared to have less in it than when I'd been in the bathroom a week earlier, so Sal seemed to be taking them. But what if they *weren't* Lexapro? Eddie had proved to have at least some minor ability to interact on the Internet, which was how he'd been able to send messages to Jak. Could he have manipulated the labels? They appeared to be fixed firmly to the bottles, no sign of tampering, but that wouldn't have been how his power would have changed them anyway. He would have changed them in the computer at the pharmacy before they were printed.

I took a few of what were labeled Lexapro, little blue pills, and stuck them in my jacket pocket.

"What are you doing?" Mom asked.

"I'm going to have Alesha test these at the lab," I whispered.

"Why?" Her eyes widened. "Wait, you're not saying you think—"

"Did his apartment look clean or dirty when you were seeing him?"

"What kind of question—"

"Just answer it, Mom."

"Um. I don't know. Clean. I guess clean. Why, what—"

"If he's not taking the Lexapro, then he's getting a mental boost from something else. Come on, let's … let's …"

My train of thought skipped on the last word, because I suddenly felt something, an uneasiness that raised the hairs on the back of my neck. By now, I knew the feeling well. I reached into my leather jacket for the Glock, but it was already too late.

The door flung open.

Sal stood there leering, his own gun already pointed at me—a .38 special that didn't have the power of a Glock, but then at this kind of range, it didn't need it.

"Don't," Sal said.

I expected to see the Ghost Reaper looming over him, or hovering somewhere in the room, but he was alone. At least that's what I thought until he stepped close and shoved his piece into my gut, so close I was looking directly into his eyes. There, in the wide, dark pupils, I saw what I'd seen in Jak's apartment a few days earlier: a filmstrip of flickering faces. They were so tiny I could barely make them out, but there was still no denying their expressions.

They were screaming.

Chapter 19

THE MAN WHO MURDERED nineteen innocent people—and perhaps more that we didn't know about—reached into my jacket and retrieved the Glock, all while keeping his gaze firmly locked on my own. The swirl of screaming faces in his eyes intensified, spinning faster, becoming a rippling blur. He stood so close I smelled his minty aftershave and just a hint of cigarettes on his breath. I saw the tiny veins on his nose and the cracks on his lips. With all the practiced skill of a lifelong cop, he took my piece and stuck it into his back pocket, then shoved the barrel of his gun even harder against my stomach. I never had a chance to make a move.

"Hand over the pills," he said.

Mom, who'd been holding her breath this entire time, finally expelled it all in one big gasp. "Sal!" she pleaded. "This isn't you! This isn't—"

"Shut up, Eleanor."

I was so surprised by the turn of events that it took me an extra second to realize that he had just spoken to a ghost. "You can see her?"

"The pills, Myron."

I took them out of my pocket and handed them to him. He gestured with his pistol for us to leave the bathroom, which we both did.

There was something about his face that had changed, something other than the eyes. Even in his darkest moments, there had always been some warmth in his face, a kindness that ran through him like an underground river, but it was gone now. The sweat on his brow glistened like glass beads. Outside the apartment, the world was silent, as if life itself had raced ahead and left us all behind. I felt a keen sense of abandonment.

"Why?" I said.

He stared at me with those crazy eyes of his, glanced at the label on the pill bottle, then shook his head. "I didn't know what Eddie had done. Not until now. I didn't know that somehow he switched the pills."

"But why, Sal? All those people—why?"

"It wasn't me."

"Who was it?"

"It wasn't me," he said again, this time giving his head a hard shake, as if trying to free himself from the thought. "It wasn't me. It was *him*. I was trying to help them. I was … He would have destroyed them. I—I took them to a better place. I kept them safe, inside. They're safe inside me."

"It can't be," Mom said. "I don't believe it!"

Sal, keeping the gun leveled at me, turned to look at her, his fierce expression melting into sadness. "It's so strange, seeing you again. He doesn't usually let me see the people on the other side unless he's … he's taking them. I wish it didn't have to be like this, Eleanor. I didn't want him to come back. I took my pills. I promised Maria I would keep taking them and I did. They kept him away. They kept him from taking control. But Eddie … he must have made a deal with—with *him*. Eddie switched the pills so he could find out who—who would be taken before it happened."

"You can't be this person," Mom insisted. "Not all those horrible things. That's not you."

"He started visiting me when I was little. He said we could be friends. I didn't know what he was then. He didn't want things until later."

"Put the gun down," I said. "Let's talk about this. It doesn't—"

"Shut up!" he snapped. A bead of sweat broke free from his forehead and dribbled down his nose. He wiped it off with the back of his arm, the movement jerkier, more feverish and uncontrolled than before. "Both of you, be quiet. Yes, I will do it. Yes! I know what has to be done. He has to die."

Mom produced a low, anguished moan, like a cat in pain. I watched Sal aim the revolver at me, felt the cold certainly of my fate hinging on his trigger finger.

"Who are you talking to?" I asked.

"Him! Him!"

"Sal, there's only you."

"No."

"Sal, if you do this, it's going to be on you. You're the one who met those kids at the school visit. You're the one who decided to target their mothers. And everyone else. You killed them all. *You.*"

"Not my fault," he said. "I didn't want him—want him in my life. I wanted to keep him away. But he … didn't … *listen.*"

"Sal—"

"STOP!"

The shout boomed throughout the apartment, so loud we all flinched, but it wasn't from Sal. It came from the front door. Even before I turned I knew the voice, that deep, resonant voice, a bit scratchy from years of disuse but still the same man. He loomed in the open doorway like some beast out of the forest, his thinning hair askew, his face smeared with mud, his trench coat covered with leaves and twigs. He stood straighter than I'd seen him stand in years, and it made him appear fuller, wider in the shoulders, more like the man he used to be than the frail thing he'd become.

Sal swung the gun from me to him, then back to me, stepping away from all of us. "Hank," he said. "Hank, you shouldn't be here."

"Oh, Hank," Mom said.

"Dad," I said, and my voice sounded as tiny as a seven-year-old's.

"Don't ... don't do this," Dad said, each word annunciated sharply. "Sal. My son, no ... I've been following him, hoping ... to protect him. I didn't think ... didn't want it to be you."

He took a few steps into the room. Sal pointed the revolver at him, his hand twitching, a spasm of muscles playing across his face. From where he stood now, the swirl of ghosts in his eyes appeared like a pulsing glimmer.

"Hank, stop."

"You ... won't do it," Dad said. He took another few steps, already bridging half the distance between them. "Won't shoot me. Won't shoot ... son."

"Hank!" Mom cried, but he did not react to her at all. "Hank, no!"

"It's not me!" Sal insisted. "I don't want to do it!"

"You won't," Dad said, his voice steadier, gaining confidence. "You won't ... do it. I was ... your partner. This is my son. You ... know us."

He took another step toward Sal. I knew what Dad was doing, that he was making a play for the gun, and I didn't want to let it happen. I felt the most powerful sense of longing that I had ever felt in my whole life, seeing him returning to himself, seeing him becoming *him* again and not just some shell, some shadow, a walking memory that only served to remind me of what was lost. He was here. He was finally here, and I could have some kind of life with him again. To lose him now? No. It would have been devastating. I'd already lost him once. I couldn't let it happen again.

"Sal," I said. "Sal, look at me. You want to do the right thing here. I know you do. You don't want to go on being this person."

"It's not me," Sal said.

"We can get you the right pills again. Get it under control. You just have to lay down the gun."

"No," Sal said. "No, I'm getting out of here. I'm—I'm going to make it look like the Ghost—I mean, like the Goodbye Killer tried to kill all of us. I can stage it. You'll all die, but I'll pull through. He'll allow me to live."

"No!" Mom cried. "I'll tell everyone!"

"You won't be around either. I'll take you to a better place."

With Sal's attention focused on Mom, Dad tried to take another step, but Sal swung the gun back around at him. "Stop!" he said. "Hank, you stop!"

"Who … who are you talking to?" Dad asked. "There's nobody. Nobody here." He took another step. He was only three or four away now.

"Hank," Sal warned.

"We were partners," Dad said, and now his voice sounded almost as smooth and confident as it did when I was young. "We were there for each other. I don't believe this is you, not all you. Come on Sal, remember all those football games? Remember … remember all the bad fast food when we were doing stakeouts?"

As Dad gained control over himself, Sal was losing his, becoming more fidgety, his body full of weird tics and spasms, his face a quivering mess. Sweat darkened the collar of his shirt. I wondered why the Ghost Reaper didn't emerge. Was Sal suppressing it, or was it afraid to come out to face us? Dad took another step, a very small one, but I saw the way Sal reacted to it—biting down on his lip, his crazy eyes narrowing, steeling himself for what was to come. It didn't take someone with the ability to predict the future to know how this one was going to play out: Dad would end up on a gurney with a sheet over him.

Sal's gaze kept flitting back and forth from me to Dad, but most of his attention was focused on Dad. That gave me an opening, a split second of surprise if I was willing to use it. I was willing. I wasn't losing Dad.

When Sal's gaze again turned to Dad, I rushed him.

I knew even then that this would be one of those moments frozen in the memory banks, burned forever into the synapses. I had the jump on him, a solid step before he knew I was coming, but I was still a long way away when the destination was a man with a revolver who knew how to use it. Dad knew this, too. He saw me coming before Sal did, when Sal's gaze was still fixed on him, and he decided to make a move.

Sal took a shot at me. Distracted by my father, his aim was off, and the bullet just clipped the sleeve of my jacket. The gunshot rang in my ears.

He spun toward Dad, getting off another shot, but this one missed the mark completely—exploding into the wall, a puff of drywall filling the air.

Dad was on him then, the two of them grappling with each other, wrestling for control of the gun. I was only a split second behind, would have gotten there in another step, but Sal was much stronger than Dad. All those years battling his mental demons had robbed Hank Vale of his vitality. He may have been coming back to himself, but his body had not yet caught up.

Dad managed to pry the gun away, but Sal, with an anguished roar, tossed my father directly into my path.

Dad crashed into me, and both of us went down. I knew he was thin and frail, but tangled up in arms and legs, trying to get back to our feet, made me realize just how little of him there was, like some twigs held together by twine. Mom shrieked, a real doozy, hands on either side of her face like a horror film. I made it to my knees in time to see Sal fleeing the apartment.

I helped Dad, who had Sal's pistol in hand, back to his feet. Mom rushed to his side, groping for his arm, but of course her hands passed right through him.

"Oh Hank," she said.

Dad, getting his bearings, didn't even look at her. I felt her anguish. All those years at his side and now, when he was at least partly himself again, he didn't even know she was there. He showed great concern about me, however, grabbing my arm and examining the ripped leather where the bullet had done its damage. The jacket was beyond recovery, but I saw no blood.

"I'm all right," I said.

He nodded, his face pink, his pupils dark, a moment of deep affection passing between us that I'd desperately wanted all these years—just one moment like this—but then he rushed toward the door.

"Let's go," he said.

"Dad—" I called after him.

"Go! He's getting away!"

I called after him again, but he was already gone. What could I do but follow? On my way out of the apartment, I yelled at Mom to call the police, not remembering until I stumbled down the stairs that she could do no such thing. I still had my phone on me, but there was no time to do it now. When I reached the sandwich shop, I saw Dad already bursting through the door onto the street. He looked right, left—then must have seen something to the left that caught his eye because he bolted in that direction.

I hit the street a second after he did, rushing to catch up with him. The gray sky, streaked with thin white tendrils, stretched over us like cracked pavement. Sal was a block ahead of Dad, another gun in hand—my gun, the Glock. He glanced over his shoulder at us but didn't fire. Not a single person other than the three of us occupied the street. A brown UPS truck rumbled across an intersection far ahead, but that was the only car. The thick air, heavy with moisture, rolled across my face. I thought I felt a few pinpricks of rain.

Then just like that, the sky opened up and flooded on us. Hard rains were rare in Portland and this was a good one, hitting the sidewalks with enough force that the impacts created tiny white explosions, sparkling ahead of us like a blanket of shiny quarters. Cold water doused my hair, blurred my eyes, and ran down my back. I caught up with Dad just as Sal, still a block ahead of us, ducked into a side alley next to the four-story abandoned warehouse—the one with the *For Sale* sign with the missing letters.

"Dad—" I began.

"Not now, son."

"We need backup."

"Call them."

By the time we reached the same alley, I had my cell phone out of my pocket. We saw Sal throw his shoulder into a side door, splintering it and ducking inside before we could get to him. I should have called

911, but I still wasn't sure how this was all going to go down, so I called Alesha's number instead. I was talking before she even finished saying hello.

"Alesha," I said, "it's me. The empty warehouse near the sandwich shop—get there. It's Sal."

She responded with a blast of questions, but I clicked off and shoved the phone back in my pocket. Dad was at the door, Sal's .38 special in hand. I grabbed him before he stepped into the opening. I saw cardboard over bare concrete, a cave of darkness beyond. Sal could have been standing right there, aiming at us.

"Dad!" I said. "You want to get shot?"

He scowled at me, but then we heard footfalls from within the building—hollow and distant, like they came from a stairwell. Dad barreled inside, leading with his pistol. I followed, stepping into a narrow hall with a low ceiling, the smell of mold and rot growing stronger as we pressed into the darkness. I reached for my gun and remembered that Sal had it. It made me feel exposed, dependent on Dad for my safety. Back to being a boy.

This wasn't smart. I was walking into darkness without my gun, dependent on a man who'd spent the past decade lost to Alzheimer's—a man who couldn't have weighed more than 120 pounds.

And yet there was the other part of me that was thrilled by what was happening—the two of us together, cops working side by side, something I'd dreamed of for years. I would have walked into a thousand dark hallways if that was the price I had to pay to have him as my partner.

"Dad," I whispered to him. "You should give me the gun."

He ignored me, wiping at a spiderweb that hung in our path. I saw light ahead where the hall turned to the left. When we reached the juncture, I saw a stairwell. Weak light, filled with motes of dust, filtered down on the stairs. I saw a small paned window, the glass mostly opaque, high above. The echo of the footsteps changed, becoming sharper, less hollow. There was an open doorway at the foot of the stairs, some kind of janitor's closet, with a wheeled yellow mop bucket in the center. As we neared, I saw two little girls huddling behind the bucket. They wore matching blue and white uniforms and red bows in their hair, and they stared at me with utter fright.

I grabbed Dad's arm. "Wait," I said.

"Son, he's up—"

"Do you need help?" I asked the girls, ignoring him.

They scurried past us and fled around the corner. When I returned my attention to Dad, I recognized his peculiar expression, the same one I'd seen plenty of times from other people over the past six years. Only this time, instead of asking the usual question, he gripped my shoulder and nodded sympathetically.

"Ghosts?" he said.

I breathed a sigh. "You know?"

"I know what you can do," he said.

"How—?"

"I've heard you. Talking to your mother. I was still in here, Myron. I wasn't—wasn't gone completely."

He squeezed my shoulder again, then started up the stairs, leaving me to grapple with the emotional wallop. Not only did I have my father back, but he knew me. He knew what I had to deal with on a daily basis, and he had always known. Yet this was no time for introspection, no time for anything other than steely resolve, so I battened down the mental hatches and followed him up the stairs. There were a million things I wanted to say to him, but they would all have to wait.

We crept to the top of the stairs, turned on a landing where the light from the window high above fell in neat rectangular squares, and continued to the next floor. A door propped open by a plastic garbage bin led into a cavernous space, dimly lit by dusty windows on all sides. The rain tapped on the roof, the overcast skies choking off much of the light.

We heard footsteps on the far end, followed by a metallic squeak.

Flanking the door, we both glanced inside. I saw Sal, a silhouette against the distant window a good hundred feet away. All that filled the space were wooden crates, a couple of metal chairs, and a single filing cabinet mostly lost in darkness, other than the occasional metal support pole. Sal struggled with the window latch.

Suddenly, Dad thrust the pistol into my hands.

"Wait five seconds, then yell at him to stop," he said. "His attention will be focused on you. I'll sneak around and get the jump on him. If he shoots, shoot back ... Goodbye, son."

He ducked inside, angling left, before I could grab his arm. I peered in after him and saw him moving panther-like along the wall. What was Dad doing? It was insane. That last word, *goodbye*, lingered in my mind, ratcheting up the fear. Why goodbye? I counted to five, listening to the squeaks, fearing Sal would get out before we could stop him, but he was still working on the latch when I leaned around the corner and yelled at him.

"Stop!"

Sal spun around and fired blindly in my direction, three shots in quick succession. I ducked behind the wall and the bullets burst through wood and plaster, dust raining down on me. I made sure the safety was off on the .38, then, rolling onto my stomach in the doorway, took aim and fired. High above Sal, the window shattered, and he dropped to the floor. I rolled back behind the wall.

Not knowing what would happen to him if he died, I'd deliberately avoided shooting him. The goal was to get him locked up, where he could be medicated again. If he died, the Ghost Reaper might die with him, but it might also be completely free of him, and then what would we do?

Neither of us fired a shot. I held my breath and listened for Dad's footsteps, but all I heard was the rain pounding on the roof—a good thing, because it covered his approach. Still, I needed to keep Sal's attention focused on me. I stood again, leaning out just a little, straining to make him out in the shadows.

"Throw the gun my way," I yelled. "Do it now, Sal, and you can walk out of here alive."

There was a pause, then: "You come in here, I'll shoot you!"

"It doesn't have to end like this."

"If you kill me," Sal shouted back, "he'll come out! He'll come out and take you both! I don't want that! Let me go! It's the only way."

"You don't want to hurt any more people, Sal. I know you don't. We can get you back on your medication—"

He fired another shot at me, blistering the wall near my head. I ducked out of sight. So much for negotiation. I knew Dad must have been getting close. I couldn't fire back blindly now or I might hit Dad, but I needed to keep distracting him. What could I do? I had to go in there—fast, zigzagging at him. If I was going to shoot at him, it was going to be with deadly aim. It would make me a target, but that would give Dad a chance. Maybe he felt responsible for Sal, for not recognizing him for what he was years ago, which was why he was so willing to put his own life at risk now, but I wasn't going to lose him when I'd just gotten him back.

Goodbye. He'd said goodbye in the way a person says goodbye when they don't expect to see you again for a long time, and I wouldn't accept that outcome. There were years ahead of us—hiking in the Cascades, laughing over local microbrews, watching Blazers games even though I had no interest in basketball—I could see all those new memories, just waiting for me. Sal was going to take all that from me.

I ran. I ran hard, straight at Sal, then veered to the right. He fired a shot. I had my pistol pointed at him, but I didn't fire. Not yet. I veered left, then right again, closing the gap between us. A hundred feet became fifty, became thirty … I was close enough now that even in the shadows, I saw him crouching there, aiming the Glock at me.

I pulled the trigger and blasted him in the shoulder.

Running and unsteady, I hadn't aimed well, but still the impact socked him backward. He didn't quite go down and managed to keep the Glock trained on me. I expected the shot to come at any second, a surefire hit at point-blank range, but once again Dad emerged out of nowhere, flying from the shadows at his old partner.

Sal got off another shot, this one right at Dad's gut.

Someone cried out in surprise, and I realized it was me. Dad took the hit but kept going, tackling Sal to the ground and fighting with him for the Glock. He was so much smaller than Sal, a scarecrow in a trench coat, and I didn't see how he could come out on top. I rushed forward to intervene, but a sudden gust of wind sent me tumbling backward. That queer feeling, the hollowness starting deep in my gut, was back stronger than ever. The rippling cloak, the swirl of darkness, the bony hands reaching—it rose straight out of Sal and seemed to engulf him.

Dad, undeterred, somehow managed to point the Glock toward Sal. They both had their hand on it, but, incredibly, Dad was winning the battle. I staggered back to my knees, aiming the pistol. Howling, the Ghost Reaper rose up like an ocean wave and crashed down on Dad, smothering him with its cyclone of darkness. I heard a scream. I didn't know who it was, Dad or Sal, and they were too entwined for me to get a safe shot.

Then a shot *did* go off, the Glock—a sharp bang, and Dad rolled backward. He lay at an awkward angle, one arm bent underneath him, one leg painfully to the side. Both Sal and the Ghost Reaper rose up with the gun, one form overlapping, a hurricane of shadows and darkness that appeared to be decaying before my eyes, bits of the Ghost Reaper disintegrating and disappearing. Something had happened to it. Something was destroying it.

Inside that raging maelstrom, Sal was still there, pointing the Glock at Dad, roaring in anguish. Now I had a clear shot and I aimed well, squeezing off three in a row.

Two struck Sal in the gut, one in the neck, flopping him backward. He spasmed like a man having a seizure, the Ghost Reaper spinning apart right on top of him, the bits of cloak flying off and vanishing into nothingness. Then Sal lay limp and still, but the Ghost Reaper continued its mad macabre dance, an undulating mass of rage and darkness.

There wasn't much of it left, just a few tatters of cloak, and with a last primal scream, the whole thing launched itself at me.

I raised my arms to shield myself, whatever good that would do, but the Ghost Reaper never made it all the way. What remained of it broke apart just as it reached me, fragmenting into nothingness, the wind dying along with its scream.

The last thing I saw of it was that horrible face—all those screaming faces inside the larger face—before they all vanished.

Shaking, layered in sweat, I crawled to Dad. The scratching of my pants on the bare tile floor was suddenly loud in the big open space. The rain drummed against the windows. On my way, I saw that Sal's eyes were wide open and unblinking, his neck soaked in blood. I prayed that Dad was in better shape than his old partner, but I knew before I got there that he had to be gone, too.

Sure enough, his eyes stared straight up, seeing nothing.

Shards of ice dug into my heart, the world collapsing around me. I felt for his pulse, both on his neck and his wrist, and couldn't find it.

I held my breath and waited, waited for Dad's ghost to appear. Where was he? Sal's ghost wasn't here either. Something was wrong. For six years I'd been cursed with a terrible gift, and I'd wished a million times that it would go away, that I could have my life back once again, but now, when I *wanted* to see a ghost, I couldn't. Was I cured? Had I lost my ability? Somehow I didn't think so. Somehow I was sure that one of the few things I'd wanted in life, to have my father back, had been taken from me. He'd said goodbye. He'd known he was leaving, and he said goodbye.

I refused to accept that he was gone. I listened to the rain and waited, watching Dad's lifeless eyes. I was still waiting when I heard a commotion behind me, a shout, hurried footsteps. I didn't look. If I looked away from Dad, I might miss him. He could be here any second.

Then I saw Alesha crouching in front of me, her face full of sympathy, and that's when I knew Dad wasn't coming back.

Chapter 20

At ten o'clock on the dot Monday morning, the familiar limo pulled up in front of my office on Burnside, where I stood waiting at the curb. The rain, which had been savagely pounding Portland the past two days, had finally stopped that night, but the gray sky bowed over us like a canvas filled with water, ready to unleash another storm at a moment's notice. I felt the thickness of the air, the moisture in it, with each breath. Elvis, working his hot-dog stand, tipped his white chef's hat toward me. Across the street, a couple of soldiers in Revolutionary War–era uniforms marched silently, saw me, and marched a bit faster.

The ghosts hadn't all come back yet, but they were starting to, and most of them were more afraid of me than ever.

My headaches, which had subsided a bit the past few weeks, were also back, a persistent ache in the middle of my skull. It was so nice that I had my life back, such as it was.

Minus Dad, of course.

When the limo stopped in front of me, I opened the door and stepped inside instead of waiting for Fist. I slumped in the leather seat and stared straight ahead, not sure why I was here, not sure why I was even willing to listen. Hopner was a compact gray shape to my left. The car continued idling at the curb.

"I'm sorry for your loss," he said.

I bit down on my lower lip, focusing on the black-tiled partition that separated the driver's area from the back. The tiles had been polished to a fine gleam, but there were flaws, tiny cracks here and there. I concentrated on a hairline crack in one of them, the way it zigged and zagged. When the silence grew uncomfortable, Hopner cleared his throat.

"I gather the money was wired into your account?" he asked.

I replied with a grunt.

"We are certainly grateful for all you have done," he said. "If there's anything—"

"I want my father back," I said.

"Ah. Yes. Well, I'm afraid that—."

I laughed sharply. "How surprising."

"Myron—"

"You knew, didn't you?"

"No."

Finally, for the first time since I'd stepped into the limo, I turned and fully looked at him, realizing how small and ridiculous he was with his white bowler hat and prim double-breasted suit, the black handkerchief sticking out of his pocket just so. "You knew what Dad was going to do. You knew that his Alzheimer's would destroy the Ghost Reaper. You knew somehow that the disease, if he absorbed Dad, would stop him. You set me up."

"No, Myron."

"You're lying."

Winston held up a finger in warning. "Careful with that word, my friend. I grieve for your loss, truly I do, but you should remember exactly who you are dealing with here."

"I know who I'm dealing with," I said. "That's why I believe you knew what was going to happen. You gave Dad a bit of his old self back, just enough for him to be a pawn in your little game."

"There was no game, Myron. We still don't know exactly how the Ghost Reaper came to be, and that troubles us greatly. And all those victims, those ghosts who'd been trapped inside him—now gone. Forever gone. That has shaken us to the core. Who would have thought that even the dead can die? But one thing is absolutely clear. There was a terrible menace that was threatening to destroy all of us—and your father bravely sacrificed himself to save us. To save *you*."

"So you admit you knew what would happen."

"No. Not me."

"The Director?"

"I can't speak for him."

"But he knew? He knew what would happen?"

"I *told* you, I can't speak for him."

I heard the grievance in his voice, saw the anger flash across his face. I knew it burned him up, being kept in the dark. He prided himself on his absolute control of his organization, on his ability to pull the strings and turn the gears, to know all that had to be done and how to do it. I saw how sensitive this was for him and homed right in on it.

"So you were a pawn, too?" I said.

"Don't be ridiculous."

"There really is only one person in the Department who has any real power, isn't there?"

"Myron, I'd suggest you—"

"I want to talk to him."

Hopner sighed heavily. "No one but me talks to the Director. I've already—"

"Get him on the phone. Call him."

"Nobody calls him! *He* calls *you*!" His face ripened, the veins on his neck bulging. "I've had quite enough of this, sir! I came to personally thank you, to express my condolences, and am made to—to—to suffer these indignities! It's too much! I *am* sorry for your loss, truly I am. I am sorry for all those poor souls who did not get to enjoy eternity like the rest of us. But it is better! Better they were not made to suffer! Your father did that. He was a—a hero! Now, if there's nothing else—"

"One last question," I said.

Hopner, trembling so violently he could barely speak, managed to spit out three words: "If you must."

"Oh, I must. Maybe you can't answer it, but I've got to ask ... If you all could bring Dad back to himself now, why not before? All those years, he had to watch himself fade away ... Why?"

Judging by the flare in his eyes, Hopner had been preparing a sharp retort to whatever insult I would toss his way, and my question was like a bucket of ice water on his rage. His expression softened, his eyes turning sympathetic, some of the red fading from his face. I liked the angry version of him better. I didn't want any pity.

"I wish I could give you an answer to that," Hopner said.

"But he has the power."

"Perhaps. I can't speak for the Director, no one can, but I do know this, Myron. There are ... balances that must be maintained. Cause and effect. Action and reaction. We *all* know this in the Department and must measure our decisions carefully, but he knows it better than anyone. And his power is not nearly as omnipotent as some would believe. A nudge here, a nudge there, yes, there are things he can do, that *we* can do, and he gave your father a nudge. Whether it would have lasted anyway ... I don't know."

"But he promised," I said. "He promised—"

"Did he?"

"What?"

"Think carefully. What did he promise? He said if you helped us, he would help you. He said he could do something about your father's condition. He did. I'm sorry, Myron, but he never promised that you would have your father back again. It's always dangerous to infer too much from what the Director tells you."

I returned to staring at the partition tiles, trying to cool my rage. "I feel cheated."

"Join the club," he said.

We sat in silence with our respective grievances, the limo idling, the city outside like a world many light-years way. If I opened the door, I knew I was throwing myself back into that world, and I wasn't sure I wanted to do that. What did it matter, if I was just a puppet on strings, if we were all just puppets—both the living and the dead—bit parts in somebody else's movie, none of our lives mattering all that much in the grand scheme of things?

Yet Mom was out there, and she'd lost the man she loved forever—in a way that few experienced the concept of forever. Alesha, my friend, sometimes more, she was out there, too. And of course there was still that beautiful blond firecracker in the hospital, awake but asleep, facing her own kind of eternity. I looked at Hopner, and he must have seen the question in my eyes. Either that, or what he said was the same answer he would have given to lots of questions.

"You just have to hope," he said.

Chapter 21

IT WAS NEARLY NINE O'CLOCK before the sky outside the window showed any blush of red and orange, and another good hour after that before the sunset finally dissolved first to lavender, then, finally, a deep shade of indigo that somehow appeared both warm and cool. The color was especially pleasing as a backdrop to the dogwoods and cherry blossoms that lined the Mistwood grounds, like a cloak draped over the shoulders of the trees. The streetlights had not yet buzzed to life, marring the scene, so this was my favorite time to watch. I put down my wrinkled copy of *Crime and Punishment*—it seemed a fitting choice of reading material, though I found myself often reading the same page for hours on end—and committed to watching the changing light.

I'd become quite a connoisseur of sunsets in the past three months. I'd discovered that there were good ones and great ones, but seldom bad ones. There were, however, lots of sunsets that you didn't notice. Sitting in this little room for hours on end, I'd vowed to notice more of them. No matter what happened, I told myself I wouldn't go through life so oblivious to such regular beauty.

In my lap, Patch purred softly. At some point, he'd showed up at the Mistwood to keep vigil with me, and the staff seemed happy to have him back. I was stroking his fine black fur when, next to me, Jak murmured—and, as I had done so often, I looked over at the bed hopefully. She stared at the ceiling, seeing but not seeing, blinking but otherwise showing no sign of consciousness, the same way she'd been since I'd moved her into the Mistwood shortly after my heart-to-heart with Winston Hopner. The tan bedspread was barely wrinkled as it passed over her body, she'd lost so much weight. Though she did eat if someone put food to her mouth, she did not eat a lot, and no one wanted to put her on intravenous tubes if she was showing any desire to eat on her own.

All progress, however small, had to be encouraged. That's what the doctors said.

Her color, though somewhat more pale, was still good. Her hair, though thinner, still had a good shine. This was what I told myself as I studied her, and of course I realized that I'd made just these sorts of rationalizations about Dad. Even when you knew deep down someone was fading before your eyes, you still lied to yourself about it.

The room was on the opposite side of the building than Dad's had been, in what they referred to as the Structured Care Center, whatever that meant, but it looked much the same: a couple of maple dressers, taupe walls that mostly, though not quite, matched the color of the bedspread, and watercolors in silver frames on the walls. Jak would have hated the decor, and I'd thought about hanging a few pulp-movie posters on the walls, but that would have been admitting that her stay was more than temporary.

Anytime now, I told myself. *Anytime and she'll wake up.*

"Do you want company?" Mom asked.

I turned and saw her standing in front of the closed door, dressed in the same black silk dress she'd been wearing since Dad died. Or vanished. I wasn't quite sure how to describe what had happened to him, since it was far more permanent than death. Mom glanced at Patch in my lap, and I saw her straining not to frown.

"No," I said.

She started to leave and was halfway through the door before I realized how harsh my tone had been.

"Mom," I called after her.

She ducked back into the room, arching her eyebrows. I was impressed that she'd gone through the door at all. It was a sign that she'd finally started to accept what she was and what she could do.

"I appreciate you checking on me," I said.

"Oh," she said. "Well, yes. I just want to make sure you're all right."

"I'm all right."

"Good. Good." She nodded.

"How are you?"

"Me? Oh, I'm fine. I'm just … I've been visiting with a nice Iranian man who just … crossed over. Helping him, um, adjust. He doesn't have anyone."

"That's good of you."

"Oh, I don't know." She shrugged, then added as if in explanation, "He's very good at bridge. Not as good as me, of course."

She smiled, a tiny smile, a bit forced, but it was still something I hadn't seen her do in months. It wasn't something she had done much alive or dead. But it was another sign of change, a sign she was evolving to be someone a little different, a little kinder, a little bolder. She hadn't even asked to move in with me, not once. *Why* it had taken Dad's leaving to prompt her to make these changes, I couldn't say, but just like Patch showing up at the Mistwood fifteen miles from the office, I thought some questions were better off unasked.

"She's going to get better," Mom said. "She's going to be herself again. Have faith."

"I know. Thank you."

"Don't give up hope. She knows you're here."

"I know."

She stood there nodding for a moment, as if contemplating what else to say, then disappeared through the door. I returned my attention to admiring the sunset, to petting the purring cat in my lap, and let my thoughts linger on the meaning of hope and faith. Most of the people who came to visit—Alesha and Tim, the doctors, and some of the residents, both living and dead—often expressed similar sentiments. Don't give up hope. Keep believing. She's a fighter, you'll see. Even Hopner, in his parting words to me, had said something similar.

The difference with Mom was, she really believed it. I appreciated the difference now in a way I hadn't before. Everyone else, I got the sense they thought that I should get back to my life. I'd already burned through much of the money Hopner had given me to take care of Jak, making sure she had the best care, the best doctors. Mom knew what it was like to bet it all on hope and faith. She knew, to really believe, it was all or nothing.

Without my quite noticing it, the sunset faded from indigo to black. Eventually the streetlamps brightened, and this I did notice, the harsh bubbles of light signaling that I should call it a day and head home. For some reason, though, I didn't, my thoughts still lingering on hope and faith, my eyes getting drowsy. The sounds of activity within the Mistwood—distant voices, footsteps, closing doors—all fell silent, leaving me with the purr of a cat. I may have dozed in the chair for a few minutes, an hour, what did it matter, but I awoke when Patch meowed loudly.

When I glanced down at him, I saw that he was looking over at the bed. Following his gaze, I saw Jak looking back at me—really looking at me, seeing me. My breath caught in my throat, and I waited, blinking away the bleariness, hoping I was seeing what I thought I was seeing, hoping it was real and not some cruel dream. Hoping.

"So," she said, her voice scratchy and weak, but still with the old ring of Jak to it, "you going to join me in this bed or what?"

Acknowledgments

I'd like to single out a few people who've been of great help in the writing and production of *The Ghost Who Said Goodbye*.

To Elissa Englund, my fantastic copy editor who once again went above and beyond the call of duty: A big thank-you for catching all the typos and miscues, as well as your thoughtful suggestions about the story. It's a testament to your ability that I almost always use all of your suggestions. The mistakes that remain, of course, are entirely my own fault.

To Annie Reed, a superb writer and consumate professional: Thank you for the early read and insightful suggestions.

To my family, Heidi, Kat, and Calvin: I know it's not always easy living with a writer, and I appreciate your support. You lift me up. I hope I can continue to do the same for you. I know I don't always succeed, but I'll try even harder.

And of course, to my readers: If my family makes me want to be a better man, you make me want to be a better writer. I can't promise I'll never let you down, but I can assure you that you'll always get my best effort.

About the Author

SCOTT WILLIAM CARTER's first novel, *The Last Great Getaway of the Water Balloon Boys,* was hailed by *Publishers Weekly* as a "touching and impressive debut" and won an Oregon Book Award. Since then, he has published a dozen novels and over fifty short stories, his fiction spanning a wide variety of genres and styles. His most recent book for younger readers, *Wooden Bones,* chronicles the untold story of Pinocchio and was singled out for praise by the Junior Library Guild. He lives in Oregon with his wife and children.

Visit him online at *www.ScottWilliamCarter.com.*

CPSIA information can be obtained
at www.ICGtesting.com
Printed in the USA
BVHW031932040619
550142BV00001B/33/P